THE ... SECRET

Jack and Lou's story

Celia Tandy

To Royena
Happy reading
Celia
x

ISBN 978-1-0685637-1-3

Chapter 1 - Lou

It's beginning to look a lot like Christmas…

Lou sang the words softly and placed the last red bauble on the rather pathetic Christmas tree she'd bought that morning from the florist along the high street. Even the assistant had looked doubtfully at her choice, but it was the only one small enough to fit in her cramped sitting room. She flicked the switch, and the twinkling fairy lights winked on. Annie would love it, and she certainly wouldn't care if none of the decorations matched.

Thinking of her daughter, a soft smile brushed her lips. She was two years old and already had bags of personality – a mix of curiosity, energy with a sprinkle of naughtiness thrown in. She was also a terrible sleeper and had woken Lou up twice in the night. Since Annie was napping, she supposed she should as well, but the temptation to have an hour to herself was far too strong.

Besides, the laundry basket was overflowing, and she was about to run out of pants. There was also a pile of dishes sitting in the kitchen sink, and she still hadn't written a single Christmas card. Sure, these days, most people didn't bother exchanging cards when a generic social media post would do, but she liked the tradition and personal touch of sending a handwritten card.

Since leaving London, life had completely changed. Now her days revolved around Annie: her nursery and nap times and having eyes in the back of her head to make sure she didn't tumble over because she always ran everywhere at alarming speed. It was funny how quickly your social life imploded when you had a small munchkin to take care of.

It was lonely too, without a partner to share all Annie's 'firsts' with. Her first gummy smiles, nonsensical words, and stumbling steps, plus the thousand other amazing things she did every day. Lou's heart squeezed at how much Annie's father was missing, but there wasn't any point crying over spilt milk, as her mum would say. Time to let go of the past and start writing all those Christmas cards.

"Mama, Mama, Mama!" Annie's insistent call came from her small nursery.

She sighed. Maybe it wouldn't matter if she gave Christmas cards a miss this year.

***

"Hey sweetie. Did you have a good nap?"

"Mama, milk," Annie chanted.

"Yes, milk in a minute, but first let's brush the tangles out of your hair and give your face a wash." Annie gave her a beaming smile, and Lou chuckled. It was good to know she was fully on board.

Five minutes later, they both went into the open-plan kitchen/sitting room. The flat was rundown and in need of refurbishing, but she was lucky to have it. The night she'd turned up at the hotel and told her mum she was pregnant and, no, the father wasn't involved, her mum had said she could stay as long as she wanted.

In fact, her mum had been amazing. Letting her bawl when pregnancy hormones and her decision to go it alone had become too overwhelming and helping her with all the practicalities that being a single parent entailed. Not surprisingly, she had lots of questions, but Lou had pleaded with her not to ask about Annie's father, and so far, she hadn't.

Her mum, Sylvie, was the owner of the Broadsham Arms Hotel on the high street in Broadsham, a pretty village in the heart of the Cotswolds. Lou's flat was at the back of the hotel in the former servants' quarters. These days, all the hotel employees lived locally, and her mum also had a house in Broadsham, so Lou's was the only occupied accommodation.

She'd landed on her mum, who had scooped her up and helped her deal with her wrecked life. Because it had felt wrecked, walking away from the only man she'd truly loved and deciding to continue with her pregnancy when well-meaning friends said it was a mistake. It wasn't a mistake, not at all. She didn't regret for one moment having Annie. No, her only regret was her terrible taste in men.

***

There was a gentle tap on the front door before her mum let herself into the flat.

"Hello darling, Reg sent me over with some leftover cottage pie he thought you might like." She put the dish down on the kitchen counter as Annie raised her arms, wanting to be picked up. Her mum was Annie's favourite person, and she scooped her up and began nuzzling her chestnut curls.

"Thanks." Lou smiled, though as her mum was the hotel owner, she imagined it wasn't so much the chef had leftovers he was trying to find a home for but more that her mum had asked him to set some aside for her.

"Ooh, how's my sweet baby girl today? Your hair smells heavenly."

"I washed it last night, though Annie's not a great fan of hair washing." Defeat edged her words because Annie hated it with a passion, and it always resulted in a battle between them.

"You look a bit tired, love. Would you like me to take Annie out so you can have a break? I could show her the lights on the Christmas tree on the green."

"Are you sure? I'd love a soak in the bath, but only if you've got time?"

"Of course, I've always got time for my favourite grandchild."

"Your only grandchild." Lou chuckled.

After bundling Annie up in her warm coat, hat and gloves and strapping her into her pushchair, grandmother and granddaughter set off, and Lou found herself alone. She loved Annie to bits, but an hour of peace was a rare gift.

Lou's phone buzzed, and a message from her friend Mordros popped up on the screen.

Mordros: Fancy a coffee?

Lou: Yes, sure. When were you thinking?

Mordros: Are you free now? I could treat you to a posh coffee in the hotel?

Lou: That sounds wonderful. I'll be over in a minute.

All thoughts of a relaxing bath flew out of Lou's head as she contemplated catching up with her best friend. They'd met when Mordros had asked Lou to organise her aunt's seventieth birthday celebration at the hotel. Mordros had also reconnected with Adam, an old flame, and now they were engaged to be married. It had been a fairy-tale ending to a romance that had begun in Cornwall fifteen years ago. So maybe there was still hope that she'd meet her own Prince Charming one day. She snorted at the thought. She didn't want a prince; she wanted an equal partner who wouldn't lie or cheat on her.

She quickly applied a spray of perfume and stared at the dark shadows under her eyes in the broken bathroom mirror. Last night, Annie had woken up teething, her cheeks red and inflamed, and she'd gently rubbed some cooling gel onto her tender gums to soothe them. Eventually, Annie had fallen back to sleep, but Lou had tossed and turned for the rest of the night until *(because the Gods were having a laugh)*, Annie had woken up at five a.m. and refused to go back to sleep again. Lou dabbed on some tinted moisturiser, but it couldn't hide the evidence of her disturbed night. Sighing, she grabbed her jacket and left the flat.

***

Lou stood for a moment, admiring the six-foot Christmas tree with its twinkling lights in the corner of the hotel lounge. The perfectly matched baubles and silver tinsel shimmered, capturing the light from the large cut-glass chandelier, which dominated the ceiling. It was an impressive sight to greet hotel guests as they walked in.

Her eyes drifted around the spacious room: the squashy, comfortable sofas, the crackling log fire and the old oil paintings on the walls. Soft Christmas music played in the background while the aroma of coffee mingled with woodsy-scent from the fir tree and strategically placed pine-scented diffusers. The hotel's history, tradition, and comfort were renowned, and Lou felt enormously proud that her mum had made such a success of running the hotel since her dad had passed away.

"Hello Henry, how are you today?" Lou hugged the elderly maître d'hôtel and kissed his pink, ruddy cheek. He'd worked at the hotel from as far back as she could remember - a part of their small family, really — and she couldn't imagine a time when he wouldn't be serving guests. But he was nearly seventy now, and every year his hair got a little greyer and his walk a little slower. She also knew his arthritis was getting worse.

As if reading her thoughts, Henry replied, "I'm very well, thank you, Miss Louise. My arthritis has been much better since the doctor put me on some new tablets."

"I'm glad to hear it." She smiled with relief. It would be a sad day when Henry retired, and neither she nor her mum wanted that day to come.

"And where's Annie today?" His eyes scanned the room.

"Mum's looking after her for an hour, and I'm here to have coffee with a friend. Do you have any of those delicious fruit scones Patrick makes?"

"Not today, I'm afraid, but your friend's already here." He waved his hand towards Mordros. "I'll be over in a minute to take your order."

She watched as he walked back towards the kitchen. That was odd. Patrick was their pastry chef, and there were always fruit scones on the menu. The hotel was famous for them.

Still, there was no point in pondering the lack of scones, because Mordros was waiting for her. She smiled and waved as she began walking towards her friend.

"This is a lovely surprise." Lou sat down after the girls had hugged. "How's the wedding planning going? I want to hear everything."

"There's not much to report, really. The only thing we've agreed on so far is that we want to get married before Christmas."

"Oh wow, a Christmas wedding will be lovely, but you'll have to get your skates on booking a venue because there'll be an enormous demand at Christmas."

"What would you ladies like today?" Henry had reappeared and stood with his pen poised over his notepad to take their order.

"Ooh, a hot chocolate with all the toppings and some of your lovely gingerbread, please." Mordros smiled up at him.

"Sounds good. Same for me, Henry."

"I'm sorry, but we don't have any gingerbread today."

Lou frowned. "Okay, a mince pie then."

"Apologies, but we don't have any mince pies either. I can only offer you a toasted teacake." Henry's cheeks had turned a shade pinker.

Lou suddenly felt annoyed with herself. It wasn't Henry's place to apologise for their lack of menu choices. She worked at the hotel too, albeit part-time, so if there were problems in the kitchen, she should have known.

"A toasted teacake is fine." She watched as he jotted down their order in his spidery handwriting and headed back towards the kitchen. She made a mental note to ask her mum why they had such a limited sweet menu, but now wasn't the time to think about that.

"I can't imagine anything more romantic than getting married at Christmas." She sat back on the sofa, smiling.

"We're so excited. And that's why I wanted to see you today because, obviously, time is short, and I'd really love you to be my bridesmaid and Annie to be my flower girl. Please say yes."

Lou's eyes widened with surprise. "I'd love to be your bridesmaid, and I know Annie will be over the moon. Ever since last summer, I think she's had a bit of a crush on Adam."

"It's reciprocated. Adam loves reminiscing about all the times Annie came running up to him with worms and snails she'd collected for him to admire. Do you remember when she picked up some dried-up dog poo and handed it to him and he was too polite not to take it?" Mordros giggled.

"Don't remind me. Last week she found a big, hairy spider in the bath and brought it to show me. I nearly died of fright." Lou shuddered.

"I hate them too, but thank goodness Adam doesn't mind. Anyway, thanks so much for agreeing to be my bridesmaid. At least that's one thing I can cross off my very long list. We're having a small dinner party on Friday night, and we'd love you to come. You'll know Nick and Sam - Nick's my chief brides-man - and you'll get to meet Adam's best man. We thought it would be fun if we got everyone together, and you'll be able to help us make plans for the wedding."

"Sounds great. I'll ask Mum if she'll babysit." Lou smiled as Henry returned with a tray bearing their hot chocolates and toasted teacakes.

"Here's to your perfect Christmas wedding." Lou raised her hot chocolate, and they clinked glasses.

Mordros grinned. "And just so you know, the best man is single, so…"

"Oh, come on, really? Please don't start matchmaking."

"Why not? Christmas is the perfect time for romance, and if you can't do a little matchmaking at Christmas, when can you?" She winked.

Chapter 2 - Jack

Jack closed his eyes and tried to block out the random thought that had just popped into his head. It felt like Susie's tongue was on a washing machine spin cycle in his mouth … in, out, up, down, twirling round and round. Now he could feel one of her hands moving slowly over his shirt and down his chest while the other one squeezed his behind.

Abruptly, she pulled her tongue out of his mouth and began reaching for his belt buckle. He concentrated hard, trying to get into the moment, but his body was having none of it, and embarrassingly, now she could tell. She was rubbing his crotch like it was Aladdin's magic lamp, but there definitely wasn't any magic happening.

"Sorry, I think the scallops I ate for dinner were bad. I don't feel well," he lied as he batted her hand away and began zipping himself up.

"Oh, that's a shame. All my exes say I'm great at –,"

"Maybe another time." He tried for a smile, but it came out more of a grimace because there wouldn't be a next time.

Extricating himself from her place as swiftly as he could, he drove back to his apartment, heading straight to the on-site gym in the basement. He rushed through his workout in half the time it usually took. Sweat poured off him, but he'd burned off his frustration. Eventually, he got in the shower and turned the setting to zero. The water was freezing, but he forced himself to stand under the spray until his body was numb with cold.

Why did he keep doing this? It was stupid. He was stupid. The only sensible part of him consistently made it clear his dates weren't right for him. It wasn't as if he didn't like a blowjob, but his body had decided it had to be with the right person. Unfortunately, that wasn't Susie or any of the other women he'd dated since Lou.

It had been nearly three years since they'd been together. Since Lou had in fact unceremoniously dumped him. For months he'd thrown himself into work, balking at the idea of another relationship. But eventually, he'd begun tentatively dating again. Wasn't the saying the best way to get over someone was to get under someone else?

Of course, it wasn't fair to compare his dates to Lou, but it was hard not to. The few women he'd dated since their breakup had all been nice, but for some ridiculous reason, his body had developed a moral conscience that he was cheating, which was ridiculous because Lou didn't want him. She had in fact made it crystal clear that she never wanted to see him again. He closed his eyes, absorbing the harsh truth, because he might as well accept that he'd spend the rest of his life celibate. It was far easier than the embarrassment he'd endured earlier.

He missed Lou so much. Her dazzling smile and her sense of humour. Her long fair hair, and that little scar on her knee, which she'd said was from when she'd fallen off her bike when she was five years old. Hearing her belt out musical theatre songs in the shower and how she loved putting her cold feet on him in bed. Actually, she was like a koala bear, always wrapping her body around his and taking up far too much of his side.

His fridge no longer contained her emergency supply of chocolate bars, and there was no need to set his phone timer for the way she preferred her boiled eggs – four minutes, thirty seconds precisely.

He'd loved Lou. Just a shame she hadn't loved him back.

***

Thirty minutes later, he was lying on his back in bed, staring at the ceiling in his bedroom. Still wired from earlier, his thoughts drifted back to Lou and the night they'd met. He knew it was self-destructive, like picking at a scab that refused to heal, but he'd do it, anyway.

He'd been at a dull corporate event at a swanky hotel in London. Usually, he made his business partner, Adam, go to these things but, this time he'd drawn the short straw and since he couldn't get out of it, he'd promised himself he'd put in a brief appearance - an hour tops – before sloping off to the pub.

He'd spotted Lou straight away. She was wearing a black sleeveless dress that clung to her perfect curves and showed off her toned arms. Bright red lipstick and honey-coloured hair fixed in a loose bun, and as his eyes slid down, high heels that made her tanned legs go on forever. She looked gorgeous, and he let his mind imagine those same legs wrapped around his waist, her feet still encased in those killer heels.

He'd quickly let the thought go because a man, probably twice her age, was leaning into her personal space, his large body pressed up against hers and his hand stroking her arm. Jack briefly wondered if they were together, but then she'd looked up and caught his eye, throwing him a pleading look, and so he'd walked over.

"There you are, darling." He bulldozed his way in front of the older man, who had grey hair sprouting out of his bulbous red nose and ears. "I've been looking for you all over the place. The babysitter's just messaged, and little Jeremiah has a tummy ache, so I think it's time we headed home." Jack stared at the man. "I'm sorry, but I'm sure you understand."

"Oh goodness yes, we must go immediately." She'd grasped Jack's hand, and he'd begun steering her towards the other side of the crowded room.

"Thank you so much. I thought I was going to be trapped with him all night," she said as soon as they were out of earshot.

"Let's find somewhere to hide." Jack grinned as he swiped two glasses of champagne from a passing server. But when she looked uncertain, he continued. "Since little Jeremiah is miraculously feeling better, it would be nice to have a drink together. My name's Jack, by the way."

"Lou," she smiled back.

He led them through the throng of people to the quieter cocktail lounge, and they found a secluded corner away from the other guests. "Who was handsy man, anyway?" Jack placed their champagne flutes on the coffee table and sat next to Lou on the sofa.

"Barret Fortesque. He's the owner of the hotel. I'm the events coordinator here, so I have to be nice to him." Lou shuddered.

"You shouldn't ever have to be nice to a man like that." Jack held her gaze.

"Easy to say, but he could make my life very difficult. I hope he doesn't work out that little Jeremiah doesn't exist." Lou laughed wryly. "Anyway, let's not talk about him anymore."

Jack nodded, fighting his desire to give Barret Fortesque a piece of his mind, but that would mean leaving Lou on her own, and he didn't want to do that. "So, you're the one responsible for organising this evening?" He grinned. "I've been looking forward to it for ages. You've done a great job getting so many entrepreneurs together in one room."

"Liar." Lou shot him a look that called out his bullshit and then giggled. "I saw you earlier, staring at your watch and wondering how long until you could escape."

"Well, I'm glad I didn't." He had the good grace to look embarrassed. "Now tell me all about yourself and exactly what an event coordinator does."

Lou was 33, single (important because Jack's one unbreakable rule was never to sleep with a married woman) and she'd been living in London for the past year. She loved the buzz of the city, the theatre, especially West End musicals - as far as Jack could tell she'd seen most of them - Italian food, and slow-paced Sundays taking in the sights and all the free museums and art galleries London offered. He'd also discovered that her favourite time of the year was Christmas. She loved everything about it – the tree and decorations, festive food, cheesy Hallmark Christmas films, carols, mistletoe and mulled wine.

He could work with that.

She was called away twice - she was still technically on duty - but once the evening had wound down, he'd bought her a coconut martini and she'd kicked off her shoes and tucked her shapely legs under her, lying back on the squashy cushions on the sofa.

Two martinis later and they were still chatting. Her mum ran a small hotel in the Cotswolds, but Lou had wanted to move to London. "I want to gain some more hospitality experience, but Mum's thinking of retiring in a year or two, so I've promised to go back then and take over."

"What's the hotel like?"

"Dark wood panelling, roaring log fires, lots of history – it's over six hundred years old, which sounds glamorous, but actually there's always something that needs fixing. And then there are dozens of restrictions about what you can and can't do because it's a listed building. Mum took over running it when Dad died five years ago, but it was Dad's passion, really. She's keeping it going until I'm ready to take over." Lou smiled. "Anyway, you've been listening to me all night. What about you? You're a lawyer, right?"

"How did you know?"

"Sixth sense." She grinned and tapped her nose. "Never fails."

"And what else does your sixth sense tell you?"

"That I should be extremely careful of someone like you."

"And why might that be?" Jack laughed.

"Because I imagine you regularly break girls' hearts, and I don't want you to break mine."

"I'd never do that." And even though her judgement was correct, and that was exactly what he usually did, he met her eyes and hoped she'd see he was telling the truth.

She giggled, and the sound was sexy and languid. God, she was pushing all of his buttons, but she'd also stifled a yawn, and he wasn't that much of a jerk to try it on when she was clearly tired. Anyway, he wanted to see her again.

"Can I see you tomorrow?"

"I'm working during the day, but my shift finishes at six, so I could meet up after that."

Jack watched, transfixed, as the tip of her tongue slid over her bottom lip. He had to concentrate hard – imagining a boring affidavit – to stop his body from taking an interest. "Um, yeah, that works for me."

Eventually, he'd walked her to her flat, which was only around the corner, and then they'd stood talking outside for another 20 minutes, neither of them seeming to want the evening to end. Maybe the night air had woken them both up.

"Do you want to find a café?" She'd nodded and fixed her gorgeous violet eyes on him, and he'd grabbed her hand before she changed her mind.

It was past midnight, but they found a small family-run place that was still open. The friendly waitress greeted them as they walked in and settled them at a small private booth. Lou ordered a fancy hot chocolate with whipped cream, mini marshmallows and a chocolate flake on top, and Jack couldn't help teasing her.

"If I drank that much sugar, I'd take off into orbit."

Lou laughed. "I have a terrible sweet tooth, and I love everything chocolate-y. I only have two vices, and that's one of them."

"And what's the other one?"

Lou laughed. "That would be telling."

"Yeah? Well, I'm definitely up for the challenge of finding out." Jack winked and tried to stop his imagination from running away with him.

"So, why did you want to become a lawyer?" Lou's eyes fixed on his as she subtly changed the subject.

"I could say it's because I wanted to help people in trouble and maybe make a difference to someone's life. I always liked the idea of saying to a client, I'm the only chance you've got." Jack grinned. "But the real reason is that my best friend wanted to be a lawyer, and I just thought, why not?"

Lou snorted. "So, you became a lawyer because of your best friend?"

"Yeah, pretty much. We were at school and then university together. After that, we did our articles and spent a year in New York. A few years later, we opened our own law firm in Cheltenham as joint business partners."

"Wow, you really are best friends."

"We've been through a lot together. And I love working with my best mate."

"So why are you in London?"

"We're looking at expanding and opening another office. There's a lot of groundwork to do first, but if we can persuade a few city businesses to ditch their existing legal firms and also attract some entrepreneurs and small start-ups with potential to make it big, well…"

"You sound ambitious."

"Is that a bad thing?" Jack looked serious for a moment.

"No, of course not. So that's why you were at my networking event this evening?"

"Your event?"

"Yeah, of course. I organised it. And for the record, I'm ambitious too."

"Well, in that case, we're going to be perfect together."

"Aren't you getting a little ahead of yourself?" She tried to smother a smile.

"Like I said, I'm ambitious," Jack grinned.

***

Two months later, Jack found suitable office premises and moved down to the capital to oversee the renovations before they officially opened. He'd also begun dating Lou.

London was a romantic city… a city for lovers, and he'd loved exploring it with Lou. They both had busy jobs, but they spent as much of their free time together as they could: lazy Sunday brunches, a boat cruise to Greenwich, a ride on the London Eye, cocktails at the top of the Shard, picnics in Hyde Park, galleries, museums, West End shows, and lesser known fringe theatre plays. Jack loved it all.

He'd also fallen in love with Lou.

Not for the first time, he wondered what he'd done wrong. They'd been happy. She'd been happy. You couldn't fake something like that. In fact, they'd only recently said they loved each other. Walking home from seeing a play at the Festival Hall, they'd gazed across the inky Thames towards the lights of St. Paul's, all their hopes and dreams tied up in those three small words. So, there was that evidence, too.

He'd even begun thinking about how he'd propose. It was still too early, but that didn't alter the fact that he wanted to.

Then, after they'd been dating for ten months, Jack woke up to a message from Lou that it was over. A sterile one-liner without explanation. He'd asked to meet up and talk… she blocked him. He sent flowers with an apology for whatever he'd done… silence. Finally, at his wit's end, he stood outside her flat in the pouring rain waiting until she'd returned from work. He wanted Lou and happy ever after. She told him she never wanted to see him again. There was no arguing with that.

He watched as she walked up the three steps that led to her flat. The rain had soaked him, plastering his hair to his scalp, but he stayed where he was because the time for talking was over.

"Whatever happened… whatever I did. I'm sorry. I'm sorry this has ended us because I really think you're amazing." He swallowed his misery. *"You're going to make someone else so happy one day. He'll be a lucky man."*

He turned and walked away.

So here he was, and he'd survived. Survived Lou. He swallowed down the familiar regret as pain, like a punch to the stomach, threatened to overwhelm him. He blinked hard, trying to stop the sting of tears. Damn it, he should be over her by now.

These days, he spent as little time at their London office as he could. They had a small team permanently based there, and Adam did most of the overseeing. It wasn't fair to him, but his best friend hadn't challenged him when he'd made up a feeble excuse why.

Well, one thing was for sure: sleep wasn't happening now. He reached for the remote control at the side of his bed and switched on his TV, searching for his favourite sports channel.

***

The next morning, Adam walked into Jack's office and handed him a coffee from the posh deli across the road. "What's this for?" He looked up from the brief he was reading. "You never buy coffee from Alfonsos. You always say there's nothing wrong with our office coffee machine."

"Well, there isn't anything wrong with it. But I was passing, and I thought of you."

"And?" Jack watched curiously as a hint of nervousness crossed his friend's face.

"And it's also because I want to ask if you'll be my best man?"

"You do?" A wide grin broke out on Jack's face.

"Well, I asked about ten other people, and they all said they were busy, so…" Adam grinned.

"Oh mate, I don't know what to say." Jack felt himself choking up. "Thank you."

"It comes with a few conditions, though. You'll have to arrange my stag."

"I can do that. I mean, we'll be going to Ibiza, right? All that nightlife."

"Absolutely not."

"Okay then, what about Las Vegas? Those gambling casinos won't play themselves."

"I was thinking about Broadsham."

"What? It'll be freezing in December. Why would you want to do that? I thought the whole idea of a stag do was that the groom could have a last hurrah before the big day. You know, indulge in a bit of sun and naughtiness before the whole marriage ball and chain."

"I don't consider marrying my fiancée to be in any way related to a ball and chain," Adam growled. "Anyway, can you really see me in Ibiza or Las Vegas?"

"No, I suppose not," Jack conceded. "At least consider having your stag abroad. I'm sure I can find a fun place we can go to."

"Jack, I just want something simple."

"But Broadsham? Really? What the hell is there to do in Broadsham on a stag?"

"Well, I'm sure you can come up with something. Plus, you'll need to liaise with the bridesmaid to ensure the wedding day goes like clockwork. Talking of which, we're having a small get-together at home tomorrow night, so you'll get to meet her then. I know it's short notice, but I really want you there."

"Sure, I'll be there. If Mordros is prepared to put up with you for the rest of her life, then the least I can do is help to make your wedding day perfect." Jack grinned and ducked as Adam threw a paperclip at him.

"Good, that's settled then. Dinner's at seven, and you'll meet everyone then, and we can start planning."

Chapter 3 - Lou

"Are you sure?" Lou handed her mum a mug of tea and then sat down at the kitchen table with her own.

"Of course, I'm sure, love. You haven't had a night out in ages. Plus, I'm looking forward to a bit of one-on-one nanny and granddaughter time."

"I shouldn't be very late… it's just dinner, and we'll be talking about the wedding, so not exactly a wild night out."

"Have they decided where they're having their wedding? You might mention that the hotel is a lovely venue if they want something small and intimate."

"Mum, I can't blatantly plug the hotel. Anyway, I imagine they'll want to get married in Cornwall, since Mordros is from there."

"Oh yes, of course."

Sylvie put down her mug, and Lou caught a look on her face, which she couldn't quite read. "Is everything okay?"

"Yes, of course. Everything's fine."

"Mum?"

Sylvie ignored the question. "What time do you want me here?"

"Dinner's at seven, but Mordros said to come a bit earlier so we can have a drink first."

"How about I come round at half-past five? That'll give you plenty of time to get ready in peace."

"That would be amazing."

"Good, that's settled then."

"Are you sure you're fine? Is there something worrying you?"

"Of course not. I'm just tired, that's all. It's been a busy day, and we're short-staffed. Patrick, the pastry chef, didn't turn up again, and one of the waitresses handed in her notice this morning. She doesn't want to do early shifts anymore."

Well, that explained why there was a limited sweet menu, thought Lou. "I'm sorry, there's me asking you to babysit when you've got enough on your plate already."

"Don't be daft. I love spending time with Annie. Anyway, it'll do you good to have a night off. Hopefully, you can let your hair down a bit. Who else is going?"

"Nick and Sam will be there, and Adam's best man."

"Sounds a perfect number of people for a dinner party." Sylvie put down her mug and smiled. "Well, I'd better get back, but I'll see you tomorrow."

Lou walked her mum to the door and gave her a parting kiss on the cheek. She watched her walk across the courtyard to the back entrance of the hotel, her mind still dwelling on the enigmatic look she'd seen on her face.

The hotel was a twenty-four-hour, seven-days-a-week job, and while her mum was lucky to have mainly loyal, reliable and long-serving employees, all the responsibility of managing the business fell on her shoulders. She helped as much as she could – when Annie was in nursery and sometimes in the evening if they had functions, and she could get a babysitter, but she knew it wasn't enough.

She sighed. There was always something to worry about these days, and her gut instinct told her that there was definitely something wrong. But her mum obviously wasn't ready to confide in her. There was also another, much bigger, worry gnawing at her. Something she tried to swallow down but kept resurfacing like a bad dose of indigestion.

Her ex was a lawyer like Adam, and he'd mentioned that he worked with his best friend. She trawled through her memories, trying to recall the friend's name. Her mum always teased that baby brain made you forgetful, but they'd both been living in their London bubble, completely focused on each other, so she was sure it just hadn't come up.

She let go of her worries. There must be hundreds of lawyers in the area, so the odds of Adam and her ex knowing each other, let alone working together, must be practically zero.

***

"Night, night baby girl. Try to sleep, and Mama will see you in the morning." Lou kissed Annie's forehead, smelling her clean baby smell, and tiptoed out into the hallway. Her mum was already in the small open-plan kitchen/sitting room, ensconced on the sofa with her book, so she went into her own bedroom and began getting ready.

She chose a simple black sleeveless dress from her wardrobe and held it up against herself. Pulling off her jeans and top, she slipped the fabric over her head, relishing the softness of the material against her skin. She'd lost most of her baby weight, and it clung to her, accentuating her figure.

Tears stung as memories flooded back. She'd been wearing the same dress the night she'd met the man she'd once imagined spending forever with. She'd been so happy… if she was honest, she'd fallen in love with him. But he'd thrown her love away. She pulled the dress off and put her jeans back on. The last thing she needed was to think of him.

Half an hour later, Lou left the flat. She hurried down the high street, clutching a poinsettia in one hand and a bottle of wine in the other. The night air was chilly, and she snuggled deeper into her coat, pulling her scarf over her chin. Broadsham was full of festive cheer, with its decorated shop windows and a large Christmas tree with twinkling fairy lights in the centre of the green. The gift shops were still busy, and the café was serving mulled wine and mince pies to any late-night shoppers in need of sustenance.

She'd always loved Christmas, but the Christmas after Annie was born, she'd sobbed through the whole twelve days of it. With baby hormones raging and the pain of her failed relationship, she'd just wanted the whole thing to be over. And now yet another Christmas loomed, and she felt the same tug of guilt because Annie's father didn't know he had a daughter.

Whatever her feelings towards him, he had a right to know. But then he'd want to see his daughter and be part of her life. And that was the crux of it. Despite trying to push her feelings away, she was still in love with him, and seeing him again…

So, the weeks and months had passed, and she'd put off telling him again and again.

I'll tell him soon; she made a silent promise as she arrived at Adam's house.

***

Mordros raised her glass of mulled wine. "Merry Christmas, everyone."

Lou had been to Adam's house a few times, and watched Mordros transform the once minimalistic masculine interior into a warm, stylish living space. Brightly coloured cushions, throws, rugs, and a couple of pieces of modern art had appeared in the sitting room. In the hallway there was a striking piece of coloured glass, from a gallery in St. Ives, and blue and white Cornishware replaced Adam's plain crockery in the kitchen.

"I'm thinking maybe a plum colour" Mordros put down her wine and reached for her iPad. "Something like this?" They all peered at the small screen as she pointed to a model dressed in a long bridesmaid's dress. "What do you think?"

"I think it'll be bloody freezing at this time of year." Nick, her chief brides-man grumbled.

"We're not getting married on top of a cliff in Cornwall." Adam laughed. "I mean, we're not, are we?" He looked at Mordros uncertainly.

"No, of course not. Though if it were a summer wedding, it would be a lovely idea. But since it's a winter wedding, what could be better than Broadsham? The honeymoon's in Cornwall, though," she smiled at Adam.

"I love the colour, and it's perfect for this time of year. Though maybe have one of those fur boleros, too." Lou imagined herself wearing the long dress, the silk falling in soft folds around her. It was a stunning colour, perfect for winter, and for once, she could leave her jeans at home.

"I can't tell you how excited I am that we're getting married." Adam reached for Mordros, linking their fingers together, and dropped a gentle kiss on her lips.

Lou shifted uncomfortably as she remembered her mum's plea. *You might mention that the hotel is a lovely venue if they want something small and intimate.* Thankfully, Sam saved her by piping up, "Have you got a venue sorted yet?"

Mordros looked at Lou. "We're hoping you have availability at the hotel. I know it's terribly short notice, but please say you do."

Lou smiled. "I'll just check the bookings calendar online. What date were you thinking?"

"The Saturday before Christmas Day." She bit her lip nervously as Lou began logging in to the hotel bookings system on her phone.

"Have you thought about what style of dress you'll wear?" Nick took the iPad from her and began scrolling through the bridal gowns.

"I've got some ideas, but would you like to come dress shopping with me?"

"Try stopping me, darling. I've always thought I'd make a terrific fashion influencer. I might even start a wedding Instagram and post our wedding journey every day."

Sam snorted. "It's Mordros and Adam's day, not yours."

"Rubbish. I'm head brides-man don't forget. Plus, I'm the most fashionable person in this room." Lou smothered a grin, because he was probably right. He certainly had a nicer set of manicured nails than she did.

"Yes, we have availability on the last Saturday before Christmas. We can only cater for up to a hundred guests, though." Lou stared at her phone screen and the hotel calendar, which only appeared to have a smattering of bookings leading up to Christmas. That was strange. The hotel was usually fully booked during the Christmas period.

"We won't have anywhere near that number. Unless you've got coachloads of friends travelling up from Cornwall." Adam looked at Mordros for confirmation.

"I'd imagine at most half a dozen friends will make the journey. Cornwall's a long way and most people don't want to travel this time of year when the weather's so unpredictable."

"Shall I reserve the date, then?" Lou smiled at them both. At least she could tell her mum that she'd got them a booking. But why weren't there any others?

"Yes, please." Adam grinned as he took Mordros into his arms. "I can't wait to marry you."

***

Sam took a handful of cashews from the bowl on the coffee table and sat down beside Nick on the sofa. "So, what else is on your list? Wedding venue booked… tick. But what about all the other stuff?"

"I mean, I know there are a few things to organise, but we want a very simple wedding. No jugglers, or trapeze artists, or fire-eaters." Mordros laughed.

"You'll need a photographer, though… and wedding flowers and …"

"The hotel can help with some of these things. You'll also both need to come in and do some food tastings so we can get your menu sorted." Lou began making a list on her phone. "Where are you actually getting married? In church or…"

"No, neither of us are churchgoers. The hotel holds a wedding licence, doesn't it? We'd like to get married there."

"I'll have to check that the registrar is available, but it shouldn't be a problem." Lou added that to her list. "You'll also need to give 29 days' notice that you intend to get married at the hotel, so make an appointment at the register office as soon as you can."

"What about entertainment? Are you having a live band in the evening?" Nick pinched a cashew from Sam's palm.

"Gosh, I hadn't thought of that." Mordros frowned. "I guess we ought to."

"How about one of those barn-dance type things where everyone joins in? I like the idea of shouting out yee-haw as I gallop by," Nick guffawed.

"Hmm, not sure about that," Adam visibly winced. "I'm more a jazz man myself."

"And you'll need to send out invitations pronto, though email would be quicker because you don't have a lot of time." Sam swiped Nick's hand away as he stole another cashew. "And a gift list. Otherwise, you'll end up with ten toasters or, even worse, ten irons."

"My brain hurts." Mordros groaned. "Let's eat dinner and come back to this later when I've had some prosecco."

"I'll just check the lasagne is ready." Adam got up and began walking towards the kitchen just as there was a loud knock on the front door. "That better be my missing best man," Adam quipped before re-routing to the hallway.

Lou smiled to herself. Mordros and Adam's excitement was rubbing off on Sam and Nick, and she half listened as they began bickering over more and more outlandish ideas for wedding entertainment as they tried to outdo each other. An adult bouncy castle… was that really a thing? Well, possibly, but not in the middle of December. And what about singing waiters, a casino or even a glitter bar?

It wasn't as though she didn't have wedding planning experience, but she'd need to up her game if the hotel wanted to attract more wedding bookings. She'd research some of their more reasonable suggestions.

There was still no sign of Adam and his best man, and Mordros had disappeared into the hallway, too. She sent a quick message to her mum to check on Annie. It was silly to worry, but she couldn't help it. She waited impatiently for a reply, refreshing the screen as each minute passed. Her mum was probably busy making a cup of tea, or Annie was indeed wide awake and, if that was the case, she definitely wouldn't be monitoring her phone.

The door to the sitting room swung open and suddenly all her concerns about Annie flew out of her mind as a tall, chestnut-haired man came into the room and for the first time in nearly three years, Lou came face to face with Annie's father.

Chapter 4 - Jack

"What the hell have you done to your hair?" Jack's eyes bored into Lou.

Adam, who had followed him into the sitting room, frowned, his eyes darting between them in confusion. "Do you two know each other?"

He ignored him and began pointing as if he couldn't believe that Lou's once long, fair hair was now cut in a short pixie style. "You've cut it."

"Jack!" Adam bellowed and pushed hard on his arm. "What on earth's got into you?"

They were all standing now, and Jack found himself surrounded by a testosterone wall of men - Adam, Sam and Nick - who were all giving him murderous looks. He felt his face warm, and then Adam began hustling him out of the room and into the privacy of the kitchen.

"What do you think you're doing? You can't come bulldozing in here and start insulting our guest. Have you been drinking or something?" Adam glared.

Jack blew out a steadying breath, trying to slow down his heart rate because he was probably going to have a heart attack if he didn't. Was it shock or anger at seeing Lou again … or both? At this precise moment, he couldn't tell. "No, of course not. But why is she here?" he gritted out.

"Well, give me a chance and I'll tell you. But if you can't act civilly, then you need to leave." Adam eyeballed him.

"Are you serious?" He stared back, but then all the fire inside him died just as suddenly as it had ignited. He took a step back, letting his shoulders slump. "Sorry."

"You should be. Now what's going on?"

"It's a long story, and not for tonight."

Jack sat on one of the kitchen stools and dropped his forehead to the granite counter, feeling the coolness against his heated skin. His emotions were all over the place, and maybe Adam was right, and he should leave. "Look, it was a shock seeing her, that's all, but maybe I should go. I don't want to ruin your evening."

"Or you could stay and just deal with whatever *this* is." Adam finally sat next to his best friend and gave him a gentle nudge. "Lou is our friend, and Mordros has asked her to be her bridesmaid."

"Are you okay?" Mordros walked in and squeezed his shoulder gently. "That was a grand entrance, Jack. It certainly woke us all up."

He had the good grace to look embarrassed, but then Lou was there too and, short hair or not, she was still stunningly beautiful and all his memories of the two of them together flooded back and with them, his anger. "I wasn't expecting to see you," he grunted.

"Well, that's plainly obvious, but here I am anyway, and with short hair, too." He wondered if she was trying to be funny, but then she glared at him. "I couldn't give a flying fig if you approve of my haircut, but I'd appreciate it if you'd keep your thoughts to yourself."

"If you want to talk privately, you can use my study." Adam's eyes flicked between them, but Lou shook her head.

"I should go."

"Yeah, you should," Jack barked, his eyes locking with hers. They were the colour of pale lilac and were glistening. Were those tears? But she was already turning away from him and moving towards the hallway. Hell, he couldn't let her leave like this. Not if she was upset.

He followed her out into the hallway as she was shrugging on her coat. "I didn't mean it."

"You said it."

"I know, and I'm sorry."

There was a long awkward silence, and he could hear the others talking softly in the kitchen. They were probably wondering what on earth was going on because he'd ruined their dinner party. "Please stay. If anyone leaves, it should be me." He watched the nervous lip-biting she always did when she was unsure, so he repeated, "Please stay."

She nodded slowly, and he helped her out of her coat again, his fingers briefly brushing against her arm. Even though she had a long-sleeved blouse on, he could feel her warm skin beneath the silk material and smell her familiar perfume. He had to stop himself from inhaling.

"You don't need to leave either." She almost smiled, and he smiled back, almost dizzy with desire for her, which was absurd because they hadn't seen each other for nearly three years.

They were still in the hallway facing each other, and he wondered what she was thinking, because his own thoughts were a jumbled mess. On the last night they'd been together, she'd been happy. He was sure of it. But then something had happened, and he still didn't have the slightest idea what it was. But the next morning, she'd ended their relationship with a blunt text.

She was speaking softly, and he dragged his mind back to what she was saying.

"We should talk."

"Agreed, but later." His voice was too gruff, but it hadn't wobbled, and he was thankful for that. He pushed his hand through his hair, conscious it was probably now sticking up every which way, but that was the least of his problems. "Come on," he jerked his head towards the kitchen, "let's get this dinner party started."

***

They were all in the kitchen now, and his cheeks were on fire as everyone focused their attention on him. "Please sit at the table, anywhere you like, and I'll bring the food in," Adam instructed as he took a large dish of lasagne out of the oven and began serving it onto plates.

They all filed into the dining room and began taking their places. Sam and Nick placed themselves on either side of Lou at one end, like a protective sandwich, and as far away from him as possible. Well, he couldn't blame them. He hadn't been exactly polite, but jealousy flared that he wasn't sitting next to her. He told himself it was simply because he wanted to apologise to her again, but who was he kidding?

There were a hundred questions in his head. *When had she met Mordros and Adam… and why hadn't he known? What was she doing in Broadsham? Hell, what had she been doing since they'd split up? Was she still single? Unlikely, he imagined. But above all… why had she left him without an explanation?*

But then Nick was beside him, pouring prosecco into his glass, and Mordros placed a plate of food in front of him. So, for now, there wasn't time to add any more questions to his list.

"Help yourself to salad and garlic bread." Mordros smiled, but Jack had lost his appetite, and it seemed also his ability to talk as everyone else tried to make polite conversation. He watched Lou check her phone, and he wondered if it was her boyfriend messaging her. There was no way she'd still be single after all this time. A heavy weight settled in his stomach, and he reached for his glass of prosecco and gulped it down. The bubbles caught in his throat, making him cough. He hated the stuff. It was far too sweet for his taste.

He got up and went back to the kitchen, taking two bottles of beer out of the fridge. "Mind if I have a beer?"

"Course not. Are you okay?" Adam clinked his bottle against Jack's and then began covering up the leftover lasagne.

No, he wasn't okay, but now wasn't the time for a heart to heart, so instead he nodded. "Look, I know I made a fool of myself earlier, but I want to make your wedding day the best."

Adam grinned. "Yeah, well, I'm counting on you for that, especially if Elizabeth turns up. Heaven help us all."

Jack chuckled. Adam's relationship with his mother was strained at best, and they barely saw each other. "Is she invited?"

He shrugged. "I've told Mordros it's up to her. I guess I can cope with her for one day."

"Isn't she living in the south of France or somewhere? Will she even want to come?"

"I don't know, but let's hope not." Adam grumbled before leading him back into the dining room.

Chapter 5 - Lou

Jack's hair was shorter than she remembered, too, though still the same dark chestnut with highlights of red when the sun caught it. He was an attractive man, tall, with a smattering of freckles on his nose and cheeks. But it was his eyes that had always captivated her the most. Pale green and sparkling with laughter and mischief. Well, except for earlier, when they'd been angry like black jade.

Tonight had at least answered one question. Jack was Adam's business partner and soon to be best man, which meant it would be impossible to avoid one another if they wanted to make the wedding the success it deserved to be. That thought excited and terrified her.

She spied Jack surreptitiously. He'd recovered from his initial shock at seeing her, and was joking with Adam, making him laugh. Her stomach flipped because she couldn't remember the last time she'd properly laughed. Not since they'd been together, anyway.

Jack was easy-going and confident in his own skin, something she'd loved about him from the first night they'd met, and he'd rescued her from the clutches of Barret

Fortesque. Even though he was sitting as far away as it was possible to get, she still felt a fizzing electricity between them - a connection that drew her to him like a moth to a flame. And Annie was a mini version of him: the identical hair colour and the same shaped nose and freckles. She was developing his cheekiness, too. There was no mistaking Jack was her father.

Guilt bubbled to the surface that she'd kept Annie a secret from him, but maybe tonight the gods were telling her it was time to tell him. She squashed the thought down because what on earth would she say and, more importantly, what on earth would Jack say?

***

"I've collected lots of dirt on you over the years, so my best man's speech will be epic."

"I can't wait. Give us some tasters, Jack." Mordros grinned at the same time Adam groaned.

"Like the time we were living in New York. After a long day, Adam finished work and decided he deserved a drink at a sports bar he'd spotted - you know, the sort of place – big screens, plenty of atmosphere and exactly the energy he was looking for.

"So, he goes in, orders a beer, and sits down to watch the game. He notices it's unusually friendly – people are chatting with him, complimenting his suit and being way nicer than any other bar he's ever been to. But New Yorkers can be nice, right?

"It wasn't until about an hour later – after several men had bought him drinks, another wanted his phone number and someone else asked him which team he played for - that he finally put two and two together. He wasn't at any sports bar. He was in a gay sports bar. But being Adam, when he finally figured it out, he didn't leave. Nope, he stayed right where he was. By the time I arrived, he was cheering for the Yankees with his new best friends."

"You're quite attractive in a buttoned-up lawyer kind of way." Nick ran a perfectly manicured nail across his lips, contemplating. "I mean, if I weren't happily married to Sam, I might be interested."

"Nick," Sam and Mordros chimed together, and Nick wiggled his eyebrows to show he was only joking.

Lou zoned out. She'd forced down most of her lasagne, and now they were eating dessert. Well, more accurately, she was pushing her chocolate mousse around her dish. She checked her phone for the twentieth time. Why wasn't her mum answering?

"If everyone's finished, let's go into the sitting room," Mordros said, still chuckling. Relieved, Lou put her spoon down and got up from the table.

Suddenly, she and Jack were the only ones in the room. How had that happened?

"I… um…" Lou looked around wildly, trying to see where everyone was.

"I think they've left us alone so we can talk," Jack answered as if he'd somehow read her mind.

Lou's phone buzzed, breaking the awkwardness.

Sylvie: Darling, I'm really sorry, but I can't get Annie to settle.

Lou: Okay, mum I'm on my way.

She walked straight past Jack, ignoring the questioning look on his face.

Chapter 6 - Jack

Well, that was rude, but from the concerned look on Lou's face, the message hadn't been a good one. Still, it had nothing to do with him.

He was alone now, though he could hear muffled conversation coming from the sitting room. He supposed he should join them, but it had been a lot seeing Lou, and he wasn't sure he could face an evening of wedding planning, at least not until he'd had time to process everything that had happened and get his emotions under control.

A minute later, Adam appeared in the doorway. "Lou's going home. Can you walk her back?"

"What? Why? Is this your way of getting us to talk?"

"No, of course not. But she shouldn't walk back alone in the dark."

"Why can't Nick or Sam do it? They live in Broadsham, don't they?"

"They do, but Nick's deep in wedding planning. Please, Jack."

"I suppose so," he grunted and followed Adam out into the hallway, shrugging on his jacket.

"Be nice to her."

"Of course, I'll be nice."

"I mean it, Jack."

"I'm always nice."

"And then tomorrow you can tell me what this thing is between you both."

He was about to argue, but Lou had joined them. "I'm so sorry, Adam."

"No problem at all. Hope everything's okay when you get home."

"I'm sure it will be, and thanks for the lovely meal." Lou began buttoning up her coat as Mordros joined them in the hallway.

"Call me tomorrow?" She gave Lou an affectionate hug, and then Adam did the same.

"Of course."

Adam opened the front door, and Lou walked down the steps onto the street. She looked back over her shoulder to see Jack following her. "What are you doing?"

"I'm walking you home."

"I don't need you to walk me home." She glared at him.

"Well, I'm not happy about it either, but Adam didn't want you walking back alone."

"But…"

"Look, I don't want to argue, so let's get going so you can deal with whatever it is you need to."

"This is ridiculous," Lou huffed, but her eyes were glistening in the glow from the streetlamp, and he watched her swallow. Great, he'd upset her again. He stuck his hands in his pockets, and they walked along the pavement in awkward silence.

The night air was frosty, and the atmosphere even more so, but it wasn't long until they reached the front of the

Broadsham Arms Hotel. Then Jack remembered her mum owned the hotel, which at least explained why she'd come back to Broadsham.

"You can leave me here." Lou broke the silence and made eye contact for the first time since they'd left Adam's house.

"I said I'd walk you home, so that's what I'll do. Presumably you don't live in the hotel?"

"Really? You're treating me like I'm five years old."

"Well, if you behave like a five-year-old…"

"Aargh, you're insufferable." Lou turned into a narrow cobbled alleyway at the side of the hotel, and he followed. It led into a small courtyard, and he could see lights in what he imagined was a flat in the facing building.

Lou stopped and turned to him. "Look, I appreciate you walking me back, but I'm fine now. See, this is my flat." She pointed to the front door opposite them.

"Well, goodnight then." Jack hesitated. "I hope everything's okay."

She gave a quick nod and inserted her key into the lock. He watched as the door opened and then he could hear… was that crying? But she'd already slipped inside.

It wasn't any of his business, but he stayed where he was, listening. There were no more sounds coming from inside, and he could hardly knock and demand to come in to check out the source of the crying.

Sighing, he turned and made his way back along the alleyway onto the high street. The shops were all closed, the chilly night air discouraging anyone from lingering outside. Two women were tottering along in strappy high heels and figure-hugging glittery dresses, obviously on their way to a party. *How on earth did they walk in those things, and why weren't they wearing coats?* His sister had been the same when she was younger. She never seemed to feel the cold or admit to it at least. The thought of Clemmie made him smile. She'd be at the wedding, and he couldn't wait to see her.

He walked purposefully towards Adam's house, his thoughts drifting back to Lou. Seeing her again had been a shock, and now he could add yet another question to his growing list.

Why was there a baby crying in her flat?

Chapter 7 - Lou

Annie was finally asleep, dosed up on Calpol, and Lou lay in bed, replaying the night's events. Jack had looked sinfully delicious in dark jeans and a black jumper, the sleeves rolled up so she could see the scattering of light freckles on his forearms. She knew what lay underneath the jumper too. She let out a deep sigh. He was every bit as attractive as she remembered.

Whatever she'd imagined his reaction would be to seeing her again was nothing compared to the resentment vibrating off him. Admittedly, she'd ended their relationship, but it wouldn't have been difficult for him to work out why. After what he'd done, she was the one whose resentment was justified, not him. Or maybe he was bitter because she was part of the wedding party. To be fair, it was going to be awkward, but neither of them could back out now. So, for the sake of the wedding, they'd just have to put their differences aside.

Then he'd pulled the short straw and walked her home and, if anything, his resentment had intensified. There was none of the fun, jokey Jack she remembered. They'd walked in stony silence, neither of them speaking until she'd told him to leave her outside the hotel. But, typical of him, he'd refused because he wanted to keep her safe. He'd always looked after her - always been reliable and trustworthy … until he hadn't. And to add insult to terrible injury, tonight he'd acted like the wronged party, as if he'd been entirely innocent and not the one responsible for their breakup.

When they'd finally reached her flat, and she'd opened the front door, Annie had been bawling as only a toddler can. Those baby teeth were really giving her trouble. She'd shut the front door quickly, but Jack wasn't an idiot, and he'd probably have questions. *Lots and lots of questions.*

She squeezed her eyes shut. What on earth was going to happen now?

***

Annie slept until seven the next morning. It was unusual, and Lou savoured her first cup of tea in peace until her daughter hollered from her nursery, letting everyone in Broadsham, and probably the surrounding villages, know she was awake.

It was frosty outside, but winter sunshine poured in from the window, bathing the kitchen in gentle warmth. Annie sat on a cushion on a kitchen chair, enjoying her eggy soldier breakfast, and she watched her daughter trying to feed herself. Some toast landed in her bib catcher, but she carefully retrieved it and re-directed it back to her mouth.

The pile of Christmas cards still lay untouched on the table, but it wasn't one of Annie's nursery days, so there would be no time to write them today. The Christmas market was on in the village this morning. Stalls full of artisan gifts: jewellery, candles, local gin and beer, cake bakes and cheeses. Mordros also had a stall selling her handmade baby knits and soft toys. The weather was bright, so they could wander around the market for a bit and end up at the church, where there was a Christmas tree festival taking place.

Annie finished her breakfast, and Lou quickly wiped her sticky hands and face and lifted her down, leaving her to play with the toys she'd laid out for her earlier. A knitted black cat with pink paws was her latest favourite, and she liked to take it everywhere. Good job it was black, considering the love, aka dribble, it got on it, thought Lou wryly.

She began clearing away their breakfast things as her thoughts returned to Jack… the surprise of seeing him again and how gorgeous and funny he still was. Then, just before she'd gone inside the flat, his eyes had searched hers as if she was a mystery to be solved, even though he'd been the one who'd kept secrets from her and who hadn't been honest in their relationship. And there went her emotions running wild again because she was still so attracted to him. Despite everything, she still wanted him, which was ridiculous, when he'd broken her heart before.

Annie was chattering away to the soft black cat, swinging him around by one of his pink paws, as her thoughts came to a juddering stop.

What if they bumped into Jack while they were out? Whatever the status of their relationship, she needed to tell him about Annie, and soon.

Chapter 8 - Jack

This was the second time in a week Adam had bought him a posh coffee from the deli across the road. Jack mumbled his thanks as Adam sat down in the chair opposite his desk and studied his face, taking in the stubble peppering his jaw and dark shadows under his eyes.

"What are you doing here on a Sunday?"

"I just thought I'd check in with you and make sure you're all right."

"I'm fine, but how did you know I'd be here?"

"You always work when you're upset."

"I'm not upset," but when Adam gave him a hard stare, he conceded: "I needed to catch up with some paperwork, that's all."

"Sooo…" Adam dragged out the vowel and took a sip of his fancy coffee. "What was last night all about?"

Where did he start? He hadn't told Adam about Lou other than he'd dated someone in London. "It's complicated." He let out a heavy breath, trying to think of what else to say. *I loved Lou, and I don't think I'll ever get over losing her.* But what was the point in saying that, because Lou was history. She'd made that crystal clear, so he needed to get a grip. "We dated for a while and then things went tits up," was the best he could come up with.

"So why were you so affected by seeing her again? You've got an enormous backlist of exes, and you never care if you bump into any of them. What about whatshername Molly or Milly?"

"Mimi."

"Yeah, Mimi. And then there was that dizzy blonde with the big—"

"Yep, I know who you mean."

"And potty-mouthed Penny."

"She was a bit." He grinned.

"Or Lexi with the lip fillers that made her pout like a fish."

"Okay, okay, you've made your point."

But Adam was on a roll. "Oh God, remember posh Polly. I thought she'd be the one to get you down the aisle."

Jack grimaced. "She was keen."

"Sooo…" Adam repeated, his eyes on Jack. "What makes Lou different?"

"I don't know. She just is."

It was tempting to share that Lou was the love of his life, and he didn't know how his heart kept beating after the enormous hole she'd left…but Adam had enough of his own problems with his awful mother coming to the wedding. So instead, he said, "It was just a shock seeing her last night, but I'm good." It was a lie, and by the sceptical look Adam was giving him, he knew it was a lie, too.

"Is Lou being a bridesmaid going to be a problem for you, because I don't want any atmosphere between you on our wedding day?"

"There won't be. I mean, not from my side, anyway." And there was the second lie out of his mouth, because if she turned up with a plus one, he couldn't guarantee his behaviour. Not that he'd ever been the jealous type, but there was always a first time.

"Did you talk last night when you walked her home?"

"No." He'd been too busy being a grump, and then there was the whole crying baby business which had distracted him, too. "You're right, though. We need to clear the air," he finally acknowledged. "I'll go to see her and make things right."

"Good, because you're our two favourite people, and we want you both to be friends."

Friends? Could he ever be just friends with Lou?

***

A couple of hours later, Jack turned off his laptop and locked up his office. Ignoring the lift, he took the stairs two at a time and headed for the carpark. It was early afternoon, and he debated what to do for the rest of the day. On the one hand, he could drive home, work out his frustrations in the gym, watch some TV, order a takeaway for dinner and drink a few beers. It was tempting, but…

He'd promised Adam he'd talk to Lou, and there wasn't any point in putting it off. Except Lou had blocked him on her phone and social media so he couldn't message to arrange a friendly meetup.

Would it be friendly, though? He doubted it. But they needed to talk and get this *thing* between them out in the open. He still didn't know why she'd left, but if they were going to make the wedding a success, then they had to sort it out. It was the civilised thing to do.

Yeah — friendly, civilised — whatever you wanted to label it, but they needed to get through the wedding and move on.

Decision made, he switched on the car engine and headed off towards Broadsham. Lou probably wouldn't like it when he turned up unannounced, but then again, she didn't like him much anyway, so there wasn't a lot to lose.

Chapter 9 - Lou

A rich mixture of scents filled the air as Lou pushed Annie around the Christmas market in her stroller. Orange, cinnamon and cloves from a stall selling mulled wine, smoke from roasting chestnuts, sweet hot chocolate, and the unmistakable festive smell of warm mince pies. There were other temptations too: freshly baked bread wafting from the bakery and fried bacon from the open door of the café.

The Christmas market was popular, locals and visitors alike shopping or simply browsing and enjoying being outdoors on a crisp winter morning under a perfect blue sky. Lou bought a couple of scented candles as gifts for Annie's nursery workers and then spotted Mordros behind her stall. She had a colourful display of knitted gifts and a queue of customers. She waved as she strolled by.

Next to the Christmas tree on the village green, a silver band played carols and Christmas songs, and Lou sat down on a bench to listen. Jingle Bells, We Wish You a Merry Christmas, Frosty the Snowman and Away in a Manger. Annie didn't know the words, but she didn't let that stop her from singing along in her own inimitable way. Lou's mood lightened. This was what Christmas was all about, and it was good to forget her problems, if only for a little while.

When the brass band took a well-earned break, Annie began fidgeting, wanting to get out of her pushchair. Time to go. Lou made her way briskly towards the church at the end of the village. The Christmas Tree Festival was a charity event, and this year there were seventy trees, each decorated and sponsored by local businesses, community organisations and schools. Even Annie's nursery had taken part, each child decorating a baby sock to their own creative design. Lou was eager to see Annie's attempt.

It wasn't difficult to find The Little Poppins' Christmas tree amongst the other more professionally dressed ones, and there was Annie's sock, covered in red and gold glitter, though what it was supposed to represent, Lou wasn't sure. She stifled a laugh as Annie spotted it too and shouted, "Mine, Mama."

"Yes, darling, it's gorgeous, just like you." Lou bent to give Annie a kiss on her nose and her daughter beamed.

After that, Annie quickly lost interest in the rest of the Christmas trees, so Lou made her way to the café, spotting her friend Julie behind the counter.

"Hello, my lovelies," Julie grinned as Annie's eyes widened at the selection of homemade bakes on the counter. If there was one thing Annie loved, it was cake.

"Which one would you like?" Lou waited as Annie dithered. There was so much choice, and it was a hard decision, but there was a small queue forming, so she tried to hurry her daughter up. "How about the one with the Father Christmas on top?" Annie shook her head. "Or the snowman?" Annie scrunched up her nose. "Then it had better be Rudolph the red-nosed reindeer." Lou was prepared to select for her when Annie firmly nodded her approval.

"Rudolph."

"And what else do you say?" Lou gave her daughter a stern look.

"Peas."

"Good girl." Lou chose her own cake and a sandwich for them to share, and ordered their drinks, which Julie quickly prepared. They'd become friends back in the summer, but there wasn't any time to catch up properly as the queue was getting bigger.

Lou paid and found a vacant table; half an hour later, they were ready to leave. Annie was becoming tired and fractious and would probably nap on the way home. Lou sighed. She should call at the hotel to tell her mum about Mordros and Adam's wedding booking, but an overtired toddler wasn't on anyone's list of welcome visitors. She'd already entered the date on the online booking system, but there was also the mystery of why the hotel didn't have more reservations leading up to Christmas to discuss. Never mind, it would have to wait until tomorrow.

The afternoon had turned colder, and the winter sunshine had vanished, leaving ominous dark clouds. They just made it home as the first snowflakes began falling. Lou shivered as she opened the flat door. The boiler was old and temperamental. Please don't play up now, she silently begged.

Annie was still awake but sucking her thumb, a sure sign she was ready to nap. Lou lifted her into her cot-bed and covered her in a pale lemon knitted blanket Mordros had given her.

"Do you want some warm milk?" But Annie's eyelids had already fluttered closed.

Chapter 10 - Jack

Jack faced the door to Lou's flat and cursed under his breath. Snow flurries whipped around the small cobbled courtyard, and he pulled his jacket tighter around his chest. The day had turned from winter sunshine to a winter wonderland as a covering of snow began settling everywhere.

His plan to drop-in on Lou had felt like a good idea half an hour ago when he'd set off, but now he wasn't so sure. Yeah, they needed to talk, but what if her boyfriend was there? Plus, she'd left Adam's dinner party abruptly because of some sort of emergency, so who knew what she was dealing with. He frowned. Chances were, she'd shut the door in his face.

Still, he was here now so, taking a deep breath, he knocked on the flat door and waited. A moment later, it opened and there was Lou, staring at him as if he was the last person she expected to see, which was probably true. He wasn't exactly on her friends list anymore.

She was in a pair of faded jeans, a smiley Santa jumper and a pair of fluffy slippers. She looked beautiful, and now that he'd got over the shock of her new short hair, he realised it was a perfect frame for her elfin face and enormous violet eyes.

"Hi, I wondered if we could talk?"

Lou seemed frozen to the spot, which was ironic because he was going to freeze to death if he didn't get out of the cold. "I would have phoned, but you've blocked me. But if you don't want to talk now, can we at least make a date for when we can? Actually, I don't mean a date …" He trailed off because he didn't want her to misunderstand his motives. "I just mean, can we arrange a time to sort things out?" He waited, but when she didn't answer, he tried again. "Please Lou. It's like the bloody Arctic out here."

Finally, she nodded and opened the door wider for him to go in. He followed her into a small hallway, which led into an open-plan kitchen/living room. The kitchen was out of a 1970s time capsule - burnt orange cabinets, bold geometric tiles and brown linoleum flooring. Fans of retro design would love it, but he knew Lou wasn't one of them.

His eyes drifted around the rest of the tired room. A small Christmas tree stood in the corner, and cut-out snowmen and Santas hung from the kitchen cupboards. Someone had decorated them using wax crayons and didn't seem to have much idea what they were doing. Stuck to the window were cut-out snowflakes, and draped above them was a red and green garland.

He noticed other things too – a small kitchen table, a worn sofa and a storage basket full of toys. A couple of throws lay folded on the sofa, and on the wall were two watercolours of the London skyline he remembered from her London flat. Her new place wasn't a patch on her old one. Why the hell was she living here? He took a breath, trying to tamp down his frustration.

"Would you like coffee, tea or some hot chocolate?" Lou took two mugs from a cupboard as he pulled out one of the plastic kitchen chairs and sat down.

"A coffee would be great. I'm frozen." He suddenly realised how cold the room was. His chest tightened… maybe she couldn't afford to put the heating on, or it wasn't working. And why did that annoy him so much? His eyes drifted back to the toy basket. Well, that explained the crying he'd heard the other night. "You should get the heating fixed if you have a child living here," he grunted.

She turned, giving him a perfect eye roll, followed by a 'mind your own business' glare. She was right. It was nothing to do with him, so he surprised himself by offering, "I can have a look at the boiler if you like? I mean, I'm no handyman, but I can try to figure it out." Instantly, a grateful smile replaced her glare, and she nodded.

The boiler was in a cupboard in the bathroom, and he had another flashback to the seventies when he saw the pink 'chicken' tiles on the walls and avocado green bathroom suite. His parents had installed a similar one when they'd been in vogue and then ripped it out a few years later. Why was she living in this flat, which was stuck in a seventies time warp?

He ignored the awful colour scheme and concentrated on his task. Twenty minutes later, the flat began warming up. Admittedly, it had been a bit of a bodge job, but at least it was working now. Once they were back in the kitchen, Lou finally handed him a mug of coffee while she added mini marshmallows to her own hot chocolate. He had a sudden memory of their first date *(was it a date?)* when she'd ordered a hot chocolate at the café the night they'd met.

"You still have a sweet tooth then?"

She nodded, her cheeks becoming a soft pink. "I read somewhere that eating chocolate every day is actually good for you." When he raised an eyebrow, she went on, "Okay, that might be a slight exaggeration, but I'm sure the feel-good factor is a benefit."

"Maybe." Jack chuckled.

"What about you – do you still like superhero movies?"

"Of course. Action, good triumphing over evil, escapism – what's not to like? Though I'm guessing you still prefer romantic comedies?"

"Oh God, remember the time we went to the cinema in Leicester Square to watch that romantic film I'd been dying to see? It had a terribly sad ending, and I sobbed all the way home on the Tube. Everyone we passed thought you'd done something awful to upset me."

"Don't remind me," Jack groaned, but he smiled at the memory of all the angry looks he'd got from passengers on the train.

When they'd arrived back at his flat, he'd kissed away her tears and then taken her to bed and made slow, gentle love to her. Afterwards, he'd held her in his arms, and she'd curled into his chest like a koala bear, and they'd talked quietly about their future.

"I want to make London my home. Be here with you. Maybe find a place to live together. Make love to you every night…"

He could feel Lou's smile on his skin. Then she'd raised her head, her violet eyes holding his. They were full of hope and love. He could see the joy in them.

"I want that too." Her lips brushed his in a gentle kiss… then not so gently as she began moving on top of him.

That night, he'd also realised he was in love with her. And that he didn't care if they only ever watched cheesy romantic films and not superhero ones.

Another memory floated into his mind. He used to love making romantic dinners and planning date nights for the two of them. Things that weren't out at a fancy restaurant or a bar. "Do you remember the time I made you a curry?"

Her face had got redder and redder as she'd valiantly tried to eat the fiery food. Until he'd finally realised and given her a glass of milk and told her he was ordering them a pizza instead.

"I can't handle anything spicy." She giggled, and he could only watch transfixed. She was so beautiful, and despite everything, he knew he was still in love with her. Sadness, a vice-like grip around his chest, made him almost wince with pain. *Why did you leave me? Why did you break my heart?*

He supposed now was the time to have the talk they needed to have. After all, that was the reason he was here. But he could feel the chemistry between them and the connection they'd always had, and suddenly the past and the reason for their split didn't matter. He just wanted to carry on chatting in this cramped seventies throwback flat and make her laugh with their trip down memory lane. Lou's warm eyes captured his, and maybe she was feeling the same. Yeah, their talk could wait, so instead, he asked, "How long have you known Adam and Mordros?"

"Since last summer. I helped Mordros organise her aunt's seventieth birthday party at the hotel."

"I see." Jack took a sip of his drink and considered this new information. He wondered why Adam hadn't ever mentioned Lou, but then he didn't know about Jack's history with her, so why would he?

"Small world, isn't it? I mean, out of all the lawyers in the area, who would have thought Adam would be your business partner?"

"Yeah," he shrugged, his eyes landing on the toy box again. There was a well-loved knitted black cat with pink paws lying on top, and this time he did wince, as he realised Lou had a whole new life now. A life she'd made without him. How had they gone from being so happy to this? "I see you've moved on… which is great because I have, too," he grunted.

Instantly, the amicable atmosphere disappeared, and she was back to glaring at him. He wanted to take the words back, but a demanding child's voice was coming from another room.

"Mama, me awake."

Lou gave him a pleading look. "I know we've got to talk, and we will, but would you mind if we did it another time? Actually, I think you should leave now." She reached for her phone. "I'll unblock you so we can message each other."

He nodded and gritted out: "Sure, you've obviously got more pressing things to do. I'll see myself out."

***

The snow was falling more heavily now, but he ignored it as he stood in the small courtyard staring at Lou's closed front door.

He shouldn't have lied and said he'd moved on because it was the furthest thing from the truth. But the last thing he wanted was for her to think he'd been pining for her when she'd clearly got over him so easily.

He'd followed her out into the hallway, and she'd disappeared into what was presumably her child's bedroom.

She'd left the door slightly ajar, and he'd stood for a moment and blatantly listened.

"Hey munchkin, are you ready for some milk now?"

Fuck. Lou had a child. His mind whirred… how had she met someone else so quickly and forgotten all that they'd meant to each other? Maybe the child had been unplanned, or maybe it was one of those whirlwind relationships – like the romance films Lou loved watching - and they were so in love with each other that the child was very much planned.

But then, where was her partner? They'd been no sign of him in the flat. No man's coat hanging up or shoes left in the hallway. No smell of a man's aftershave or cologne. There weren't any photos either. Of course, he hadn't seen the rest of the flat, but still.

Something didn't feel right.

He was tempted to bang on the front door again and demand an explanation. But whatever his feelings, there was a child to consider now, and that thought was like a knife cutting through his heart.

Chapter 11 - Lou

"Why are there so few bookings in the lead-up to Christmas?" Lou peered at the hotel's booking screen and then at her mum.

"We've had a few maintenance problems, which has meant some bedrooms aren't usable." Sylvie shifted in her seat.

"What sort of maintenance problems?"

"The roof needs fixing in a couple of places. The gutters too. There's damp coming through the ceiling in several rooms, so they can't be occupied. But it's all easily sorted."

"And what about the staffing issues?"

"I told you about Patrick not turning up. Apparently, he's got another job. It would have been nice if he'd worked his notice, but there we are." Sylvie sighed.

"Have you advertised for someone to replace him?"

"To be honest, I don't think I can afford to with all the other maintenance bills."

"Are things really that bad?" She watched as colour flooded her mum's cheeks.

"It's just everything's come at once. I've got a couple of quotes for the roofing work and … well, it's more expensive than I'd thought, and being a listed building, everything needs to be approved in triplicate."

"Can we manage without a pastry chef, though?"

"It's not ideal, but I think we'll have to." Her mum sighed again.

"Why didn't you tell me sooner? You've been dealing with this all on your own, and I could have helped."

"It's just a blip, and the money from Mordros and Adam's wedding will help a bit. But we won't be able to accommodate our usual number of overnight guests."

"How many rooms are out of action?" They had twenty-six rooms, so having any of them unoccupied was financially serious.

Sylvie gave a helpless shrug. "It's all the bedrooms on the top floor."

She did a quick calculation - there were fourteen rooms on the first floor, which left… "That's twelve rooms."

"Yes," Sylvie said quietly.

"Oh, fur balls." Lou used one of her favourite child-friendly curses even though Annie was at nursery. She'd developed quite a collection of them.

Sylvie opened a buff folder and passed her a quote for the roofing work. "This is the cheapest quote. The other quote is almost half as much again."

"Have we got that sort of money? I know Dad left some, but…" The highlighted figure at the bottom of the quote glared out from the invoice. "That's a mind-boggling amount of money."

"I'll need to look at some finance options with the accountants because there's not just the roof and damp to sort. The rooms affected will have to be refurbished, too."

She studied the quote again. Her mum said the roof needed fixing in a couple of places, but from the detailed estimate, it was a lot more serious than that. And the price… she blew out a breath, trying to get her head around the eye-watering figure. "Okay, Mum, let me know what they come up with."

***

Lou pushed the sample menus across the table for Adam and Mordros to look at. "These are just some suggestions, but nothing's set in stone, and if you have some ideas of your own, we can put them in the mix, too. Once you've made a few choices, we'll organise some tastings."

Hot or cold, meat or fish, vegetarian and vegan… and that was just the canapés options. Dietary and religious requirements were equally important. The last thing you wanted was for any guest to end up in hospital because they'd eaten something they were allergic to.

There was also a broad range to suit all tastes and budgets. Sharing boards with a Mediterranean, Asian or a British theme or a more classic dinner menu. In the summer, there was an alternative BBQ option, but nobody wanted to be outside eating sausages and burgers in bitterly cold December.

Lou's favourite was the sumptuous dessert menu, full of traditional or more modern options. Couples could choose full-sized portions or, if they preferred, a trio of mini ones. The hotel also offered an old-fashioned dessert trolley so guests could help themselves, though since they currently didn't have a pastry chef, it might just be her mum's apple crumble on offer.

Mordros and Adam's eyes began glazing over, and Lou smiled because there was a lot to take in. "I'll leave you in peace. Take your time and highlight the ones you'd like to try."

She ordered them a tray of tea and then went into her mum's small office. She'd check back in twenty minutes in case they had questions, but in her experience, it was best to let couples mull over their menu choices alone.

Every couple was different and often had very specific requests. One bride had asked for traditional fish and chips wrapped up in newspaper, and a groom once requested chicken nuggets. She smiled at the memory. Yep, literally that. Thankfully, the bride persuaded him to add a variety of salads and quiches, so at least the other guests had more choice. It was their special day, so whatever they wanted, she would try her best to accommodate them.

Lou sat at her mum's desk, her mind returning to Jack. He'd reached out to her, wanting to talk and make things right between them. He'd fixed her boiler too, albeit it was a temporary solution. Afterwards, they'd reminisced about the great times they'd had together in London… and they had been great until he'd done something she couldn't forgive. Seeing him again, she'd almost forgotten she was supposed to be angry with him.

Since then, she'd heard nothing from him. She guessed he was waiting for her to contact him since he'd made the first move, and she'd sent him packing when Annie had woken up.

I see you've moved on… which is great because I have, too.

The words still stung, but she could hardly blame him since she'd been the one to leave him. And even if he had moved on, he still had a right to know about Annie.

She found his number on her phone and began typing.

Lou: Hi

Lou: Are you free tonight to chat?

Lou: I could meet you for a drink at the hotel at 8 p.m. L

It was short and to the point, but what else could she say? She added an x and then deleted it.

She stared at her screen, waiting, but there was no reply.

***

Mordros handed Lou their menu choices as Adam rose from his chair. "I'm afraid I have to get back to work, but I'm sure you've got lots of wedding stuff to chat about. I'll see you at home, love." He bent to kiss her and then gave Lou a brief hug before leaving.

"Come on, let's have a proper drink and you can tell me all about Jack." Mordros began walking towards the hotel bar, not waiting to see if Lou was following her.

It was mid-afternoon, and the hotel bar was quiet, except for the muted Christmas music playing in the background. They found a table, and Lou went to the bar to order mulled wine for them both. Cinnamon and orange – the smell of Christmas – made her mouth water.

"Cheers." They clinked glasses, and Lou took a sip of the spiced wine, tasting its sweetness and warmth. "I guess you've already figured out that Jack and I know each other."

She set her glass down and looked at Mordros. "But we haven't seen each other for nearly three years."

"Did you date?" Mordros put her own drink down as her kind eyes held Lou's.

"Yes… yes, we did. For about ten months, actually."

"Do you want to talk about it?"

Did she want to talk about it? She hadn't told a soul what had happened. Not even her mum. But if she and Jack were going to put their differences aside because of the wedding, maybe now was a good time.

"We met in London when Jack was searching for some new office premises." She smiled at the memory. "I guess it was a bit of a whirlwind romance."

Mordros nodded and waited.

"I was in love with him." Her voice was barely above a whisper, but it felt good to say it. To finally admit it.

"What happened?" Mordros squeezed her hand, and that simple act gave her courage to continue.

"I thought Jack was in love with me, too. I really thought he was the one…" Lou's voice broke, and she blinked back tears.

"Oh, sweetheart." Mordros squeezed her hand again.

She let out a breath, steeling herself for what she had to say next. "He cheated on me."

Mordros looked at her aghast. "Jack cheated on you?"

"Yes". Her voice cracked, and a lone tear slid down her cheek, which she wiped away with her thumb.

"Jack? I mean, I know he's got a reputation as a serial dater, but a cheat… are you sure?" Mordros shook her head in disbelief. "Sorry, that was really insensitive of me. Of course, if you say he cheated…" Her words trailed off.

"I have proof."

"What kind of proof?"

"Someone sent me some photos. They were of Jack and another woman taken at the same time we were dating, and a message saying that they thought I should know."

"Are you sure the photos are genuine? I mean, if someone sent them anonymously, then maybe they were trying to stir up trouble."

Lou shook her head. "Whoever it was didn't want to give their identity, but yeah, there's no doubt the photos are real."

Mordros still didn't look convinced. "What did Jack say?"

She pressed her lips together because she hadn't confronted him, or even screamed and shouted at him. She'd just eradicated him from her life.

"Lou?"

She took a shuddering breath. "I didn't tell him. I didn't see the point because he'd have only denied it." The emotion in her voice wrapped around her words.

Mordros gave her a look that spoke volumes, her eyes wide with disbelief. *You didn't give him a chance to explain?* But she'd been through this once before, admittedly not with Jack, but with a previous ex, who'd cheated on her. He'd denied it, and idiot that she was, she'd believed him. At least she had until he'd cheated on her again. "I know Jack's Adam's best friend, and you don't think he's capable of cheating, but he did, and I couldn't get past that."

"I'm so sorry." Mordros looked contrite.

"The thing is…" She stopped. God, this was difficult.

"What is the thing?" Mordros said softly, trying to help her.

"Annie," she whispered, and Mordros nodded.

"Yes, I see that now."

Of course, it was obvious once you connected the dots. *Jack and Annie. Annie and Jack. They were like two peas in a pod.*

"It's all such a mess." She was crying now, and Mordros pushed her chair next to Lou's and put her arm around her.

"It is a bit, lovey. I guess he doesn't know."

"No." She took the tissue Mordros offered her and blew her nose. "I wanted to tell him, but I didn't know how, and the longer I've left it, the harder it's got. Then seeing him at yours the other night…" She trailed off.

"No wonder you were both shocked at seeing each other again."

"I should have told him, and now he's going to hate me for keeping Annie a secret from him."

"Finding out he cheated on you and then about your pregnancy - that's a lot to deal with."

"It's no excuse. Not really. I've been such a coward."

"Do you still have feelings for him?"

There was the million-dollar question, because when they'd been sitting in her grotty flat, and reminiscing, she'd still felt the same aching attraction towards him she always had. *She could so easily fall back in love with him. In some ways, she'd never stopped loving him.* But he'd cheated… and a cheater was always a cheater.

"I can't forgive him for what he did. But then I guess I've done something far worse. I've kept Annie from him, though maybe when I tell him, he won't want anything to do with her."

"I'm sure he will," Mordros said softly.

She was right. Whatever her own relationship with Jack was — and by the sound of it, he'd moved on — of course he'd want to be a father to Annie.

"When are you going to tell him?"

There was a sudden bleep on her phone, and she peered at the message on the screen.

Jack: Yep, 8 works for me.

Jack: I'll see you at the bar. J

"I'm seeing him tonight." Lou's stomach twisted with worry.

Chapter 12 - Jack

"Turn that bloody thing off." Jack glared at Shona, the office receptionist. "We're a serious legal firm, not Tesco."

"It's Christmas." Shona gave him one of her dazzling smiles, which he'd once foolishly fallen for. "It's just a little background music to make the ambiance more relaxing."

Jack ran his fingers through his thick hair, which was a habit he had when things weren't going his way. Even though he was her boss, the reception was Shona's domain, and he knew even before opening his mouth that he was onto a loser. "Well, at least play something more traditional. Baby, It's Cold Outside isn't the vibe we're aiming for."

"Oh, and what vibe is that?" Her seductive voice, which had once enamoured him, now left him wondering what the hell he'd ever seen in her.

He swallowed his annoyance because it wasn't her fault that after a handful of dates, he'd broken up with her. No, he was totally to blame because he'd ignored the number one golden rule… don't dip your pen in the company ink or, in layman's terms, don't date one of your employees.

Afterwards, he'd felt awkward about the whole thing and, privately, hoped she'd leave. But four years later, she was still here and taking every opportunity to make sure he knew what he was missing.

He shrugged. "Just find something more appropriate."

He strode across the reception and took the lift to the top floor, where both his and Adam's offices were. Adam's door was open, and without knocking, he walked in and plonked himself down on the leather chair facing his antique mahogany desk. Along one wall was a bookcase of old legal books - where furnishings were concerned, they were quite different. Adam was a traditionalist, whereas his own office reflected his more contemporary taste.

Adam was reading something on his laptop, his reading glasses perched on his nose, but he looked up as soon as Jack shoved his shoes on his desk. "Get them off now," he growled, but Jack just grinned.

"Can you have a word with Shona? It's not even the middle of November, and she's playing cheesy Christmas music. And she's put up every tacky Christmas decoration she could find. Reception looks like Santa's bloody grotto."

Adam, who knew about Jack's brief fling with Shona, raised one eyebrow. "I quite like it, but if you don't, do your own dirty work. Anyway, where's your Christmas spirit?"

Jack huffed and sat back in his chair, closing his eyes. He knew his grouchy mood had nothing to do with Shona playing Christmas music or putting up decorations too early. After two days of waiting for Lou to message him, she finally had, and he didn't know how he felt about it. On the one hand, he still wanted to know why she'd left him without a word of explanation. But did it matter anymore because she was obviously with someone else now and had a child to boot?

So here he was in Adam's office because they'd always been there for each other. It was a solid friendship going back to when they'd first met at school. If he were going to open up to anyone about Lou, it would be him.

As if sensing his need to talk. Adam got up and went over to his coffee machine and programmed it to make two coffees. "Come on, out with it." He turned to look at Jack.

"I'm seeing Lou tonight." He finally opened his eyes.

"Good. And if you could at least try to be civil to each other in the run-up to the wedding, that would be great." Adam chuckled.

"I guess."

"So, what's got you so wound up?"

"I'm not." He hesitated before adding. "Is Lou with someone?"

"No."

"Are you sure?"

"I could ask her during school break if you like." Adam smirked and then took pity on him. "I'm pretty sure, unless she's met someone in the last couple of weeks, though she'd have told Mordros if she had."

Jack sat up and digested this new information. "Does she have a child?"

He watched as Adam shifted uncomfortably from one foot to the other. "I think that's Lou's information to share."

"I'm not asking for her bank account password," he grumbled.

But, thankfully for Adam, his intercom buzzed, announcing his next client's arrival and saving him from further interrogation.

***

At five o'clock, Jack drove back to his apartment, spent an hour doing his usual workout in the basement gym, then showered and changed. At seven forty-five, he was in the bar at the Broadsham Arms Hotel, drinking a well-earned beer, waiting for Lou to arrive. He imagined how the evening might play out. Maybe they'd order some bar food and reminisce some more. At the very least, he wanted to know about the child she appeared to have living in her flat.

Three quarters of an hour later, and Lou was a no-show. Fine, if that was how she wanted to play it. He tapped out an irate message.

Jack: You could have told me you weren't coming. Guess I'm not worth an explanation… same as London! J

By now, he was starving, so he ordered a sandwich and wolfed it down. Twenty minutes later, he settled his bar tab and headed back out to his car. Snow had settled a couple of days before, and it glinted like diamonds in the glow of the streetlights. He stood for a moment, staring.

Bugger it.

He walked down the side alleyway to the courtyard where Lou's flat was. The lights were on, so she was clearly at home. He huffed out a breath of frustration, which turned to fog in the frosty night air. She didn't have far to come to meet him at the hotel. It was just across the courtyard.

He rapped on her flat door and waited.

***

The last thing he expected when the door opened was to see Lou in floods of tears. "I'm sorry, but I'm a little busy right now." She looked up at him and then began closing the door, but he shot out his foot.

"Lou, whatever's happened, let me help."

She began shaking her head, but then seemed to change her mind. "It's Annie. She's bumped her head, and I don't know what to do."

"Okay, let me have a look." He followed her into the kitchen and saw a small child sitting on the sofa sucking her thumb.

"Annie, this is Jack."

He smiled at the girl, whose enormous green eyes were watching him. "Hello, I'm a … um… friend of your mum's." He could see a lump the size of a small egg on the side of her forehead. It was red and livid.

"I don't know what happened. One minute she was sitting at the table, and the next she was on the floor screaming." Lou was trying hard to hold in her tears, and he reached for her hand and squeezed it. "I tried putting a cold compress on it. Well, it was a bag of frozen peas wrapped in a cloth, but Annie just screamed."

"She needs a proper child seat." He realised he wasn't being very tactful, especially as Lou was already upset, so he quickly added. "Let's try again with the cold compress."

She nodded and went to the freezer to retrieve the bag of peas before wrapping it in a tea towel.

"No, Mama, cold. No, no," yelled Annie as she batted the tea towel away, and Lou looked at Jack helplessly.

"Okay, Annie. How about I do it first and then you have a go?" Jack took the cold compress and placed it on his own forehead, and she watched as he attempted to make a funny face, scrunching up his nose and then sticking his tongue out. Annie giggled.

"Has she been sick?"

"No. No, she hasn't."

"Okay, Mama's turn now." He handed the compress to Lou, and Annie watched as she put it on her forehead and blew out an enormous raspberry, making Annie snort with laughter.

"My turn, Mama."

"Good girl." Lou placed the compress on Annie's forehead, and she screwed up her face and then grinned. Lou turned to Jack and mouthed, "Thank you."

"We can take her to A&E if you want to get her checked out, but I think she's okay. It probably looks a lot worse than it actually is. But if she vomits or gets a headache, then she should definitely see a doctor." Jack went over to the small kitchen area to fill the kettle. "I'll make us some tea. What does Annie have to drink?"

"Some warm milk, please. There's a sippy cup in the cupboard."

Jack began making their drinks. At least there was a reason she'd stood him up, but now he had questions that needed answering… like where was Annie's father?

Chapter 13 - Lou

Having Jack here - his solid strength and presence - made Lou feel instantly better. He'd walked into the flat and handled the situation with Annie without batting an eye, whereas she'd been a hot mess. As soon as she'd heard the hard thump and saw Annie sprawled out on the floor screaming, her heart had almost stopped because her precious baby girl was hurting. She'd scooped her up and tried to calm her, but Annie was having none of it. She'd screamed the flat down.

Ten minutes later, once the worst of Annie's tears were over, she'd hastily cancelled her babysitter. Jenny was a college student who lived in the village and was studying to be a nursery nurse. She worked weekend shifts at the hotel to supplement her income and, being one of five sisters, a pizza was payment enough if she could study alone in Lou's quiet flat.

She'd debated calling her mum, but it was her book club night, and she knew how much she enjoyed her one precious night off. And then, like a knight in shining armour or, in his case, a dark green chunky jumper under a well-worn leather jacket, Jack had rapped on her flat door and come to her rescue.

There had been no shock or surprise on his face when he'd met Annie. *When he'd met his daughter.* Maybe he hadn't realised who she was, but to Lou, it was obvious. They had identical hair and eye colour, the same shaped nose with a scattering of light brown freckles. And they'd both tilted their heads in exactly the same way, studying one another. She'd almost stopped breathing because she was certain he'd realise. But he hadn't.

After their drinks, Annie seemed almost back to her usual self, albeit with a small lump on her forehead. It was late, and her eyelids were dropping with exhaustion, so while Jack washed up their mugs, she put Annie to bed. When she returned to the kitchen, he was standing waiting for her.

"I should go. But if Annie wakes up in pain or is sick, please call me and I'll take you both straight to A&E."

His green eyes held hers – the same green as Annie's – and God, she didn't want him to leave. Before she lost her courage, she blurted out. "Can you stay for a bit?" He nodded, and she led him over to her small sofa. Was this the right time to tell him he was Annie's father? "Thanks for everything you did tonight," she said instead.

"No problem. I'll get a proper booster seat for Annie tomorrow. She'd not old enough to sit at the table on her own."

He was right, but the implied criticism still stung. Embarrassment warmed her cheeks, and she snapped, "I'm trying my best."

"Hey, I'm not blaming you. You're doing a great job, Lou."

A band of tightness squeezed her heart because she didn't feel like she was doing a great job. Not at all. Tonight, through her carelessness, Annie had fallen and hurt herself. She was a terrible mum. "It is my fault, though. She's my responsibility, and I should have bought a proper seat, and now she's hurt."

"Stop beating yourself up. All kids have accidents sometimes."

"She's my daughter, not just some kid. Anyway, what would you know about parenting?"

"Well, clearly nothing." Jack stood up, his body rigid with annoyance.

"I'm sorry. I'm sorry. That was a terrible thing to say."

He hesitated and then sat down again.

"I'm sorry," she repeated. "It's just so hard being a mum, and Annie keeps waking up at night, and I can't keep asking Mum for help when she's got a hotel to run. And I'm so tired." A single tear fell down her cheek.

"It sounds tough," he said softly. He leant over and gently brushed the tear away with his thumb. "I know I've only just met Annie, but I can tell she adores you."

She snorted and shook her head. "I feel so inadequate most of the time. It's a battle to get her to eat any vegetables, and she always screams blue murder when I wash her hair. Yesterday, she had a meltdown at the supermarket when I wouldn't buy her some dog treats. We haven't even got a dog," Lou grumbled. "I know what they say about the 'terrible twos', but she's so difficult sometimes."

"You're doing the best you can, and even I know that two-year-olds can be hard work."

"Thanks". She gave him a weak smile.

"Lou…" Jack inhaled. "I'm sorry for what I said in my message earlier. I was upset because I thought you'd stood me up." He carried on softly, "and I just want to say that I had a great time with you in London. I loved every moment.

And whatever happened… whatever I did to make you leave. I'm sorry."

She took a shuddering breath. *I loved every moment, too.*

He gently squeezed her hand. "It's late. Get some sleep and let me know how Annie is in the morning. If anything changes, ring me, even if it's the middle of the night." He gave her hand another quick squeeze.

She nodded, but she couldn't trust herself to speak. Long after he'd gone, she sat on the sofa as sobs racked her body. *Why did you cheat?* The words repeated on a loop.

Chapter 14 - Jack

Jack hadn't heard from Lou overnight, which he took as a good sign that Annie's bump on her head wasn't more serious. The next morning, he stood outside a popular out of town retailer waiting for it to open. He'd already done his research to find the best toddler seat, reading and comparing customer reviews, and knew exactly which one he wanted to buy.

Also on his shopping list were several more items. Lou said Annie hated having her hair washed, and from his investigations he figured a hair-guard might prevent water from getting into her eyes. He also couldn't recall seeing any children's bath toys in Lou's avocado green bathroom. Maybe if Annie had something fun to play with, it would distract her from hair washing and make bath time more fun for both of them. He briefly wondered if he was overstepping, but last night Lou had seemed at the end of her rope, so maybe these gifts would help make her life easier. He hoped so.

Even though it hadn't been the best of circumstances to meet Lou's daughter for the first time, Annie had been adorable. Sitting on the sofa in her pyjamas, she'd turned towards him, her tear-stained face an absolute mirror image of the way Lou was looking at him. God, they were so alike, and he felt completely powerless under their gazes… almost like he was falling under their combined spell. He had, in a way, because when Lou confessed her feelings of inadequacy, he'd wanted to make things better. Hence, being outside the retail store at stupid o'clock so he could get back to work before his first appointment.

He wondered who Annie's father was, but he clearly wasn't around anymore, so in some ways, it didn't matter. His blood pressure rose just thinking about that, because how could anyone abandon Annie? If she were his, he'd count every one of his lucky stars and cherish her every single day.

***

He had appointments all morning. At noon, he sent his clerk out to buy a sandwich from the deli, and, between mouthfuls, he'd ploughed on throughout the afternoon.

At five o'clock, his pile of yellow legal pads was gaining height, covering the clean lines of his desk. He regularly stayed late to finish work, but this evening he had somewhere else to be. He powered down his laptop, grabbed his jacket from the hook behind his door, and headed out.

"Hey, have you got a minute?" Adam called out from his office.

He shoved his hands in his pockets and leant against the open door. "Not really."

"Are you seeing Lou again?"

"How did you know?"

Adam grinned. "Well, apart from the fact that you're leaving on time, and you haven't asked me if I want to go to the pub?"

"Okay, guilty as charged." He grinned back.

"If you're seeing Lou, can you ask her for some ideas for our sten-do?"

"What the hell's a sten-do?"

"It's a combined stag and hen. Like a joint celebration."

"I thought the whole point of a stag and hen was having your last night of freedom away from one another."

Adam shook his head. "We have a group of shared friends, and we love the idea of everyone celebrating together. It's also gender neutral, so will work well for Nick and Sam."

"What about the Cornish contingent? Presumably, Mordros has friends coming up?"

"No, she's only inviting them to the wedding. She thinks it's too much to expect them to travel for both events, especially with the potential for bad weather at this time of year. To be honest, I feel the same about our university friends."

"Quality over quantity," he grinned. "Okay, I'll talk to Lou, and we'll come up with some suggestions. Can you make a rough list of people you want to invite?"

"Will do." Adam smiled. "So, what are you two doing?"

He hesitated because he didn't have a clue. His usual dates were out to a bar or restaurant, but with Annie to consider, that wasn't happening. Anyway, it was hardly a date. He was just dropping off Annie's booster seat and a few more extras he'd bought. "Don't know yet," he admitted.

"Well, have a good night, whatever you get up to," Adam chuckled.

***

Would it be a good night, though? He sat in his car, debating. Maybe turning up unannounced at Lou's with all his shopping wasn't the best idea. He pulled out his phone.

Jack: Just wondered if you're around. I have a few things for Annie. J

He added a smiley face and then deleted it.

Thirty seconds later, a reply popped up on his screen.

Lou: Yes, please come over. We're baking biscuits. L x.

He put his phone away. A kiss, huh! Well, that was a distinct improvement between them.

Thinking of them baking together made him smile. He remembered doing the same thing with his own mother when he was a child. He couldn't wait to see them both, but rush hour traffic slowed him down. By the time he got to Broadsham, it was nearly six o'clock, and he was starving. Maybe he could take them both out for dinner to somewhere child-friendly… a pizza place, maybe? Did two-year-olds eat pizza? He guessed they did unless Lou had strict food rules. She'd mentioned getting Annie to eat vegetables … he could always order a veggie pizza, though he doubted she'd think that counted. He chuckled because he was obviously overthinking. She probably wouldn't even invite him in.

He needn't have worried. When he knocked, both Lou and Annie came to the door, and he grinned when he saw their pink flushed cheeks and floury faces. "You look like you're having fun."

"And making a terrible mess, too." Lou giggled, and God, he'd missed that. It was the first time he'd seen her look genuinely happy. Without makeup and with something green staining her fingers, she was beautiful…and it was on the tip of his tongue to tell her, but he swallowed the words down because it wasn't his place. Not anymore.

She moved to the side so he could enter the small hallway, and he noticed that she and Annie were wearing identical Santa aprons. It was cuteness overload and felt like he'd just stepped into one of the heartwarming Christmas movies that Lou loved so much.

"Hello Jat." Annie gave him a beaming smile, and he beamed back.

"It's Jack, darling," Lou gently corrected before he could say anything.

"J A T," Annie repeated carefully.

"Yeah, that'll do." He winked at Lou.

She was right. The small kitchen was a mess: the table covered in flour and sugar and what looked like small green holly leaves and red berries made of icing. Cooling on a wire rack were star-shaped biscuits, each one haphazardly decorated. He watched as Annie pointed to the ones she'd made, giving him a wide grin.

"They look amazing, Annie. Well done, you."

Lou stood beside him as they admired Annie's handiwork. "Would you like one? They're a lemon shortbread mixture."

"Absolutely." He made certain to choose one of Annie's and saw the look of pride on her face when he took his first bite. "Annie, this is delicious. In fact, I think it's the best biscuit I've ever tasted."

"Mama try."

Lou nodded, and a warm feeling of belonging … or coming home floated over him. It was perfect being in her messy kitchen eating lemon biscuits. In fact, he couldn't think of anywhere else he'd rather be.

Chapter 15 - Lou

Jack set down the three bags he was carrying beside the sofa, and she kept sneaking glances, trying to guess what was inside them. One bag probably contained the booster seat he'd promised Annie. But the other two …?

First things first, though, Annie was sticky, and they both had food colouring staining their fingers. She whisked her reluctant daughter to the bathroom to clean up and dropped their aprons in the laundry basket. It was past Annie's bedtime, and she was yawning, so a bath would have to wait until the morning. She found some Winnie the Pooh pyjamas and helped her put them on.

"Time to brush your teeth, sweetie." She squeezed a tiny, pea-sized blob of toothpaste onto her daughter's toothbrush and held it out for her.

"No mama. More biscuits," Annie protested.

Please don't play up. Not tonight. Not with Jack here. She let out a calming breath. "You've had three. That's enough. We'll save the rest of the biscuits for tomorrow. And then maybe we can take nanny one."

"Take nanny one," Annie repeated.

"Yes, and you can have one then, too."

Annie shook her head. "No, Mama, want one now."

"Fur balls," Lou silently cursed as Annie's face and ears began turning pink, a sure sign that a tantrum was looming. "Brush your teeth, and then I'll read you a bedtime story. You can choose which one," she spoke briskly.

But Annie was shaking her head more vehemently now, her cheeks growing redder by the second. "Want a biscuit."

"Annie, please be a good girl."

"Biscuit, Mama! Biscuit!" she repeated more insistently, and she saw the first fat tears slide down her daughter's cheeks.

"No. No more biscuits. Now please brush your teeth." But Annie was having none of it. She was howling now, and her own tears began falling, a mixture of crossness at Annie's tantrum, embarrassment that Jack was hearing it and disappointment at herself that she'd let this stupid stand-off escalate.

Chapter 16 - Jack

"Hey, Annie. I have a present for you, but you can only have it if you do what your mama tells you." Jack leant against the bathroom door and observed his girls glaring at each other. *His girls… where the hell had that come from?*

It was like a switch. Annie's enormous eyes, which only a moment ago had been brimming with tears, zoomed in on his face, and he nodded at her. "Say sorry to your mama and brush your teeth, please. Then I will find your present."

It was bribery, and he wondered if Lou would pull him up on it. He hadn't any idea what the rules were in a situation like this, but he imagined bribing a toddler was breaking one of them. Still, drastic times called for drastic measures, and Lou had looked wrung out, and he couldn't stand listening to the two of them bawling. Not to mention the noise. Thank God Lou didn't appear to have any close neighbours. They'd either need to be stone deaf or wear industrial ear defenders.

Annie sniffed and nodded back at him. *Okay, so far, so good.* He waited, counting down the seconds in his head, and then she whispered shakily. "Annie's sorry."

He blew out a breath and watched as Lou knelt down and pulled her into a hug. "I love you, sweetheart. But it's time to go to sleep now, so let's brush your teeth and then do snuggles in bed."

Annie nodded, sniffing again. "And Jat's present."

Lou smiled. "Yes." Her eyes locked onto Jack over Annie's shoulder. "And Jat's present."

***

Jack looked around Annie's small bedroom, taking in the furnishings. Someone, presumably Lou, had painted an old wardrobe and chest of drawers white, and then stuck Winnie the Pooh characters on them… Piglet, Tigger and Eeyore. There was also a giant Winnie the Pooh sticker on the wall. *Annie obviously likes animals, then.* He made a mental note and filed it away.

Annie sat propped up in her cot, her thumb firmly lodged in her mouth as he placed the gift bag onto her lemon blanket. He'd bought the booster seat, the hair guard and the bath toys, but they could wait. He'd found something far more special for Annie. She withdrew her thumb and looked at the wrapped gift, her light green eyes focused as she began tearing at the tissue paper.

"This is Simba," Jack explained. "He's a young lion prince, and he's from your mama's favourite musical, the Lion King. When you're a little older, I'll take you to see it too."

"Sim-Ba," Annie sounded out the syllables, and he nodded.

"Yes, Simba." He stole a look at Lou, and her violet eyes met his. "We saw a lot of musicals," he chuckled.

"What do you say, Annie?" Lou prompted.

"Thank you, Jat."

"You're very welcome, honey." He forced his eyes away from Lou's and smiled. Annie's eyes slipped shut, and Lou pulled the soft blanket around her as she snuggled down with her new friend.

He left them to it and went back to the kitchen. By the time Lou joined him, he'd cleaned up the baking detritus and had made them both mugs of tea.

"You didn't have to clear up." Lou's eyes scanned the tidy kitchen.

"I know I didn't, but you look shattered."

She nodded and sat down at the table, and he placed the tea in front of her. "Thanks."

"Are you okay?"

"Yes, of course."

He knew her and when she was lying. "Look, I'm starving. How about I order us a takeaway? My treat."

Chapter 17 - Lou

Jack ordered Italian food from a place he knew in the village and left the flat to collect it. While he was out, she laid the small kitchen table and put two plates in the oven to warm. Besides her mum, she couldn't remember having anyone over to eat dinner since she'd moved in. Mostly, she ate early with Annie and spent her evenings trying to keep on top of the never-ending cycle of laundry and cleaning that an active toddler created. To have dinner, albeit a takeaway, with Jack felt grown up and all kinds of dangerous…

Dangerous, because she needed to keep her guard up to protect the walls she'd built brick by brick to protect her heart, because if she didn't, he was going to bulldoze right through them.

Dangerous, because she wanted him to.

When he was back, they put the containers in the middle of the table to share - a selection of antipasti, several types of pasta, sauces, and Italian breads. The smell of slow-cooked ragu, garlic, tomatoes and herbs filled the kitchen, and her mouth watered. He knew Italian was her favourite, and his thoughtfulness made her tummy do a little flip. Along with the food, he'd bought a bottle of red wine, which he began opening.

"Do you have wine glasses?"

"Umm, no, sorry." She reached for two glass tumblers in the cupboard instead. "Will these do?"

"Of course, though maybe I'll get you some."

His words made her smile because he'd done so much for her already. She stared at the unwrapped gifts on the sofa. "Thanks so much for these."

"You're very welcome. Now let's eat. I'm starving."

Sitting companionably together, drinking the rich red wine, which perfectly complemented the Italian food, she felt herself relaxing as the tension of the day and Annie's tantrum faded away.

Jack had always been great company, and she realised how much she'd missed that as he began entertaining her with funny stories about his work. She'd also missed the way his broad shoulders and chest filled out the white cotton of his shirt and how his muscular thighs looked in his dark suit trousers. He'd rolled up the sleeves of his shirt, and her eyes kept drifting to the scattering of light freckles on his powerful forearms. He was gorgeous in jeans and his usual casual leather jacket, but tonight, in his suit, he was on a whole different level.

What was the matter with her? She shouldn't be ogling him or letting her imagination wander into dangerous fantasies about what lay beneath his suit… *and wasn't that number three on her dangerous list?* No, she should still be furious with him for blowing up their relationship with his infidelity. But in a funny way, it was also reassuring to know that her dormant libido was finally waking up. She supposed a painful labour would do that, as she recalled swearing to her midwife that she'd never have sex again, thank you very much.

Jack helped himself to some focaccia. "Has Mordros mentioned anything about having a joint hen and stag do in Broadsham?"

She let go of her rambling thoughts because now wasn't the time to analyse her feelings. "No, but I love that idea, especially as Nick and Mordros are so close. She'd definitely want him at hers."

"Any ideas of what we could do? Adam would be mortified if I took him to a lap dance club." He chuckled at the thought. "Not that I know any," he hastily added when she frowned.

"I can't see Mordros being thrilled about it either." She took a sip of her wine, thinking. "We could make it more of a friends' weekend break, and just do some Christmas-themed stuff together."

"Good idea, but we'll need somewhere to stay. What about hiring one of Nick and Sam's holiday cottages for a weekend? I can ask them what they have available."

"Ooh yes, and then we could have a themed dinner party… maybe 1920s Gatsby? Or even make it into a murder mystery night where we all dress up."

"And make cocktails." Jack grinned. "Actually, there's a new restaurant that's just opened near Broadsham. I was reading the reviews…God, what's the name of it? The Blue something? Anyway, they do dinner and dancing – we could try that if you like?"

"I think that's much more their kind of thing." She nodded, but then it suddenly occurred to her - hiring a cottage, even at mates rates, not to mention the activities they'd end up doing, was going to cost a lot of money. Money that she didn't have. "Umm, this all sounds great, but I don't think I'll be able to afford it." Her cheeks flushed with embarrassment.

"Don't worry, we'll work something out."

"I don't want to be a charity case," she blurted.

"Hey, nobody would ever treat you like that." He reached out and squeezed her hand before letting go. It was a small gesture, letting her know he was on her side, and maybe it was the wine or the fact that for once she felt relaxed, but her whole body craved more.

It had always been like that between them. Whenever her head was in a tailspin about something, just the touch of his hand in hers or his calm voice had made her feel better. And hadn't he proven that earlier? He didn't even know Annie, and yet he'd taken control of her spiralling tantrum and her own emotional meltdown. Of course, she shouldn't condone bribery, but the promised present had been music to Annie's ears, and he'd meant well.

Her thoughts drifted to another time, another place. In this different life, they were still together, and this was just a typical night, eating dinner after Annie had gone to bed and exchanging news about their day. Later, she'd fall asleep wrapped up in his arms like she used to do. *She'd love that life.*

A hundred if only's from the past began pulling her apart.

"Are you okay?" He'd noticed she'd disappeared into her own thoughts, and she quickly nodded.

"Yes, I was just thinking about stuff."

"Stuff?"

"Like how gorgeous this wine is. I rarely drink these days because I always need to be alert for Annie." She met his green eyes and hoped that her half-truth was enough to convince him not to probe further.

"I completely understand, but I'm sure one glass won't hurt, especially as we're having food with it."

She nodded as he sipped his own wine appreciatively and then set his glass down. "You still love Christmas, then."

She watched as his eyes scanned the room, taking in the pictures of a rather wonky reindeer and a Christmas tree stuck to the fridge door that Annie had coloured in at nursery. Red, green, and gold paper chains had also joined the other decorations hanging from the cupboards. "Of course, what's not to love - and I'm teaching Annie to love Christmas too. She's not quite got the hang of it yet, but next year…" She puffed out her cheeks as if to say, just wait.

"I wouldn't blame her for thinking your flat has turned into Santa's grotto on steroids," he teased.

"Next year, I'll have even more decorations," she shot back.

"Just to spite me, huh?"

"Of course, anything to wind you up." She relaxed back in her seat, enjoying their banter about her love of Christmas. Plus, the red wine had made her feel pleasantly squiffy.

"So, tell me more about Annie?"

Fudge — where had that come from? "What do you want to know?" she asked carefully.

Maybe he sensed her hesitation because he said instead. "She's adorable and bright as a button."

"She can be a little terror, too, as you saw earlier."

"I think she's just feisty, like her mum."

She couldn't help her wide grin because there was no arguing with that.

"You're doing a great job, Lou."

She felt the sting of tears, but she blinked them away. "Thanks for saying that."

"I imagine it's hard work being a single mum. Do you get much help or a chance to get a break?"

"Not really. I mean, Mum's amazing, but the hotel is a full-time job, and she doesn't have a lot of spare time." She suddenly felt the need to defend her. "She helps me whenever she can, and she adores Annie."

"I'm sure she does." His eyes locked on her. "So, who is Annie's father?"

Well, of course he wanted to know that, and this was the perfect time to tell him. But nerves held her back. It was such a huge thing to admit that he was, and she'd kept it a secret from him. He'd be furious, and rightfully so. She took a gulp of wine, stalling. She was being a coward, but right now, she didn't want to spoil their evening. "Can we leave this topic for another time?"

He sighed, but his light green eyes remained on her. "Look, whoever he is, he should at least be helping you and contributing financially towards Annie. Does he?"

She felt herself becoming defensive. "Really? You want to talk about my finances?"

"If you're struggling with money, then yeah, I think we should talk about your finances. And if Annie's father isn't paying maintenance, then my question is, why not?"

"Look, can't we just enjoy our meal and—"

"All I'm saying is that he has a responsibility to look after his daughter. If you contact the Child Maintenance Service, they'll calculate how much maintenance he should pay and arrange the payments."

"It's not that simple."

"Lou, this is important. You're entitled to maintenance and—"

"I know I am, but, like I said, it's not that simple. Please, can we drop this and talk about something else?"

"Okay, if you don't want to talk about Annie's father, then maybe we can talk about us and why you left?" Jack's expression hardened, and she finally looked away.

The questions were coming thick and fast now, and the relaxed atmosphere between them had morphed into something quite different. She abandoned her food and frowned. "Isn't it obvious?"

"No, of course it's not obvious. If it were, I wouldn't have spent nearly three years wondering what the hell I'd done wrong."

"Oh, come on! You know exactly what you did." She felt her anger rising. "At least be man enough to admit it."

"Admit what? What are you talking about? One minute we were making plans for our future and the next you didn't want to see me again."

"Yet here you are," she spat out.

Jack's eyes darkened with shock. She couldn't blame him. It was a horrible thing to say, and she immediately regretted it.

"Yeah, well, that's easily rectified." Anger curled into his words. He got up from the table and reached for his suit jacket. "When you feel like having a proper adult conversation, call me." Strained silence hung between them, and when she didn't reply, he huffed out, "Good night, Lou."

Just as the front door quietly shut, she called out to him, but it was too late. She stared at the Italian food, now cold and congealing on their plates. It was a waste, but she'd completely lost her appetite. In fact, she felt like throwing up.

***

Much later, she lay tossing and turning in bed, reliving their terse exchange. He'd seemed genuinely at a loss about the cause of their breakup. Yet, why deny he knew what the reason was? Surely it was better to admit it and then they could move on… maybe not as a couple, but as friends.

She grabbed her phone from the bedside table and scrolled to the folder containing the photos. She hadn't looked at them in months – why pick a scab and make herself miserable? Yet, something had stopped her from deleting them.

There were three pictures. The first was a selfie of Jack and a nameless woman. The woman was kissing his cheek as they both smiled into the camera. She looked like the cat who'd got the cream.

But it was the other two photos that shattered her heart. In both, he and the woman were in bed and… she quickly closed the folder. *She didn't want to see that.*

Had she been wrong… but the proof was there, wasn't it?

Chapter 18 - Jack

Jack sat back in his leather recliner behind his desk, looking at the photos of the property he'd found for their friends' weekend. It was one of Sam and Nick's holiday lets in the Cotswolds, and since they were friends of Mordros and Adam, it made sense to hire from them.

According to the description, it was an immaculately presented holiday home sleeping fourteen guests in seven individually designed bedrooms, all with spacious ensuite bathrooms. On the ground floor were two elegantly presented reception rooms, each with character features, including wood burners and exposed beams. It also boasted a modern open-plan kitchen/dining room with bi-fold doors leading out to beautiful landscaped gardens, a large patio and plenty of outdoor seating. It was perfect.

He'd immediately asked Nick to reserve it, but when he'd proffered his credit card, Nick insisted he'd take care of it since Mordros was his best friend. That just left the rest of the weekend expenses, which he'd cover. He could afford it, and that way, Lou and the other guests wouldn't need to contribute a penny. In legalese, it was a favourable outcome for everyone.

Thinking of Lou and how their evening had imploded, his mood turned frigid. She was clearly worried about money and when she'd said she didn't want to be a charity case, he'd had an overwhelming urge to kiss her and fix whatever financial problems she had, including finding a flat for her and Annie with a boiler that wasn't on its last legs. But instead of doing that, he'd opened his big mouth and prattled on about claiming maintenance from Annie's absent father.

After that, the evening had plummeted. Lou clearly didn't want to talk about Annie's father, and frustration, or maybe irritation, made him fire off questions which had been festering inside him about why she'd left him. He blew out a heavy breath, reproaching himself for how much of an arse he'd been.

"How's it going?" Adam poked his head around his office door. "Are you okay?"

Distracted by his miserable thoughts, he jerked his head up in surprise at the interruption. "Yeah, I'm bloody marvellous." He rolled his neck trying to fight off the headache that was threatening.

Adam smirked. "Like that, is it… What's up?"

"Nothing." But when Adam gave him a hard look, he conceded. "Okay, I have one major problem, and her name is Louise James."

"I thought you two were fine now."

"We were, but then I opened my big mouth and now we're not."

Adam grinned. "Well, it's not the first time your mouth has got you into trouble. Remember the time you said how nice it was that a client had brought his daughter along to lunch, and it turned out she was his wife?"

"She was at least twenty years younger than him, so it was an easy mistake," he grumbled. "He wasn't happy, though."

"Furious more like."

He grimaced at the memory. "Don't remind me. I felt terrible, and the waiter almost choked trying not to laugh."

"Well, there you are then. You should always think before you speak."

"Oh great, thanks for that. Just what I needed to hear."

"So, what got you into trouble with Lou?"

"I basically gave her a lecture about her finances and told her she should apply for maintenance from Annie's dad."

"And what did she say?"

"She didn't want to talk about it, so then I bombarded her with questions about why we broke up."

"Nice one."

"Don't," he groaned, lowering his head to rest on the desk. "I've really screwed up, haven't I?"

"Hopefully, nothing an apology and a decent bunch of flowers can't solve. On second thoughts, why don't you take her out on a proper date?"

"What about Annie?"

"Well, I believe they have things called babysitters. In fact, I'm almost sure of it. Look, why don't you fix things with Lou, and then Mordros and I will come round and babysit one evening?"

"Really? You'd do that?"

"Of course. Annie knows us, and we need to get some practice in looking after kids if we're going to produce our own one day."

"Yeah? I didn't think you were into the whole baby thing?"

"I wasn't, but then Mordros showed me the error of my ways."

"Glad to hear it. You'll make a great dad."

"You will too." Jack began shaking his head, and Adam grinned. "You just don't realise it yet."

"Not funny. I'm actually envious of you and Mordros finding each other."

"It'll happen to you one day."

He nodded, but the truth was it had already. Lou was who he wanted, but she'd accused him… of what exactly? And there went his mood, turning dark again, as the pain behind his eyes doubled in size. He tore his hands through his hair trying to think what the hell he'd done to make her leave.

***

After Adam left, he mulled over the list of names for their friends' weekend. There weren't many of them because Mordros wasn't from the area and hardly knew anyone in the village, and Adam was a grumpy bugger, so his friendship list was even smaller: Nick and Sam, of course, because Nick was best friends with Mordros. Their mutual friends Matt and his wife Rosie, plus Lou, himself and his sister Clemmie. Also, some random guy who Mordros had made friends with at the bakery and wanted to invite as well. A grand total of ten of them. There'd also be Annie, because he didn't imagine Lou would want to leave her for an entire weekend, and Rosie and Matt's newborn, Mae, and their elder son, Toby.

He sat for a long moment, thinking. Since just before his fifteenth birthday, when he'd had a growth spurt, he'd been a magnet to girls. Maybe it was because he'd been tall for his age, good at sport, and had a wicked sense of humour, but high school dates had always been easy to come by. Since then, nothing had changed except girls had morphed into women, and he'd become more experienced. Dating was fun and not to be taken too seriously.

Then he'd met Lou, and he didn't want to date casually anymore. For the first time, he'd fallen deeply, madly, crazily in love, and he'd wanted to settle down and build a future with her. So, what the hell had gone wrong?

Whatever it was, he needed to fix it. He also wanted to get to know Annie more - after all, she and Lou came as a package now. His chest tightened because Annie wasn't his, but if her biological father wasn't around, then he'd be a father figure if Lou would let him.

A couple more hours at work and then he'd drive over to Lou's, apologise for giving her the third degree last night and ask her out on a proper date.

Then they'd talk properly, like the civilised adults they were. It was simple, really.

Chapter 19 - Lou

Lou spent the morning writing Christmas cards at the kitchen table, assisted by Annie, sitting on her new toddler seat, adding her own unique scribble signature and some Christmas stickers. After lunch, they danced around the small living area to some Christmas songs, Annie shaking a small tambourine Lou had bought her from a charity shop.

It wasn't one of Annie's nursery days, and the weather was cold and overcast, not at all like the perfect bright winter days always depicted in Christmas movies she so loved watching. Annie was becoming fractious because they'd been stuck in the flat for most of the day and she was rapidly running out of ideas to entertain her. On the spur of the moment, she decided they'd walk over to the hotel. At least it would be a change of scene, and Annie might nap while she helped her mum with paperwork. Maybe she'd have some news about the repairs to the hotel roof, too.

Her mind drifted to Jack and the horrible way their evening had ended. He'd been so thoughtful, buying gifts, defusing Annie's tantrum, as well as providing dinner for them. But instead of showing how grateful she was, she'd repaid him by being defensive and difficult. Her shoulders sagged with regret, an idea forming. Whatever he'd done in the past, he deserved an apology.

"Come on, sweetheart, let's go over to the hotel and see the big Christmas tree."

"Christmas tree?"

"Yes, and we can take nanny some of your Christmas biscuits."

"Biscuits." Annie's eyes lit up in understanding.

"Yes, biscuits." She chuckled because that was Annie's favourite word.

***

While Annie tucked into a star biscuit and a few segments of satsuma, Lou looked over the latest repair quote for the hotel roof.

"This is a ridiculous sum. Do you even have this amount of money?"

Her mum frowned. "I have some savings and I've spoken to my financial adviser, but he doesn't think I'll be able to extend my business loan… so, no, I don't have enough to cover the repair bill."

"What are we going to do?" Lou continued staring at the figures, which were swimming in front of her eyes. "What else does your adviser suggest?"

"He's looking into whether we can claim on the building's insurance, but of course they have lots of caveats, so that's not looking very promising either. Otherwise, he's suggested selling."

"What? You mean selling the hotel?"

"Yes."

"But…" Lou began, her mind racing. "You can't sell."

"We might not have any choice."

"Who would want to buy a hotel that needs a new roof, not to mention all the other work that needs doing?"

"Apparently, there are hotel chains that are always interested in buying up family-run hotels, especially when they're in a popular tourist location. He's going to put out feelers and let me know."

"But…" she began again, shaking her head. "Surely you're not seriously considering selling?"

"Well, unless we can come up with a better plan, we won't have an option."

Lou put down the quote and quietly studied her. There were fresh worry lines on her face, and her eyes were shiny with tears. "I'm so sorry."

"The hotel was your dad's dream, and he wanted me to keep it going until you could take over. But now…" she trailed off. "I'm sorry, darling, I've really let you down."

"Of course you haven't. It's not your fault that the roof is in such a state."

"I'm afraid the hotel is old and tired. There's so much that needs doing, and I just don't have the funds." Her mum looked heartbroken, and Lou couldn't blame her. The hotel had been such a big part of their lives, and it would be devastating if they were forced to sell it.

"Then we'll have to look at some creative ways of raising the money."

Her mum laughed wryly. "Well, unless we win the lottery or the premium bonds come up, I don't see what else we can do."

She picked up the quote again, staring at the amount. "We'll think of something."

***

"I wondered if I could borrow your car?" Lou finished paying the last of the supply invoices and began filing the paperwork away. They'd both been working diligently for the last hour while Annie napped, but now she was awake and helpfully tidying (aka untidying) her mum's stationery drawer.

"Of course, darling. That's why I put you on the insurance. I hardly ever use it these days. In fact, it spends most of its time sitting on the drive, so you're more than welcome."

Her mum gave her a curious look. "I know you're dying to ask…" she hesitated. Should she tell her about Jack or not? "I met a friend I haven't seen for a while, and I wasn't very nice to him, so I want to apologise."

"Him?" The tease in her words made Lou smile.

"I knew you'd pick up on that. Yes, he's a friend."

"A friend you like?"

"Mum!" she groaned. "He's just a friend."

"Would you like me to look after Annie while you apologise to this… umm, friend? We could have tea together, and if you're not back for bedtime, I can take care of that, too."

"That would be amazing. It's been playing on my mind all day, so I was sort of hoping you'd say that."

"No problem at all. Annie and I will have a lovely time together, won't we, honey? I might even find some more biscuits."

"Biscuits," Annie repeated, her green eyes lighting up.

"Yes, biscuits," they both repeated, laughing.

***

The road was busy with heavy traffic as Lou crawled along towards Cheltenham in her mum's old Mini, and it was past five o'clock when she finally pulled into the carpark of Lewis, Reid and Associates. She shut off the engine and got out of the car hurriedly, hoping Jack hadn't left his office already, because she didn't have a clue where he lived.

Now that she was here, she began doubting herself. Was it stupid, turning up like this and expecting him to forgive her? She wouldn't blame him if he gave her a mouthful, although another part of her instinctively knew that he wouldn't.

It was completely dark now, and standing in the carpark, the cold air made her shiver. She pulled her wool scarf more tightly around her neck and debated what to do. She could turn around and drive home, but then what? An apologetic text message seemed a cop-out when he deserved a face-to-face apology after her rudeness last night. He also deserved answers to his questions, and now was as good a time as any to give them to him. She gathered up her fragile courage and headed into their plush offices.

"Can I help you?" The badge on the receptionist's tailored jacket stated her name was Shona. Her heavily made-up face (far too much makeup, in Lou's opinion) stared at her sceptically as if she didn't imagine for one moment that she could.

"Yes, please." Lou smiled, noting the lack of reciprocal friendliness on the woman's face. "I'd like to see Jack Lewis, please."

"And do you have an appointment?"

"No… no, I don't, but–"

"Then I'm afraid that's impossible."

Lou felt her cheeks grow warm with irritation. "Excuse me?"

"Mr Lewis doesn't see anyone without an appointment."

"I'm sure he'll see me," she shot back, her annoyance growing. "I'm a friend of his, and I've driven all the way from Broadsham to see him. Can you please ask him?" She put on her *I'm not taking any nonsense* voice, which she'd sometimes used in her old job if clients were being difficult.

Shona looked about to argue but then gave an audible sigh, her glossy pink mouth forming a perfect pout. Lou bit back a laugh. Surely the first skill a receptionist required was helpfulness and a friendly way about them. She must be good at other office-y things because her people skills were zero.

She watched as Shona typed quickly, her long painted nails tap, tapping on the keyboard in front of her. There was something familiar about her face, her hazel eyes outlined with just a little too much eyeliner, her blusher, just a little too heavily applied, and that impossibly shiny pink mouth. Then there was her long wavy hair, almost the same fair colour as her own.

What was it?

Lou was good at putting a name to a face. As an event planner, it was a useful skill, so each client felt valued and special. She racked her brain. Did she know her? No, she didn't think so, but there was definitely something gnawing at her memory.

She wasn't someone from school or university, so why was her face so familiar? She'd never visited Jack's office before, so she couldn't have met her there. Perhaps she'd seen her at the hotel in Broadsham, or at an event at the hotel in London where she'd worked before. Either way, she definitely recognised her.

And then, in a blinding flash, it came to her.

"Lou? What a lovely surprise." Adam's friendly voice jolted her thoughts, and she whirled around to face him. "Jack's been in a horrible mood all day, so I hope you're here to cheer him up."

"No," she blurted. "No, I'm not… actually, I need to go." She began walking out of reception, through the revolving doors and back onto the pavement. Adam gave Shona a questioning look, but she merely shook her head.

"Lou, stop," he called out as he began running after her, but that was the last thing she wanted to do, tears blinding her as she raced back towards the car park.

***

Lou dropped her car keys, and as if that wasn't annoying enough, Adam was approaching her warily, like she was a wild animal that was spooked and needed calming down. He wasn't wrong. Her heart hammered from shock, and she desperately wanted to climb into her mum's car and drive away as quickly as possible.

As he got closer, she noticed he was talking to someone on his phone. He looked worried – not that she could blame him - she wasn't exactly behaving rationally.

"Are you okay?" he asked tentatively after pocketing his phone. "I don't know what just happened, but why don't you come back inside, and we can try to fix it?"

He was trying his best to help, but she didn't want to go back *in there,* and then she saw Jack at the entrance to the carpark striding towards them. Adam must have seen him too, because he bent to retrieve her car keys and silently handed them to her. And then Jack was there, pulling her into his comforting arms, and even though that was probably the last thing she should allow, she clung to him as if her life depended on it.

She didn't know how long they stood there, but when she finally looked up, Adam had gone, and they were alone in the deserted carpark.

"What on earth's the matter?" He finally pulled back and wiped his thumb down her tear-stained face as she began shivering. "You're freezing. Let's go back inside, and then we can talk." Before she could argue, he began pulling her along towards the entrance to his office.

"No, please, not in there… anywhere but in there."

"What? Why?" He turned to face her, and maybe he could see something in her expression because there was no way she was ever going back into reception again if that woman was there.

"Okay, then we'll go somewhere else. Where's Annie?"

"She's with Mum."

He nodded. "Then let's go back to mine for a bit and talk, but we'll leave your car here. You're in too much of a state to drive."

She thought about arguing, but he was right. Shock or cold or both were making her shiver uncontrollably, and she certainly wasn't in the right frame of mind to drive anywhere.

But still she hesitated until he repeated softly. "Come on. You can't drive like this. Let's get you out of the cold."

As soon as she got into his car, he put her heated seat on and turned up the temperature to full blast. They crawled along in the town traffic, and she allowed herself to lie back against the plush leather seat and closed her eyes.

They were both silent on the drive, and she wondered what he was thinking. Her own thoughts were like a pneumatic drill in her head.

You cheated… repeated over and over. *And now she'd met the person he'd cheated with.*

Chapter 20 - Lou

She followed him into the lift and watched curiously as he pressed the button to take them to the top of the building… the penthouse floor. The lift rose soundlessly, and seconds later the doors slid open, and Lou walked out into a black and white tiled foyer.

"Come on, I'll show you around." Jack took her hand, and she allowed herself to be led into a spacious sitting room with floor-to-ceiling windows along the whole of one wall, and views of the golden-glow of the town lights scattered against the night sky. The gold blurred as her eyes re-focused on a Christmas tree in someone's garden, providing a kaleidoscope of changing colours, its twinkling lights dancing in the darkness.

"Wow." She couldn't stop herself because it really was.

"I know. When I first saw the view, I knew I had to buy this place."

"How long have you lived here?"

"Almost three years. When we split, I didn't want to stay in London, so I sold up and bought this instead." He smiled as Lou continued staring at the lights against the dark night sky. "Do you want a drink – tea, coffee, hot chocolate … though I don't have the marshmallow or flake extras?"

"Tea is fine." She eventually tore her eyes away from the striking view, and when he walked towards the kitchen area, which was part of the open-plan space, she followed him.

"Look around if you'd like. I don't have any secrets." He began filling the kettle, knowing that she wouldn't be able to resist.

There were two large double bedrooms, each with its own ensuite. The master (presumably Jack's) had a TV on one wall and, like the sitting room, floor-to-ceiling windows with more incredible views towards the warm lights of the town. She wondered if anyone could see in from pavement level because there weren't any blinds… not that they were going to do anything that required privacy. The last room was an office, but from its lack of clutter, it didn't look as though he used it much. And then she was back in the spacious sitting room, which contained two comfortable leather sofas, a large glass coffee table and another TV.

"Where are your Christmas decorations? In fact, where's all your stuff?" she couldn't help asking.

"Stuff?" He looked puzzled as she joined him in the kitchen area.

"Yeah, you know, like what normal people have, like pictures and knick-knacks and books? You used to have stuff in London."

A shadow passed across his face. "Yeah, I used to, but then I decided I didn't need them. Anyway, from what I've seen of your flat, you don't have a lot of stuff either."

Well, that was true. But her flat was small — pokey, in fact — whereas the surface area of his penthouse was at least treble hers, so it was different. The only belongings she had room for were Annie's. "Where's your Christmas tree?"

He'd finished making their tea and handed her a mug. "I haven't bothered." She gave him a horrified look, and he chuckled. "Not all of us have an addiction to Christmas. Anyway, there's only me."

She took her tea back to the large window and stared out towards the town lights again. "You should get one. You can't celebrate Christmas without a tree."

"Maybe you're right. You and Annie could help me choose one." He pointed towards the sofa. "Come on, let's sit down and talk."

Chapter 21 - Jack

When Adam had rung him and told him to get down to the carpark because Lou was there and something was wrong, he'd almost had a heart attack. And then when he'd got there, Lou was shaking and clearly in a state, and Adam had given him one of his *what the hell have you done* looks as if it was his fault. Well, it was, because he should have gone round first thing and apologised for his behaviour the night before and not let things fester between them.

As soon as they'd got into his car, he'd turned the temperature up and also programmed the thermostat in his flat to come on, so by the time they'd arrived it was warm and welcoming.

She'd finally taken her coat off and stopped shaking. He watched as she sipped her tea, and he wondered if she'd finally open up and talk to him or whether she'd change her mind. He'd let his frustration get the better of him last night, but that had got him nowhere, so this time, he'd be patient and not bombard her with questions.

"I owe you an apology for last night." He put down his mug on the coffee table and turned to face her on the sofa.

"I'm sorry I gave you the third degree about Annie's father. It's none of my business."

"No, it's me that should apologise. That's why I came over to see you. I was horrible last night, and after you'd been so kind with the gifts and helping with Annie and everything." She paused, putting her own drink down. "I also think you're right, and we should talk about us and what happened in London."

"Okay," he said softly, his heartbeat flying as his long wait for answers was finally ending. *Confusion, worry, hurt, frustration… a sprinkling of anger too that she'd left him without an explanation.* He took a breath, trying to centre himself for what was to come.

"I was in love with you." Her words were soft as gossamer but still pierced his heart.

"I was in love with you, too… I'm still in love with you." Pain wrapped around his words as he corrected himself.

"Then why did you cheat?"

And there it was… the reason she'd left. All the times he'd lain awake trying to figure it out… trying to understand. He stared at her unblinking as he took a moment to digest what she was saying. "What?" he finally managed, and then almost laughed at the complete absurdity of her accusation.

"I know you cheated, so please don't deny it." Her voice wobbled, and he realised that whatever pain he was feeling, she was feeling it too. He wanted to reach out and comfort her, but now wasn't the time.

"Look, whatever you think you know, you're quite wrong," his voice hardened.

Her eyes drifted to the window and the town lights in the distance, and slowly back to him. "Fine, fine. You want to keep denying it, then that's your call. But I have proof."

He stared at her in shock, unable to compute what she'd just said. He swallowed his shock, replacing it with anger. "I don't know what proof you can have when I didn't cheat. I would never cheat on you, Lou… never."

Tears began rolling down her cheeks as she pulled out her phone. "Then please explain these photos." Her voice was so pained, it hurt to hear.

He took the phone from her and began scrolling.

Chapter 22 - Lou

Lou's heart pounded as he began looking through the photos. He couldn't deny it now, and the realisation made her feel sick. For a long time, he didn't look up, but kept scrolling through each picture and back again until finally he met her eyes.

"Lou, I swear I never cheated on you. These photos…"

"You don't deny that you know her?"

"Of course not."

"Well, that's something, at least."

"That explains why you didn't want to come back into the office, because you recognised Shona from the photos."

"I did."

He sighed. "I swear, Shona and I–"

"Please, I don't want any details."

"Look, I don't deny we dated, but it was way before us. And it was brief… maybe – I don't know – four or five dates. And that was it."

"Oh, come on. The date on these photos proves they were taken while we were together."

"Please listen to me," the command burst from his lips. "I finished with her a few months before we got together. I actually felt awkward about it because she was an employee, and I should never have got involved with her. "

"And the date stamp?"

"I don't know, but I imagine it's possible to change a date stamp."

"That sounds unlikely." She gave him a sceptical look.

"Maybe, but I don't have another explanation. Who sent the photos to you?"

"They were sent anonymously."

"Right." He finally handed back her phone. "Can you send them to me, please, so I can do some digging?"

"Why? What for?"

"Because I don't know why Shona, or whoever it was, would do this, and I mean to find out."

He sounded so reasonable, and she desperately wanted to believe him… to give him the benefit of the doubt, but she couldn't just ignore the evidence in the photos that were burned into her brain. She began shivering again, and he got up from the sofa and a minute later returned with a blanket, which he tucked around her.

"Why didn't you tell me?" he asked as he sat down heavily beside her on the sofa. "Why keep this from me?"

Why didn't you fight for us? She heard the implicit meaning behind his words and felt her cheeks warm with embarrassment. She hated talking about her ex. In fact, she tried her best never to give him any headspace at all, but it was time to tell Jack the truth.

"Someone cheated on me before… actually, twice." She cringed at how gullible she'd been. "He was my fiancé, and he swore he hadn't, and the first time I believed him. But then I realised I was being taken for a fool, and I decided no one would ever do that to me again. I didn't want to go through the same charade with you… all the denial and gaslighting, so I decided I'd just leave."

His eyes widened. "You never told me about your fiancé."

"We dated just after university, and we were together for two years. The funny thing was, he was the one who pushed to get engaged, whereas I thought it was too soon." Her fingers tightened into fists on the blanket. "It was a good thing it happened… not the cheating bit, but I mean, we weren't right for each other, and I'm glad we didn't end up getting married."

She let her thoughts drift, recalling when he'd cheated on her for the second time. The damage from his gaslighting had stayed with her for years. He'd made her a more cynical person, and her self-esteem and trust in her own instincts had withered and died too, so receiving those photos had only reinforced her belief that all men were cheaters if they thought they could get away with it.

But maybe she'd projected the actions of her ex onto Jack and if she'd told him about the photos sooner … if she'd trusted him and not doubted him and not assumed that he was the same liar as her ex – maybe they'd still be together.

"Lou?"

She dragged her thoughts back to the present, shocked by the raw pain in his eyes. "I'm sorry I didn't tell you about the photos," she whispered, her throat tightening as fresh tears began falling.

"I understand why you didn't, and I realise the photos are pretty damning, but I didn't cheat on you Lou. I'm not the same as your ex and I would never behave like he did, and all I ask is that you give me time to prove it to you."

"I don't know what to think."

She watched his jaw tighten as he nodded. "That's fair enough, I suppose." He reached for her hand, and she let him take it as he began rubbing his thumb back and forth against her skin. She felt awful for continuing to doubt him, but seeing those photos of him with Shona… his hands on her… and doing a lot more, it was difficult to ignore.

But what if he was telling the truth? In fact, when she thought about it, in all the time they'd been together, he'd never once given her the slightest cause to doubt him. On the contrary, he'd always made her feel loved and respected and wanted.

He must have read her mind because he cupped her cheek. "I'm so sorry, Lou. This was an awful burden to carry around on your own for so long. I know you're hurt and upset and confused, and I could kill whoever did this for putting you through this, but I promise you I will get to the truth."

He finally let go of her, and immediately she missed his touch and wanted it back. She also still needed to tell him about Annie - that he was her father - but it was getting late, and maybe there'd been enough revelations for one night. "I should get back. Annie will be missing me."

"I'll drive you."

"If you could just drop me at your office carpark?"

"You've been through an emotional wringer, so I'd feel better if I drove you home. I'll bring your car back to you tomorrow."

He was probably right… and there he was, taking care of her again, as he always had. They both got up, and then he pulled her into his arms, and she could feel the steady beat of his heart beneath his shirt, and the woodsy scent of his aftershave, so achingly familiar.

"I love you, Lou. I've always loved you, and I always will. Please trust me to sort this mess out." He finally let her go and kissed her forehead.

She nodded. There was nothing she wanted more in the world.

Chapter 23 - Jack

Lou sent him the photos and then fell asleep in the car almost immediately as he drove them back to Broadsham. The roads were quieter now, and the journey didn't take long. He parked outside the hotel, and when he switched off the engine, she awoke with a start.

"Sorry, I didn't mean to nod off."

"You needed it. Come on, I'll see you to the door."

"Jack…" She reached over to grab his arm. "I… my head's such a mess, but I want to believe you."

A gentle smile brushed his lips. "I know."

He walked her to the flat, and she got out her key. "I'd invite you in, but Mum…"

"It's fine. I'll drop your car back tomorrow morning, okay?"

"Yes, thank you."

He kissed her cheek and watched as she opened the front door and disappeared inside. He stood in the small courtyard for a few moments longer, breathing in the chilly night air as anger began burning through his body.

Why had Shona wanted to destroy his relationship with Lou?

Not for the first time, he berated himself for getting involved with her, albeit briefly. Yes, she'd been fun to flirt with, but he should have kept it at that, except a few drinks after work one Friday night had clouded his better judgement. A short while later, he'd come to his senses and broken up with her. His thoughts drifted back to that night… she'd taken the news relatively well, but it had still been awkward as hell at work, and Adam hadn't been too pleased either. The cowardly part of him had hoped she'd leave – there were plenty of jobs around for competent receptionists - and he'd felt even worse for being so gutless, but eventually things had settled down… or so he'd thought.

He was half-inclined to go round to her place now and demand an explanation, but a late-night angry confrontation was never a good idea. No, far better to wait until the morning when his head had cooled down.

He left his car where it was and jogged to Adam's house, which was at the end of the village. If Adam was surprised at his unexpected arrival on his doorstep, he didn't show it, but he must have noticed something serious in Jack's expression because he showed him straight into his home office.

"What's up?"

He could hear the muted tones of soft jazz playing in the sitting room, and he immediately felt guilty for disrupting Mordros and Adam's evening. Mordros had moved in with Adam a few weeks ago, and he still wasn't used to her being here.

"Jack?" Adam gave him a gentle nudge

"Sorry," he blurted. "It can wait until tomorrow." He turned to go, but Adam put his hand on his shoulder to stop him.

"Don't go running off now you're here. Anyway, you'll get me out of some more wedding planning if you stay," he joked but then grew serious as he read Jack's mood. "Let's have a beer."

They moved to the kitchen, and he noticed a portion of leftover pie on the granite counter. He hadn't eaten since lunchtime, and his stomach growled with hunger, but he had more important things to think about than food. Instead, he took the beer Adam offered him and, half an hour later, he'd finished explaining all about the damning photos and the reason Lou had left him. Mordros had popped in once to say hello but had tactfully left them to it.

"God, what a mess." Adam blew out his cheeks.

"I'm not a tech expert, but even I know that with the right skills, it's relatively straightforward to alter the date stamp on a photo."

"Though clearly Lou didn't."

"No. But that's not really the point. Shona sent her the photos anonymously with the sole intention of breaking us up."

"You don't know for certain it was Shona."

"No, but how likely is it that someone else would have access to these photos?"

"Do you think they could be fake?"

He thought for a moment. He'd assumed not, but… "I don't recall the photos being taken, but I was quite busy at the time."

"I can see that," Adam smirked. "And so could Lou."

"Don't," he groaned. "Look, Lou knows I wasn't a monk before I met her, but I never cheated on her."

"What are you going to do?"

"I'll confront Shona tomorrow morning, but I wanted to warn you first."

"You need to get your facts straight because if it turns out it wasn't her, she could sue you for defamation."

"I know, but who the hell else could it be?"

"Maybe it's one of your disgruntled clients who's holding a grudge against you because you lost his case?" he teased.

"I don't lose cases," Jack grumbled, but at least he'd lightened his mood.

"Look, instead of going off half-cocked, why don't you get an actual tech expert to look at the photos? Then they can give you their professional opinion."

"I guess so," he conceded.

"Now, do you want another beer?" Adam gestured towards his empty one.

His stomach growled again. "No, but I'd love some of that leftover pie if it's going spare?"

Chapter 24 - Lou

"So, what do you think?"

They were in a small bridal boutique in Broadsham, and Nick held up the ivory Crepe de Chine silk dress. "It's got a bias cut to highlight your curves, with a flattering draped cowl neckline."

Mordros frowned. "It's not really me."

"Then what about this one? It's floral-patterned tulle, and the sheer corset gives it a beautifully structured fit, and the dainty tie waist adds a feminine touch. The pouf sleeves make it seem playful."

"I'd look ridiculous," she snorted.

Nick was in his element, so the assistant had tactfully left them, promising to return with more prosecco. "Yeah, you're probably right… so what about this one? It's got a modern plunge neckline and an open back."

"No, definitely not." She shook her head. "These are all way too fancy."

"Okay, then let's leave yours for a moment. What about Lou and Annie's dresses?" Nick picked up one of the plum-coloured silk dresses hanging on a hook in the changing room. "Lou, what do you think?"

Lou took a deep breath. "Well, I…"

"You hate it, don't you?" Mordros interrupted.

"I don't exactly hate it," she tried to be diplomatic.

"Mama hates it, and Annie hates it." Annie chose that moment to chime in, and she felt her cheeks flush.

"Hate is an unkind word, Annie. We should say that we don't really like it," she gently chastised her.

"That's it. I've had enough," Mordros announced firmly. "None of these dresses is remotely suitable."

She was right, thought Lou, glumly. Mordros must have tried on a dozen dresses, and despite Nick's helpful commentary, none of them were her style at all.

"I agree. They're not you," Nick echoed Lou's thoughts. "We'll just have to find a different bridal shop," he said brightly.

"No, I'm going to make my dress, and I'll make Lou and Annie's dresses, too."

"Whoa! Are you sure? The wedding's in three weeks… do you have time?" Nick raked his fingers through his dark hair so that it stuck up.

"I just want to wear something that doesn't make me look like a meringue." She waved her hand toward the discarded dresses she'd already tried on. "Something that's the opposite of all these."

Thank God for that, thought Lou. Getting married looking like a meringue wasn't what she wanted for her friend at all.

***

Nick had gone back to work, and Lou and Mordros were drinking tea in Lou's small kitchen after their unsuccessful shopping trip. Annie was in her nursery, napping.

Mordros carefully dipped her custard cream into her tea and then took an appreciative bite. "Mmm, that's good."

"Oh, you're a biscuit dunker," Lou grinned. "Aren't you scared of losing half of it if you leave it in the tea for too long?"

"There's an art to it, depending on which biscuit you eat. Rich Tea, Hobnobs and chocolate digestives all have their own crumbling points. There's even been scientific studies done on the best biscuit for dunking."

"You're not joking, are you?"

"Of course not. No one wants half a soggy biscuit at the bottom of their mug. Now, my own personal favourite is a chocolate bourbon because it has quite a long breaking point, whereas Adam prefers a shortbread. And Nick likes a Jaffa, though that's not technically a biscuit. I bet Jack's more of a Jammie Dodger dunker… by the way, how is he?"

"Well done, that's a smooth segue." She laughed. "I'll have to ask him next time I see him."

"So, you two are seeing each other, then?"

"You're incorrigible, but yes, we are … though not like that," she hastily added.

"Like what?" Mordros probed innocently.

She felt her cheeks flush. "Like romantically." But when Mordros held her gaze, she felt the need to clarify. "We're just friends."

"Well, that's progress, I guess."

"I told him about the photos."

"Oh goodness, what did he say?" Mordros finally put down her tea and gave Lou her full attention.

"What I knew he'd say… that he hadn't cheated."

"And you don't believe him?"

"I want to, honestly, I do. He thinks that it's possible to change a date stamp on a photo, but why would someone do that?"

"Maybe someone who didn't like you and him being together?" She hesitated, and Lou could tell she was debating whether to say more. "Look, I know it's none of my business and I can't explain the date thingy, but since Adam and I got back together, I've got to know Jack a lot better, and I think if he'd wanted this woman, he'd have broken things off with you first."

"These photos tell a different story."

"Forget what you see in the photos. Focus on what you know about Jack and who he is as a person. Do you really think he'd cheat on you?"

She wanted to say no so badly, but could she discount them and ignore what she was seeing with her own eyes? "No, but it's hard to reconcile what I feel in my heart with what these photos are showing me." She swiped her palm down her face trying to hold on to her emotions. "He doesn't deny dating her, but he says they broke up before we got together. He thinks she sent them to me."

"That would make sense if she were upset about their breakup."

"I guess," she tested out the theory in her head. "It just seems a very malicious thing to do, going to all the trouble of altering the date and then finding my mobile number to send them to me."

"True, but perhaps she still had feelings for Jack and couldn't stand seeing him happy with you. Or maybe she thought she could make you doubt him enough to leave, so she'd have another chance to rekindle their relationship."

"Well, she succeeded then." She felt the sting of tears but blinked them away.

"Of course she didn't. He's not with her, is he?"

"No," she conceded, but it had still led to their splitting up. "Do you really think she'd be that manipulative?"

"Yes, if she felt wronged and wanted revenge and to hurt you both. Plus, some people just love causing chaos."

Lou watched a shadow pass across her friend's face, and she instinctively knew that she wasn't talking about the photos anymore. "What's the matter…are you okay?"

A flicker of a smile crossed her face. "Yes, but I'm a little worried about Adam."

"Why? What's the matter? He's not having second thoughts about the wedding, is he?" she teased.

"No, it's not that, though he's driving me mad with his wedding spreadsheet. Every night after dinner, he makes us go through it to see what progress we're making." She groaned.

"That sounds like fun," Lou chuckled. "So, why are you worried about him?"

Mordros sighed. "I don't think I've ever told you about his mother, but she's an evil witch, and unfortunately, she's coming to the wedding."

Lou's eyes widened because she'd never heard Mordros speak with so much venom. "Wow, you really don't like her, do you?"

"No, I don't. Adam doesn't either, but I still felt obligated to invite her. We were hoping she'd decline, but we found out yesterday that she's coming."

"Do you have to have much to do with her? I mean, it's your wedding day, so can't you put her next to your great auntie, or someone?"

"That's the plan," she laughed wryly. "But knowing her, she'll want to be the centre of attention, and I'm scared she'll upset Adam."

"Is that likely? I mean, from what I've seen, he can take care of himself."

"Yes, usually he can, but she's always been his one weak point, and she knows that and how to manipulate him. Well, she did when he was younger, but now Adam's got me in his corner, so she'd better not try."

Lou blew out a breath. "Well, good luck if she does."

"Sorry, you must think I'm horrible, but one reason Adam and I originally broke up was because of her. I'm sure he won't mind my saying, but he didn't have a great childhood, and he had to grow up far too quickly. Jack was the one person who really helped him, inviting him to spend the holidays with his family when they were both at school, and that's why they've become such great friends."

"So, his mum turning up…"

"Is the last thing Adam needs. Except I think deep down he's still hoping that she'll turn into 'mother of the year', which Jack and I know won't ever happen, but inside he's still that 10-year-old child looking for unconditional love."

"That sounds… difficult."

"Yes, and the worst of it is that she doesn't have any idea about how toxic she is. She just swans through life, causing chaos and mayhem wherever she goes."

Lou nodded and thought how fortunate she was to have her own loving mum. Not everyone was so lucky. "And what about your parents? Are they coming to the wedding?"

Her friend's face softened. "Ma died when I was a baby, but Pa will definitely be coming. Actually, that's something I was hoping to talk to you about. He wants to book a room at the hotel for a few days during the wedding period. We've told him he's welcome to stay with us, but he's adamant he'd prefer his own space. Plus, if Adam's old bat of a mother is staying with us, he'll want to avoid her at all costs because they were a *thing* once."

"A thing?"

"Yeah, but that's a story for another day, or at least until I've got several glasses of prosecco inside me."

"Okay, though I'm still intrigued."

"Do you have a room available?" Mordros deftly changed the subject.

Lou thought for a moment. The whole of the top floor of the hotel was out of action because of the leaking roof, but that still left rooms on the first floor. "Let me check, but I'm sure we do."

"That's great news, and something Adam can cross off his spreadsheet," Mordros giggled.

Chapter 25 - Lou

It had been three days since she'd seen Jack and shown him the incriminating photos. As good as his word the morning after, he'd posted the car keys through her letterbox. She noticed that he'd topped up the tank with fuel, and also put it through a car wash, so the paintwork was gleaming. Her mum noticed too, because she gave Lou an enigmatic smile that spoke volumes.

She stared at her phone screen, willing a message from him to pop up. *Please trust me to sort this mess out*, he'd told her, and she did... sort of. But she wasn't the most patient of people, or used to relying on others, and it was frustrating as hell waiting for him to get in touch. *Where was the man?*

She pulled up the photos on her phone again. At first glance, they appeared genuine, but what if the date stamp had been altered? That would give a completely different interpretation from the one she'd so hastily jumped to.

Why didn't you tell me? Why keep this from me? His words had accused her, because instead of giving him the chance to put his side of things, she'd run away from him. And maybe that was why he'd been silent for three days, because he was angry at her for the way she'd behaved and, honestly, she couldn't blame him.

It was nearly five o'clock, and Annie was on the sofa engrossed in a children's Christmas programme. It was time to get her tea ready, but she couldn't draw her eyes away from the damning pictures. She'd felt blindsided when she'd recognised the woman in Jack's office, but instead of confronting her and perhaps finally getting to the truth, she'd bolted…again. She needed to stop doing that.

Regret was going to crush her, a single tear making its way slowly down her cheek. She wiped it away as Annie began complaining she was hungry. "Let's have mac and cheese. I know that's your favourite." She faked the brightness in her voice.

"Mat and keys," Annie repeated gleefully.

"Mat and keys, it is." She gave her daughter – *Jack's daughter* - a gentle kiss on her cheek, and there was her regret again wrapping itself around her heart, because he still didn't know …but *their* daughter was hungry, so she needed to concentrate on that task instead.

It wasn't only Annie's favourite, but hers, too. Half an hour later, the cheesy pasta deliciousness was ready, as well as a salad she'd made to go with it.

"Sugar," she muttered as she heard knocking on the front door. "That better not be carol singers." She left the dish of pasta cooling on the kitchen counter and huffed her way out into the hallway to answer it.

"Hi." Jack stood on the porch, smiling. "I'm sorry for just turning up, but I wondered if you've got a minute?"

Relief whooshed through her at the sight of him. She smiled back like a teenager about to go on their first date. "You'd better come in."

Chapter 26 - Jack

"Hello Jat," Annie greeted him as he followed Lou into the small kitchen. She was sitting on her new booster seat at the table, already wearing an all in one apron that was clearly designed to protect her clothing from food spillage. Small red Santas decorated the coverup, which he guessed was another nod to Lou's love of all things Christmas.

"Hi Annie, what are you having for tea?"

"Mat and keys." She gave him a dazzling smile, and before he could work out what she meant, Lou came to his rescue.

"What Annie means is that we're having mac and cheese for tea. Would you like to stay and have some with us?"

He couldn't help chuckling. "For a moment there, I was worried, but mac and cheese sounds amazing… if you're sure there's enough?"

"I always make tons. Also, there's some leftover wine from the other night." She waved her hand in the vague direction of one of the kitchen cupboards. "Help yourself."

He slipped his jacket off, found the wine, and poured them both a small amount into two glass tumblers. "I know you said you prefer not to drink when you're looking after Annie, but a small glass won't hurt."

"What you mean is that it'll make my food taste a lot better," she teased.

"I wouldn't dream of saying that, and from what I remember, whenever you cooked for me in London, your food always tasted great."

"Except for the time I tried making pancakes, and they turned into scrambled eggs."

"I'd forgotten about that," he grinned. She'd used up a box of eggs trying to get the recipe to work and finally abandoned the idea. "But you can buy great readymade ones, so problem solved."

"Do you always look for solutions to problems?" She began piling their plates with the cheesy pasta.

"Of course. That's what my job is all about." He turned serious. "I have some news, but maybe I should tell you later, once Annie's in bed."

"No, not bed, Jat." Annie began shaking her head vehemently, and her bottom lip stuck out into the beginning of a pout. "I want mat and keys."

He bent to kiss her cheek. "Of course you do, and I can't wait to try your mum's mat and keys, too."

***

It was delightful having tea together and listening to Lou encourage Annie to have some of the salad she'd made - not a great success - and correcting her when she talked with her mouth full, which she quickly forgot again a few minutes later.

Annie had her own small cutlery set, and Lou praised her when she used her knife and fork properly, though some of her pasta still fell down her front, so he saw the sense in using the coverup. The meal was full of chatter and laughter, and Lou seemed relaxed and happy. He couldn't remember a mealtime he'd enjoyed more.

There was yoghurt and fruit for dessert, and then Lou took Annie off for her bath while he tidied the kitchen and washed up. He could hear Lou singing to Annie in the bathroom, and then a few minutes later, she popped her head around the door to invite him to say goodnight.

Annie was lying in her cot-bed sucking her thumb, which he now recognised as a sign she was tired and ready for sleep. She was cuddling the Simba he'd bought her, her eyelids growing heavy and almost closing.

"Good night, Annie, sleep well." He bent to give her a kiss on her warm cheek. "Sweet dreams."

"Jat?" Her eyes suddenly flew open and found his.

"Yes, sweetheart."

"Do you love Mama?" The green in her eyes was intense and totally focused on him.

"Annie, I don't think–," Lou began, but stopped when he didn't hesitate.

"Yes, I do."

As if satisfied with his answer, her eyes began closing again. "I love Mama, too." She murmured sleepily as she drifted off.

"I know, sweetheart. I know."

***

Out of the mouths of babes. Lou had gone the colour of beetroot, but he wasn't about to pass up the chance to tell her what he was feeling, because he'd wasted too much time already.

Annie was asleep, and they were sitting together on Lou's small sofa drinking tea. He quietly observed her, wondering what she was thinking. She looked tired, and he wondered how much sleep she was getting. Not a lot, he guessed, but probably not the right time to ask about that. He needed to focus.

"I gave the photos to our IT guy at work. He's called Ed, and what he doesn't know about computers and techie stuff isn't worth knowing."

"Oh?" Lou looked at him, and he could see he'd got her full attention, and she was waiting for him to continue.

"He says not only is the date stamp fake, but the photos are too."

"Really?" Lou put down her tea and stared at him. "What, like photoshopped?"

"No, not photoshopped. This was far more sophisticated and from someone who knew what they were doing."

"I see," but when he raised his eyebrows, she admitted: "Okay, I don't have any idea what you're talking about."

"I'd like you to meet him because he can explain all the technical stuff much better than I can. I wondered if you were free tomorrow." He waited. "Lou?" he gently prompted when she didn't respond.

"Sorry… I… I mean, would whatshername… Shona be capable of doing that?"

"Well, she's a competent receptionist, but as far as I know, she doesn't have those sorts of technical skills."

"So, where do we go from here? I mean, I still can't get my head around someone wanting to do this. But if it wasn't Shona, then…?"

"I don't know, but maybe Ed can throw some light on things."

"I guess," though she didn't sound convinced.

"So, can I take you to meet him tomorrow?"

She nodded. "And now that's settled, shall we watch a Christmas film?"

"Hmm, let me guess… you're thinking of a slushy, romantic one, aren't you?"

"Of course, and if you're lucky, we can watch one every night until Christmas."

He fake-groaned as he tracked the line of her smiling mouth, his thoughts turning to other things he'd rather do with her than watch a film, but for the time being that would have to do.

Chapter 27 - Lou

It was Annie's nursery day, and the three of them ambled slowly along Broadsham High Street towards the Little Poppins Nursery, which opened at eight o'clock.

Jack had arrived a few minutes earlier and was holding onto Annie's hand while also carrying her Winnie-the-Pooh backpack, which contained an emergency change of clothes, and her small lunchbox. That left Lou pushing the empty pushchair. They were making slow progress because Annie insisted on stopping and looking in every shop window they passed.

"Look, Jat, a star." She pointed towards the Christmas tree on the green. The pompom on her red bobble hat bounced enthusiastically as she turned to face him. It was a bright, crisp morning, and her cheeks were pink from the cold, her green eyes shining with excitement.

"Yes, I see," Jack grinned, tugging at her pompom, which made her giggle with delight.

"Come on, we'll never get there if you both keep stopping," Lou gently scolded.

"But Mama, we need a star on our tree, too."

"You're right, we do. How about we make one when you get back from nursery?"

"And Jat help make one, too?"

"I think he'll be busy at work, sweetheart."

"I'd love to, if your Mama doesn't mind." Jack gave her one of his winning smiles, and she couldn't help laughing.

"If you'd like to come for tea and make a star for the Christmas tree, you're very welcome."

"Great. I'm looking forward to discovering my creative side." He winked, and she felt her insides melt into a gooey puddle because he wanted to spend more time with them.

Twenty minutes later, they'd finally made it to the nursery, and Annie flung herself into Jack's arms for a goodbye hug. "I'll see you at home, sweetie." He gave her a kiss on her cheek and tweaked her pompom again. "Have a great day."

"Bye Jat. See you at home." She giggled and waved as Lou took her into the building to find her nursery worker, while Jack remained outside with the pushchair. A few moments later, Lou came out again, and when he greeted her with a warm smile, she imagined all the parents standing near them would assume that he was Annie's father. The thought made her heart sing.

She just needed to find the courage to tell him.

***

The walk back was a lot quicker without the constant Annie stops, and they were soon in Jack's car and on their way to Cheltenham. Nerves chilled her at what hand grenade the tech guy would throw at them about the photos – though maybe dwelling on hand grenades wasn't helping her nerves much either.

She sensed Jack's nerves too because he was holding the steering wheel in a death grip, his knuckles white with tension. "Are you okay?" She reached across and squeezed his arm.

"I don't understand why anyone would fake those photos and send them to you. It feels like one of us has an enemy." The growl in his voice and the hard features on his face made her sit up straighter.

"I know what you mean, but hopefully whoever did this has moved on. It was nearly three years ago, after all."

"Does a psychopath move on, or do they just wait for their prey to become vulnerable again?"

"Seriously? I think you've been reading too many thrillers. Surely, it's just someone who was jealous and got a bit carried away."

"That was more than getting carried away, Lou. Faking those photos was deliberate and manipulative and deceitful."

"Yeah, I agree with all that. But don't you think it's all water under the bridge now?"

"No, I don't. Those photos made you think I'd cheated on you, which led to us splitting up. I won't forgive that. Whoever did this, I promise I will find out and make them pay."

The man she knew was always good-humoured and didn't take life too seriously, but the determined look on his face showed an entirely different side – *the lawyer side, maybe?* - and one that told her he wouldn't rest until he knew who the culprit was and used every instrument of the law to punish them.

"I don't doubt it," she whispered.

For the rest of the journey, she gazed out of the car window, watching the apple orchards surrounding Broadsham shift to a more urban landscape as they approached the outskirts of Cheltenham. The thought that there was someone out there – in Jack's words, a psychopath – who wanted to split them up was unnerving and made her stomach squeeze with fear.

***

Jack parked his car in the small car park she'd used a few days earlier, and they walked the short distance to his office building.

The last thing she wanted was to see Shona again, but when she glanced around, there was someone else sitting behind the reception desk. She felt a surge of relief and then annoyance because she'd allowed herself to be intimidated by a woman who was obviously a troublemaker. Not happening, she told herself off.

"Ed's already waiting for us in my office," Jack told her as they took the lift to the top floor of the building.

"I hope I can understand him. I'm not exactly au fait with computer jargon."

"He's a bit of a geek, but you'll like him. We have many debates about the best sci-fi films to watch. Ed's really into Star Wars, by the way."

She chuckled, "I guess if the tech stuff gets too complicated, we can always chat about that instead."

His office wasn't at all what she was expecting: light and modern, with a view towards the park. A couple of comic cover artworks hung on the walls, and a Batman figurine perched on the glass and chrome coffee table. It didn't look like a stuffy lawyer's office, but it was very Jack.

"This is Ed Grace. As well as running a company that looks after all our office computer software, he's also a digital forensics specialist. And this is Lou," Jack hesitated before continuing, "my good friend."

She almost laughed because Ed Grace was as far removed from being graceful as it was possible to get. Tall, thin, and gangly with a lime green Mohawk haircut, he wore a Star Wars T-shirt and leather Doc Marten boots. Her eyes zoned-in on the intricate ink symbols covering his arms, which extended up his long neck. She guessed he was in his early thirties, but despite his relative youth, his skin was pasty. He didn't look like a guy who ventured outside into the fresh air very often.

"Pleased to meet you." Ed put away his phone and held out his hand.

Lou snapped her mind back into focus, smiling at the incongruity between his posh public school accent and his appearance. "I'm pleased to meet you, too, Ed."

"Can you tell us what you found out about the photos, please?" Jack got straight down to business.

"Yes, of course." He began pulling up the photos on his laptop, which was resting on the coffee table. "Someone has digitally manipulated these photos using advanced photo editing software. They've combined two different photos to make it look like a compromising moment happened when it actually didn't."

Lou's eyes widened with shock. "But they look real… two people tangled up together in bed." She stopped because she didn't want to think too much about the image of Jack and Shona in bed.

"The photos are good fakes, but when I forensically tested the images, they have subtle mismatches. For example, a faint blur where the woman's hair meets the man's shoulder. Also, the light and shadows are inconsistent. The shadows fall in different directions, and the angle of the woman's hand doesn't quite match her body. These images are a composite; someone has merged two separate photos to create a fake image."

She realised he was being tactful by not mentioning Jack or Shona by name, though he must have recognised who they were since he worked for Jack.

"Is there anything else to prove these photos are fake?" Jack queried.

Ed nodded. "Yes, the metadata doesn't match."

"Can you explain what that means?"

"Every photo has hidden data that includes when and where it was taken. In these photos, the metadata was erased. Whoever sent it didn't want anyone to know when it was really taken. I also did a pixel-level analysis… parts of the photo had been saved differently, like they came from separate sources."

"Thanks. That's really useful information. We really appreciate your expertise."

Ed nodded and began closing down his laptop, almost falling over the coffee table in the process and sending the Batman figurine flying. "Sorry." He scooped it up from the floor and placed it back on the table.

Lou smothered a laugh… he definitely didn't live up to his name.

***

"So, where do we go from here?" She sighed heavily as she considered what Ed had told them. "You've already said you don't think Shona has the skills to manipulate these photos, so where does that leave us?"

"Honestly, I don't know." Jack raked his hand through his hair.

"What don't you know?" A familiar voice from the doorway interrupted them, and they both whirled round. "Sorry, I didn't mean to startle you." Adam grinned.

"Hi." Lou walked over to give him a hug.

"We're just talking about the results of the photo analysis." Jack explained. "I showed Adam the photos, Lou. I hope you don't mind."

"Of course not. I just want this all to go away."

"I know you do, and it will … I'll make sure of it."

"So, what did Ed say?" Adam brought them back on topic.

"That the photos are fake, and someone went to a lot of trouble to make it look like I was cheating on Lou when I wasn't."

Her cheeks flushed with embarrassment. "I feel terrible for ever doubting you now."

"Hey, anyone who saw those photos would think the same," he quickly defended her.

Adam nodded. She knew they were just trying to make her feel better, but nothing could take away her guilt and self-loathing. If she'd confided in him and shown him the photos in London, they'd probably still be together. Her eyes blurred with tears, and he must have noticed because he was suddenly beside her, pulling her to his side. "I'm so sorry," she mumbled.

"Shush," he bent to kiss the top of her head softly.

"Look, guys, I know you want to find out who did this, but it's our wedding weekend celebration soon. Why don't you put your investigation on hold and have some fun?"

Lou looked up and met Jack's eyes. "Sounds good. I could do with forgetting about these stupid photos for a bit."

"Great. Then let's go shopping."

"Shopping?" Adam and Lou chimed at the same time.

Jack grinned. "Yep, we need to buy some party stuff to make it a weekend to remember."

Adam groaned. "Please don't buy something either of us will regret."

"I'm afraid I can't guarantee that," he smirked.

Chapter 28 - Jack

Taking a day off during the week was a novelty for Jack. Being a partner in a successful law practice often demanded long hours, and he was used to working six and occasionally seven days a week as his job became his solace after Lou left him. But earlier he'd instructed his personal assistant to clear his diary, so the rest of the day was theirs to do whatever they wanted.

Their shopping trip had been hilarious, as they'd dared each other to find the funniest games for the weekend. Jack had to give it to Lou because she'd been completely up for some of the ruder ones: naughty bingo, a dirty mind guessing game, and toss the willy hoopla were all going to embarrass Adam and he couldn't help wondering if his best friend would survive the weekend's entertainment.

Armed with their purchases, they ate lunch at a small bistro, which he knew was the sort of place Lou liked. It had a sheltered walled garden at the rear, with terracotta pots filled with pale pink winter cyclamen and bright splashes of purple and yellow pansies. There were blankets for those brave enough to sit outside in early December, though today it was warm enough without them. Despite the intense blue of the sky and the winter sunshine, they were the only customers choosing to eat on the patio, which he was secretly pleased about because he wanted to be alone with Lou.

They shared small plates of appetisers and then Lou ordered a fancy chocolate dessert and two spoons while they chatted about everything and nothing. As if by tacit agreement, neither of them brought up the fake photos, letting the subject rest while they enjoyed their day out together. As their lunch wound down, and after a glass of wine, Lou relaxed into a happy state of giggly-ness. He'd stuck to soft drinks and coffee since he was driving.

"Do you ever think about us in London?" Lou tipped her head back and closed her eyes.

"I do." He smiled as he realised from her flushed face, she was more tipsy than he'd originally thought - no doubt because she wasn't used to drinking now, especially in the middle of the day.

"I miss those days."

He swallowed, trying to think of a response, because she had Annie now, so she'd been with someone after him. Was this the time to ask about Annie's father? He wanted to, but… "What do you miss?" he asked instead.

"You."

It was one small word, but laden with meaning. Even so, he imagined the wine had loosened her tongue, and she'd regret it once she sobered up. Her eyes opened and found his, and he reached across and gently squeezed her hand. "I've always been here, Lou."

"I wish I could turn back time. I wish I hadn't been so horrible to you." Her voice cracked with guilt.

"Shush sweetheart. No one blames you for being taken in by those photos."

"I blame myself, though. I should have trusted you."

"Whoever sent you these photos wanted you to think I'd cheated. That's on them, not you."

"When I left you in London, my world flipped upside down. I wanted to hate you… and I tried really hard to move on, but I still couldn't get you out of my head. Every day you've been in my thoughts, and I dream about the life we could have had if only I hadn't believed those photos." She was on a roll now, and he watched as she gathered her courage. "Maybe we still can?" She held his gaze, waiting.

God, her violet eyes would always be his undoing, and they were looking at him full of hope and a thousand possibilities if only he'd take them. Slowly, he leant over, letting his lips gently brush against hers for the first time since they'd been together in London. He could smell her perfume, a little faded now, and his chest tightened with emotion as she tugged on his shirt to bring them closer.

And when he deepened the kiss, the old familiarity came flooding back … the taste and feel of her intoxicating his senses as she kissed him back. Relief surged through him, but more than that… a feeling that all the pain from being apart was now ending. He'd thought he'd lost her forever, but maybe this was their second chance?

After a minute, he reluctantly pulled away. The patio wasn't exactly private, and he didn't want an audience for what he wanted to do. "Let's head home."

He went inside to pay their bill, but as soon as they made it back inside his car, they lunged for each other. His hands cupped her face, tugging her close. Hungry and desperate, their kisses matched their need for each other as she almost climbed into his lap. If they kept on kissing like this, he was going to rip her clothes off and haul her into the back seat. He jerked back, breathing hard.

"Not here." His voice was an octave lower as he growled over each word.

Lou nodded, and he put the car into gear, and they began the drive back to Broadsham. It felt like forever, but eventually they pulled up outside the hotel and clambered out of the car, almost running towards Lou's flat. Her hands shook as she fumbled with the key to let them in while he stood behind with his hands on her waist, breathing in the citrus scent of her hair.

And then finally, they were inside, and he pulled her to him as she wrapped her hands around his neck. Their lips met, and he steered her towards what he guessed was her bedroom, his kisses becoming hungrier and more demanding with each step.

Chapter 29 - Lou

Nearly three years since they'd last made love, but it seemed to Lou the lapse of time faded to nothing as they lay wrapped up in each other's arms afterwards. Being with him had been the same as in London, but also different, as they spent the afternoon rediscovering each other. His body was stronger… fitter, as she trailed her fingers over his defined muscles. He'd always been in good shape, but he must have been spending a lot more time in the gym since they'd split.

Her own body had changed as well; a soft layer to her tummy, which she hadn't quite lost from being pregnant, and some silvery stretch marks. But his gentle kisses peppering her skin as he moved lower, swept her self-consciousness away, his touch making her dizzy with desire as the colours of the afternoon softened and the shadows lengthened.

The second time had been slower… more gentle as they'd taken time to explore each other again - her only reality was his lips, his kisses, the feel of his body moving against hers. Nothing else existed beyond the two of them, and she'd never wanted him so deeply. Her heart almost burst with love for this man and the joy of finding him again.

Kissing each other, breathing each other's breath, she lost herself in him, his weight surrounding her until she couldn't think, only feel. He'd always ensured sex was good for her, but this was another level, beyond pleasure, as she tumbled into ecstasy again.

Afterwards, she laid her head on his broad chest, and they talked softly as the light faded and the time to collect Annie edged closer. He trailed his fingers through her hair until it was impossible to delay leaving any longer. He helped her find her jeans and top in the heap of clothes they'd abandoned earlier, and between yet more kisses, they finally dressed.

While he used the bathroom, she stared at her reflection in the small mirror on her chest of drawers. Had this afternoon really happened? Her hair was a mess from his finger combing, and she looked exactly like she'd spent the afternoon in bed… her flushed cheeks and sparkling eyes a sure giveaway. Slowly, her smile grew. Making love had been the perfect ending to a perfect day. So, did that mean they were back together now? Of course, there were things to talk about – especially Annie – but what they'd done this afternoon had to mean something.

A curl of fear wrapped around her heart. At the restaurant, she'd opened up to him, telling him exactly what she wanted. *I dream about the life we could have had if only I hadn't believed those photos. Maybe we still can?*

But he hadn't replied.

No, he'd never take advantage of her like that. In fact, just before they'd stumbled into bed, he'd questioned whether she was sober enough since she'd had a glass of wine with lunch. She'd worried he'd change his mind until she told him not to be an idiot.

Her smile grew once more. She needed to stop overthinking because finally they were on the right track and things would only get better.

***

"Annie, no!" Lou hissed as she watched a tornado of glitter splatter everywhere. Annie was decorating the Christmas star with the help of Jack, who, in Lou's opinion, was more of a hindrance. It was like having two naughty two-year-olds, not a toddler with a competent adult supervising.

"It's my fault." He gave her a sheepish grin. "I misjudged the direction the glitter was heading."

She groaned as she took in the disaster zone. Glitter covered the Christmas star, the top of the kitchen table, Annie and Jack's faces, and the rest sparkled up at them from the lino floor. At this rate, she'd be finding glitter in random places for the next six months. *Fur balls!* "Glitter should be banned until at least the age of sixteen," she huffed.

"Bah humbug. Annie and I are having a great time, and don't worry, I'll clear up the mess. Why don't you relax and leave Annie to me?"

"Yes, Mama, Jat look after me." Annie gave her a wide goofy grin showing off the two new baby teeth that had appeared in the last couple of weeks, and she couldn't help snorting as they ganged up on her. They were like two peas in a pod, both covered in glue and glitter, with their identical grins and matching green eyes sparkling with mischief. She was amazed Jack still hadn't noticed the similarities between them.

"Okay, but I expect this kitchen to be spotless by the time it's bath time. And don't think I won't inspect your cleaning either."

She sat down on her small sofa and closed her eyes as the sounds of laughing in the background lulled her to sleep.

***

"Hey Lou?" Jack's low voice floated into her dream… something to do with teeth or glitter, or maybe the tooth fairy? The trouble was, once you started waking up, dreams somehow melted away, and now she couldn't remember.

"What time is it?" her voice was groggy.

"It's time to say goodnight to Annie."

"What?" Shaking off the last vestiges of sleep, she realised that other than the lights from the hotel across the courtyard, it was pitch-black outside.

"Don't worry, I've fed her and she's already in her room waiting for you."

"You've fed her?" She tried to keep up with what he was saying.

"Well, it was only beans on toast, but she seemed fine with that. Look, why don't you say goodnight, and I'll make some for you?"

She gave herself a mental shake and got up slowly from the sofa. What a sight she must have looked napping – no doubt her mouth was open, and she'd dribbled - not the image she wanted him to have of her. The last thing she remembered was the glitter incident, but looking at the kitchen now, everywhere was spotless. Well, if you didn't look too closely at the cracked lino and faded paintwork, but that wasn't Jack's fault. And there at the top of her small Christmas tree sat the glitter bomb star that he and Annie had decorated.

He was still looking at her, his face uncertain, as if he'd done something wrong, but on the contrary, his words warmed her heart because they'd spent daddy and daughter time together. She reached for him and wrapped her arms around his neck, giving him a gentle kiss. "Thank you. I was completely out of it."

"You needed it. Annie ratted on you and told me she often has middle of the night stories."

"She said that?"

"Well, not those words exactly, but I got the gist."

An unladylike snort escaped her. "That's one way of putting it."

"And after our afternoon activities, I thought you deserved a rest." A lopsided smile formed on his lips as he cleared his throat.

She kissed him sweetly again and laughed. "Having naps and beans on toast…I could get used to this."

***

"So, what's this phobia you have about glitter?" He handed her a mug of tea and sat down on the sofa beside her. She'd polished off the beans on toast he'd made, and then they'd shared some apple pie her mum had brought over from the hotel kitchen and left in the fridge with a note, "Eat me," beside it.

"I don't have a phobia. I just don't like it because it gets everywhere, and it's really annoying after a week when you still keep finding it in random places. "

"And?" he pressed because he knew her, and he recognised there was more to it than just not liking the mess.

"Okay, glitter always reminds me of Paul."

"Your ex-fiancé?"

"Yes."

"Sorry, I don't get the connection."

"You're going to think I'm crazy, but he typified glitter… all fun on the outside, especially to other people, but without substance or meaning on the inside. Actually, he was a lot worse because he was manipulative and lied and gaslighted me for so long I thought left was right and up was down. And that's why when I received those photos, I had so much trouble trusting you because I thought you were turning out like him."

"I'm sorry you went through that."

She chuckled, "You asked."

"I did. But I hope you know that I'm not like that."

"I do now." She gave him a mischievous grin. "Actually, you also remind me of glitter, because you're all colour and joy on the outside but, more importantly, on the inside, too. I know you once said you only became a lawyer because of Adam, but I don't believe it was just that. I think you like helping people because you care about them. You've certainly shown you care about Annie and me."

"I never realised glitter could have so much hidden meaning." A sexy smirk touched his lips, but she could tell her words had touched him. "So now we're back together, does that mean you might start loving glitter again?"

His words were so matter of fact; she almost missed their meaning. Joy, relief, excitement … a glitter fountain of emotions burst inside her that, despite everything that had happened, he wanted to try again. He smiled, his eyes crinkling at the corners, and tears caught in her throat before she could reply.

"Maybe if it always involves you and Annie."

He pulled her into his arms and kissed her. "I'd better buy some more then."

Chapter 30 - Jack

Maybe it hadn't been one of his better ideas, Jack thought bleakly as they stood on the freezing train platform, a bitter wind whipping through the station. Despite being bundled up in her warm winter coat, fur boots, mittens and her red pom-pom hat, Annie looked cold, and Lou was doing her best to entertain her while they waited for the Santa Express to arrive. There were a few other families on the platform, mostly in good spirits and excited at the prospect of a train ride, though one little boy was grumbling next to them, his whiny voice grating on his nerves. He tried to block out the sound and concentrated on willing the train to arrive.

A few minutes later, the smell of burning coal and oil filled the air as finally the steam train pulled into the small station, and he watched Annie's inquisitive eyes widen. The beautifully restored steam train was not something she'd have seen before, let alone travelled on. Lou carried her safely into the thankfully warm carriage while he stowed the pushchair and found their seats. Then the stationmaster whistled, and they began winding their way through the Cotswolds countryside. Even in the depths of winter, it was beautiful, and today, with a hoar frost covering the trees and hedgerows, it was a perfect Christmas landscape.

"Are you ready to go on a magical journey, Annie?"

"What's mag-i-cal?" She sounded out the syllables carefully.

"We're setting off on an adventure to the North Pole, and when we get there, we're going to have some food, and you're going to meet Santa and the elves who help him."

"Santa?" Annie repeated the key word from his convoluted explanation. He clearly needed to make his sentences more two-year-old friendly.

"Yes, and if you're very lucky, you might get a gift from him, too."

"Mama?" Annie turned to Lou as if she didn't quite believe what he was saying and needed confirmation.

"He's right, sweetheart. Every little boy and girl on the train will meet Santa. It's going to be awesome."

"Awesome," Annie repeated as she turned back to him. "It's awesome, Jat."

"You're right," he agreed, smiling.

In the heated marquee, they had hot food and drinks, and Annie dictated her Christmas wish list, which Lou wrote on a postcard before they posted it through the Santa Express letterbox. The cheeky elves dressed in bright green and red outfits entertained them while they waited their turn to see Santa.

Finally, the 'ho, ho, ho… Merry Christmas' of Santa's jolly voice beckoned them inside his grotto, and when Annie received her gift – a colouring book, stickers and crayons – her beaming smile was all the confirmation he needed that his idea to see Santa had been a good one. She'd certainly inherited Lou's love of all things Christmas gene, and for a moment he let himself imagine she was his, and his heart shattered that she wasn't.

Then it was time for photos — one with a white-bearded Santa on his sleigh, another with his naughty elves, and a final one with a rather bored reindeer. He bought all the expensive professional photos and snapped his own phone ones too. Then Lou patiently explained that no, Annie couldn't take the reindeer home, or ask for a real reindeer for Christmas, which resulted in a wobbly moment until the train arrived to take them back.

"Did you have a good time?" he asked as soon as they'd settled in their seats.

"It was awe-some," Annie carefully repeated Lou's words from earlier as he stifled a laugh. "I got presents, Santa."

"You certainly did and, you know, if you're good, Santa will bring you another present on Christmas Day." Having seen her wish list: a friend for Simba, a pair of sparkly princess shoes and a strawberry jam sandwich, he was confident he could deliver his promise.

Annie's eyes widened as she digested what he'd said. "I good Mama?"

"Yes, you are, honey."

"Are you good, Mama?"

He was losing his battle not to laugh as he held Lou's gaze. "Your Mama is very good, and I'm going to make sure Santa knows that for sure."

"Are you good, Jat?"

"Let's ask your mama that… am I?" He side-eyed her, winking as her cheeks flushed pink.

"Well, I'm not sure, but maybe you can try to convince me later."

"I'll definitely do that." The colour of her cheeks deepened, and he thought she'd never looked more beautiful.

She'd also been absolutely right, because every moment of their day trip had been awesome.

And there was still the evening to come.

***

"Are you sure?" Lou asked for the umpteenth time.

Adam's voice was gentle. "Of course, we're sure. Annie's worn out from all the excitement of seeing Santa today, so she's very unlikely to wake up. But even if she does, she knows us, so it'll be fine."

Jack gently squeezed her hand, adding his own persuasion. "Mordros will message if there's a problem. The restaurant's only up the road, so we can literally be back in 10 minutes."

The nervous lip-biting was back, and he could see uncertainty in her eyes. "We could just order a takeaway and have an evening in all together."

"We could, and as nice as that would be, you both deserve a meal out, which doesn't involve wedding planning," Adam stated matter-of-factly.

"He's got a point," Mordros smiled. "It's our wedding, and we're both fed up talking about it, so goodness knows you guys must be too. Go out and have a lovely meal."

Lou looked between the three of them. "Okay, but promise me you'll message if you need us."

"Just go." Mordros gently ushered her out of the front door as Jack took her arm.

***

He'd booked a table at the local pub restaurant. It was a friendly, popular place with a reputation for good, hearty food. Importantly, it was also within easy walking distance.

They both opted for fish and chips, which were freshly cooked and delicious. By the time they'd finished, Lou was relaxed enough that she wasn't checking her phone every couple of minutes, trusting Mordros and Adam's babysitting skills.

"Do you remember little Jeremiah?" His eyes sparkled with mischief.

"Our son? Thank God, you rescued me from the clutches of Barret Fortesque."

"That's him - I was trying to remember his name. Still, if he hadn't been so handsy, I might not have met you, so maybe I should thank him."

"Please don't… awful man." She shuddered before breaking into a smile. "But apart from him - that night and meeting you was wonderful."

There was shyness to her words, and he reached across to link their fingers together. "Maybe it was fate that brought us together?"

"Do you believe in that kind of thing… fate… destiny, whatever you want to call it?"

"Maybe… I don't know, but it's a nice thought."

"That's a typical lawyer answer, hedging your bets."

"I can't argue with that, since I am a lawyer."

"Today's been a wonderful day, too." She squeezed his hand. "Thank you."

"You're welcome. I loved watching Annie's face light up when she met Father Christmas."

"I very much think that had more to do with the gift she was expecting."

"Well, maybe, but I also think your love of Christmas is rubbing off on her."

"I am kind of brainwashing her, aren't I? But it couldn't have been much fun for you, taking a toddler out for the day. I imagine your usual days off don't involve that kind of thing."

"No, but I love spending time with Annie. I know I haven't known her long, but she's a great kid." He paused as the rest of the restaurant noise faded away: the background chatter, the laughter, the festive music. "Actually, I know it's probably too early to talk about this, but…", he swallowed, suddenly wondering if he was making a mistake bringing up the subject of Annie's father when the day had gone so well but he'd got this far so… "I was thinking maybe I could be a kind of father figure to Annie since her dad isn't on the scene."

A complicated look crossed her face that he couldn't read, so he added hastily. "Hey, I get that it's far too early for this conversation because we've only just got back together." He watched curiously as her cheeks flushed pink and her violet eyes skidded away, avoiding his. God, he'd put his enormous foot in it, hadn't he? "Sorry, forget I said anything." What was the matter with him? Hadn't Adam said he needed to think more before he spoke? And this evening, which only a few minutes ago had been so relaxed and fun, was now nosediving into awkwardness because of his big mouth.

"I think that's a lovely idea." She finally met his eyes, but the flat tone of her voice wasn't reassuring him at all.

"Okay, then that's good." But his senses were telling him there was still something bothering her. "We can leave if you want to get back?"

"No, I'm fine. I just don't leave Annie very often, so it's hard for me to relax."

"I get it - I just thought it would be nice if we had a meal together and …" He trailed off as he realised she wasn't listening. "Lou?"

"Sorry… I've just had a message from Mum. She's received an offer for the hotel."

"As in someone wants to buy it?"

"Yeah."

He waited as she rapidly typed out a reply. This was the first he'd heard that the hotel was up for sale, and he could tell from her expression that she wasn't happy about it.

"Sorry," she said again as she put down her phone. "Mum says it's an excellent offer, and they want to complete just after Christmas."

"I didn't know your mum wanted to sell up."

"She doesn't. But the hotel needs a lot of restoration work, and the repair bill for the roof repairs alone is through the roof – excuse the pun – so there doesn't seem to be another viable option."

"Can she take out a mortgage or increase the finance she already has?"

"She's already at her limit. So, unless we win the lottery, I've completely run out of ideas."

"I'm sorry. That sounds grim."

"I grew up there; it was a hotel, but it was also our family home when Dad was here. I remember him teaching me to ride my bike in the courtyard, and I can't tell you the number of times I fell over and scraped my knees on the cobblestones. When I was older, I had my first after-school job working in the kitchen, and sometimes Dad would let me help in the dining room. The hotel was his dream, and he worked so hard to build it up. He'd be so upset."

Sadness laced her words, and instantly he wanted to promise that he'd save the hotel from being sold, but he wouldn't make a promise he couldn't keep. Still, he could make sure the contract was fair. "I'd be happy to look over the legal paperwork if you'd like, just to check everything's okay?"

"That would be a great help, thanks."

He could tell she didn't want to talk about the hotel sale anymore, and he certainly didn't want to talk about his enormous 'foot in mouth' moment over Annie - not after her reaction, anyway. Still, he knew a surefire way to reset the mood and cheer her up.

"Do you want a dessert? Silly question, of course you do." He picked up the menu and offered it to her.

She began scanning. "I fancy something very chocolaty and calorific."

He grinned. "I'm with you all the way."

Chapter 31 - Lou

"This mince pie is amazing!" Lou enthused between mouthfuls of rich, fruity filling encased in light buttery pastry. It was late afternoon, and they were sitting in her mum's office having tea before she had to pick Annie up from nursery. "Have you finally found a new pastry chef?"

"No, but I've had a stroke of luck." Her mum took her own bite. "Tom, who owns the bakery on the high street, has agreed to provide all the hotel's bread, cakes, and pastries over the Christmas period."

"Is that the guy who took over from old Mr Harris?"

"Yes, Mr Harris retired. He was well into his seventies, and he's gone to live near his daughter in Warwick. Tom took over the bakery a few weeks ago."

"Mum, that's a genius answer."

"I know. I was rattling my brain trying to come up with a solution, and when I popped into the bakery for one of his doughnuts – you know how I love a doughnut – I got talking to him. He's a really nice guy, and when I explained I was having a problem trying to find a pastry chef… well, he offered."

"I hope the rest of his baking is as delicious as this." She savoured her last mouthful.

"And this is my second stroke of luck." Her mum handed over the sale contract and hovered while she perused the buyer's offer for the hotel. "It's almost the whole asking price, and they want to complete within six weeks."

"I see that." She put down her plate and began reading the fine print.

"I can't actually believe it. They didn't even haggle."

"That's surprising … but good." She carried on reading as her mum waited impatiently.

"What do you think? It'll dig us out of a huge financial hole. Plus, there'll be plenty of money left over to buy somewhere decent for you and Annie."

She looked up and met her mum's excited face. The idea of selling the hotel made her stomach sink. It wasn't just a business. It had been her home, the place she'd grown up and, more importantly, where all her memories of her dad were. "Do we really have no other option but to sell?" She handed the paperwork back. "There's got to be another way." *Please let there be another way.*

"I can't think of one. Look, I know it's upsetting. God knows your dad would be sad, but we have no money left."

There was no sugarcoating the facts. "Okay, but we'll need some legal advice. Jack's offered to look over the paperwork."

"Jack?"

"Yes, he's the friend I went to see the other day. He's Adam's partner and best man, and he's helping me with all the pre-wedding planning."

"Oh, *that* friend."

"What's that supposed to mean?" but she knew exactly what her mum was getting at when she rolled her eyes.

"Okay, he's more than a friend. I knew him in London, but then things went wrong between us. It was a stupid misunderstanding, but now–"

"Now you've worked things out."

"Yes." She felt her cheeks heat.

"Well, that's marvellous, darling. I'm pleased for you both. And is this *thing* between you serious?"

"Yes … but it's complicated."

"Hmm, is that because he's Annie's father?"

"How on earth did you work that out?"

"I'm your mum, and I know you. You came back from London pregnant and broken, not wanting to talk about what happened or about Annie's father. You've been upset for a long time, but recently you've been like a Christmas tree, all lit up and full of sparkle. Now, it doesn't take a genius to put two and two together."

"He's a good man, Mum, and it was my fault that we broke up." She let out a shaky breath, trying to stop her tears.

"Why do I get the distinct impression there's more to this story?"

Her mind drifted back to what Jack had said at the restaurant the previous night. *I was thinking maybe I could be a kind of father figure to Annie since her dad isn't on the scene.* It had been the perfect time to tell him he was Annie's father. But she'd stupidly got all flustered – panicked if she was being honest - and, pretty much, shut down the conversation, so he'd probably never raise the topic again.

Her conscience pricked because she'd lied to him. Okay, not a calculated one, but certainly a lie by omission because she hadn't immediately corrected him when he'd assumed Annie's father wasn't involved.

The problem with keeping a secret was it just got bigger and bigger until it became like a ticking time bomb, just waiting to explode and cause maximum damage and destruction to everyone involved. Her stomach twisted with regret that she hadn't told him the truth.

"Lou?" Her mum's voice reminded her she was stuck in her head.

"Sorry… the thing is… he doesn't know."

"Oh sweetie. Why haven't you told him?"

"I don't know." Tears finally spilt over her cheeks, and her mum pulled her in for a hug. "I just… every time I think about telling him I sort of freeze."

"That's not like you. You're usually very upfront and honest about things. Why are you holding back?"

"I'm scared he'll be upset or angry or hurt… or all three, and honestly, I wouldn't blame him."

"I'm sure he'll be over the moon, and Annie will be, too. Every time I see her, she babbles on about Jat this and Jat that. He's certainly made an impression on her."

"You're right. I'm just overthinking." Lou sniffed into her mum's hug.

"Well, even if he doesn't react the way you hope, at least you'll know. Much better to rip the plaster off and get it over with."

"I guess so."

"Come on, let's have another mince pie and celebrate our good news."

"The hotel sale, or Tom's awesome baking skills?"

"Both, but mainly because my granddaughter has finally got her father back in her life. I can't tell you how pleased I am."

Chapter 32 - Jack

"Are you okay in there?" Jack's deep voice rumbled through the closed bedroom door.

It was the first night of their friends' weekend break, and Annie was already downstairs with Matt and Rosie and their young son, Toby, whom she'd immediately taken a shine to.

"Won't be a minute… I'm just having trouble with my zip," she called out.

He grinned. "Do you need any help?"

"No, I'm good…be out in a sec," her reply came back instantly.

It was just as well, because they'd both agreed that until they'd told Annie they were officially together, they wouldn't be sharing a room, so for the duration of the weekend her bedroom would be strictly off limits.

A few moments later, Lou emerged wearing a figure-hugging dress that showed off her new fuller curves and cleavage since having Annie. Desire flared, testing his weak resolve to keep his distance, but she was already tottering towards him on outrageously high heels, and looked about to lose her balance.

"You need practice wearing those things?" he teased while offering her his hand to steady her.

"Yeah, they feel sort of weird after wearing flats for so long."

"You look beautiful." He allowed himself to stare at her for another long moment before his brain registered that she looked nervous. "Is something wrong?"

She shook her head, but he could sense she was lying, and he lifted her chin to maintain eye contact. "Are you sure?"

She nodded, then licked her lips, making his desire to kiss her overwhelming, and since she was technically now outside her bedroom, he didn't fight it. Sliding his fingers into her thick hair, he dropped his mouth over hers and used his tongue to urge her lips to part.

"The minibus has arrived," Nick's voice hollered from downstairs, breaking the moment.

"Damn," Jack grumbled as she pulled away laughing, but he could tell their brief kiss had settled her nerves.

"Come on, let's go. I'm starving." She kept hold of his arm as they made their way carefully downstairs.

***

The restaurant was in the next village, and he'd arranged for Jenny, the student babysitter Lou occasionally used, to look after the children while they were out. Although she was only nineteen, she seemed responsible and trustworthy. But before they left, he gave her his mobile number and told her to ring him if there were any problems.

The restaurant was busy with Christmas revellers, but the owner showed them to a table towards the rear, which was quieter and offered a little more privacy. As soon as their drinks were served, he raised his glass.

"To Mordros and Adam and an epic pre-wedding weekend."

Emotion tugged at his throat. They both looked so in love, and after enduring fifteen years apart, they deserved their happy ever after. He wondered if he and Lou would have the same… he hoped so. He'd almost lost her over those damn fake photos until she'd finally opened up and told him about them. But who the hell had sent them, and why? No matter how long it took, he'd find out. He let his anger go because tonight was about Mordros and Adam and giving them a weekend they'd always remember.

His eyes landed on his sister, Clemmie. She'd had a rough couple of years, but seeing her laughing and chatting with Tom made him wonder if she'd finally turned the page… or begun a new chapter or even an entirely new book. Okay, he'd stretched the analogy to its limit, but she was a prolific reader and had a serious book addiction, so it kind of worked. And Tom was clearly keeping her entertained; her face was flushed and her eyes sparkled. Maybe it was the beginning of something between them?

He inwardly chuckled at how ridiculous he was being, matchmaking the two of them because they were unattached and it was Christmas… *classic!*

His eyes continued roaming the room. Nick and Sam were flirting outrageously… they'd drunk a couple of cocktails at the house before leaving for the restaurant and were in their own little bubble. And Matt and Rosie were another pair with eyes only for each other. It was probably their first date night out since having their baby.

"You good?" Lou squeezed his arm.

"I was just doing a little imaginary matchmaking between Tom and my sister. They look good together, don't they?"

"You never know… the magic of Christmas and all that, but don't let your imagination run away with you, or you'll have them married with two kids by the end of the weekend."

He grinned, letting her words ground him. He imagined everyone around the table was of an age when they'd be thinking about having children or, in Matt and Rosie's case, had them already. Even Adam had told him he'd changed his mind about having kids, and he knew Nick and Sam were looking into adoption.

Lou had Annie, of course, but when he'd brought up his idea of being a father figure to her, Lou's reaction had thrown him off, so he hadn't mentioned it again. Maybe after this weekend, he'd sit her down, and they'd talk about it properly because he wanted Annie to be his, especially if they had a baby at some point.

Had he just admitted that he wanted to have a baby with Lou? He'd never considered becoming a father before, but now it seemed like a great idea.

"Do you want to dance?" Lou snagged his attention, "because I do."

"Yes, so long as you realise that I have two left feet."

"You just need to sway from side to side. It's really easy."

He got up from their table and guided her to the small dance floor. There were several other couples dancing to the soft bluesy jazz, and he pulled her into his arms as her hands found their way to his neck. She leant into him, closing her eyes as they swayed to the music, letting the sounds of Nick and Sam's laughter and the noise from the other diners fade into the background.

Nothing else existed but the two of them.

Holding Lou in his arms, he felt the luckiest man in the world. The night when he'd first met her in London had changed his life … but what if he hadn't gone to that function and Adam had instead? Or what if Lou had been working at a different hotel or had stayed in Broadsham? The randomness of their meeting terrified him.

The other night, Lou had asked him if he believed in fate, and he'd dodged the question, but now… Of course, it was fate because even though his lawyer brain only worked with logic and facts, no other explanation was acceptable.

"I love you," he murmured into her hair.

She opened her eyes and looked up at him. "I love you too, and if you're lucky, I'll sneak into your room later to show you just how much."

He chuckled. "I can totally get on board with that."

Chapter 33 - Lou

"Fur balls!" Lou looked around wildly.

The minibus taxi had just pulled into the restaurant carpark, and they were about to get on board. The others were chatting among themselves in a happy state of tipsy. "I've lost my purse." She scanned the pavement as if it would magically appear. "I must have left it inside the restaurant."

"Don't worry, I'll go back and have a look."

"No, I'll go… sorry everyone, I won't be a minute." She almost ran back inside, but he caught up with her and put his hand on her arm.

"Slow down. I'll help you find it."

It was almost midnight, and the evening was finally winding down. As they went back inside, a few people were putting on coats ready to brave the bitter night air. There was still one couple on the dance floor and some late diners reluctant to leave. He led her back to their table at the rear of the restaurant.

"Here it is." The strap of the offending black diamante purse was still hanging over her chair, and he handed it to her with a grin.

"Thank you." She reached up and gave him a quick peck on his cheek. Her lips grazed his stubble, and excitement fluttered inside her at what they'd be doing later. She grabbed his hand, and they began making their way back towards the entrance… the sooner they got back, the better.

Have Yourself a Merry Little Christmas … she focused on the couple on the dance floor, swaying in time to the music. There was something about them… or maybe it was the song. It was one of her favourites – a Christmas classic - and the pair looked so in love, and totally wrapped up in each other.

Christmas was such a wonderful time to be in love. She stopped walking as her eyes focused more closely on the man. He was tall, with sandy-coloured hair, and maybe he realised she was staring at him because he suddenly looked up, his intense blue eyes locking onto hers, freezing her feet to the floor.

"Oh, my God!"

"What is it?" Jack's eyes followed her gaze to the dance floor, and he cursed under his breath. "Isn't that Shona?"

Somehow, she unglued her eyes from the man and refocused on the woman standing beside him. Yes, he was right. It was Shona, but it was the man who sent chills racing up her arms and her stomach dropping to the floor.

***

"Hey, fancy seeing you here." She flinched as Paul pulled her into a hug.

He was smiling at her with his perfectly straight, too-white teeth that he'd paid a fortune for in Turkey. Not the time to think about that, she scolded herself. "How many years has it been? Must be, what ten?"

"Umm, hello Paul. Yes, something like that." She took a step back quickly, but Jack must have put two and two together because he put his arm around her, all his protective instincts trying to shield her from her ex.

With Jack's arm slung over her shoulders, she instantly felt braver and allowed her eyes to travel over the man standing in front of her. He was older, of course, but apart from the Turkey teeth, he was still handsome in a 'rough around the edges' kind of way. But it was his intense blue eyes that she remembered most because they'd stared into her own suspicious ones and lied to her repeatedly.

Her gaze landed on Shona. She looked just as shocked as she was, and there was something else … was that fear? But she masked it quickly and held out her hand. "Hi, I think we met the other day when you came into reception. I'm Shona."

"Yes, of course. Nice to meet you properly."

Paul smirked. "Well, this is awkward. I'm Lou's ex."

Jack ignored him. "Look, as much as we'd love to stay and chat, we have a taxi waiting. Shona, I'll see you back in the office on Monday." His arm slid from her shoulder to the small of her back, guiding her purposefully towards the front entrance, but before they went outside, she couldn't stop herself from glancing back.

Neither of them had moved, and the expression on their faces sent more chills racing up her spine, which had nothing to do with the night air from the open front door.

"See you around, Lou," Paul called out, and did that sound like a threat?

Jack turned back scowling, and she wondered if he was going to say something, but he continued gently propelling her through the open door and out into the carpark.

***

"Are you okay?" Lou realised that was a silly question because neither of them were. The others were in the sitting room, and raucous laughter was drifting upstairs as they sat on Jack's bed talking in whispers.

Thankfully, Annie had remained asleep, and once Jack had called an Uber for Jenny, the rest of them had cracked open some bottles of fizz in honour of Mordros and Adam's love of the stuff and started whatever game they were all now playing. They'd both made their excuses – to catcalls and wolf whistles - as they'd gone upstairs.

"What the hell are my ex and your ex doing together?" he gritted out. She knew it was a rhetorical question, but she still racked her brain trying to make sense of the weird scenario of Paul and Shona being together. *And looking so in love.*

It had been ten years since she'd seen Paul. Ten years for him to meet and fall in love with someone else. It just felt all kinds of weird that the '*someone else*' was Shona, but stranger things happened all the time, didn't they? Except…

"Are you thinking what I'm thinking?" Jack must have read her mind.

"It seems a bit of a coincidence …" She left the sentence hanging because it was hard to put into words what her gut was telling her.

"A fucking big coincidence, if you ask me," he growled.

She could feel the tension vibrating through his body, his muscles rigid as his mouth tightened into a hard line. It wasn't the way she'd wanted the evening to go, but she couldn't blame him for being wound up, because she was, too.

Maybe they both needed a distraction?

"I'm going to change. Why don't you do the same?" She got up and went next door to her room. She checked on Annie and quietly put on her pyjamas. They weren't sexy … more the fun kind, but hopefully they'd do the job.

When she returned to his room, he was sitting exactly where she'd left him… *so much for relaxing.* Lost in thought, he didn't notice she was back, but then his head jerked up, taking in what she was wearing.

"Lou." He lifted a brow as his eyes narrowed in on her skimpy shorts and then drifted upward, to her shocking pink cami top decorated with candy canes. Her heart began hammering at the way he focused in on her body, his eyes studying her from the top of her head to her tippy toes like he wanted to devour her.

Good, because she wanted him to.

But it was also her turn to have some fun. Her eyes landed on his shirt. That had to go… but he was already moving towards her, his body consuming the space between them. "Do you know what you do to me?" His voice was dark, like cognac.

"I can guess." She began undoing the buttons on his shirt.

"What do you want?" *And was he teasing her now too, because surely that was obvious?*

"I'm looking for a distraction," she managed as his hand skimmed her collarbone before landing on her shoulder, and he began sweeping his thumb in lazy circles there. *Well, two could play at that game.* She pushed his shirt back over his shoulders and began kissing his chest, her teeth biting gently into his pecs as he let out a low moan. They came together in a fever of kissing as their hands worked over each other.

Somewhere in the bedroom, his mobile rang.

Definitely not the distraction she'd been aiming for.

"Damn," he cursed.

"Who is it?" She watched as he read the message, and the tension was back in his body, which wasn't a good sign.

"It's Shona. She wants to meet up tomorrow to talk."

"Talk about what?" *She was clutching at straws, but maybe it was something innocent like she'd found a café that did amazing hot chocolate, or she wanted some Christmas gift ideas for two-year-old girls… yeah, right!*

"I don't know. She wants us to go to her flat tomorrow morning at eleven. She said that she'll explain then."

"That's a good thing, right? Maybe we'll get some answers?"

She watched him type out a reply and then lay his phone down. "I think we need to talk."

And there went her libido… like someone had chucked a bucket of icy water over it. And clearly, he felt the same because he began buttoning up his shirt.

***

"So, our two exes are now together," he bit out. "That's a big coincidence, don't you think?"

"Agreed." *A Grand Canyon sized coincidence.*

"What does your ex do for a living?"

She knew exactly where his mind was going and, yep, that would be another big tick in the coincidence box. "He has a degree in photography and computer science."

"Which means he had the skills to fake those photos." He stole her words before she could say them, and while she carried on piecing the jigsaw of coincidences together, he added another one. "And how did he take your breakup?"

"Not very well." Bile rose in her throat, because that was a massive understatement. "He was livid, actually, because I'd finally stood up to him and all his bullshit. I'd given him the benefit of the doubt so many times over his cheating, but I suppose I just hit my limit. So… yeah, he was mad, but I think it had less to do with losing me and more because he'd got his eye on the hotel, which he knew I'd inherit one day."

"But your dad was still alive then, so…"

"Dad was quite a lot older than mum and I guess he'd done the maths." She really was going to be sick if she dwelt on how calculating he'd been, wanting an inheritance that wasn't his.

"So, after you left him, he had the means and motive to get revenge." Jack finally spelt out the harsh truth.

She blinked back tears. "Yes."

"Oh, sweetheart." He finally pulled her into his arms.

There was a hell of a lot to process, but there were more questions that needed answering, too. "I don't understand why he waited so long?" She lifted her gaze, forcing a weak smile.

He huffed out a breath. "I don't want to ask this question, but I think it's important. Did you have any serious relationships after Paul and before we met?"

"You want to talk about my sex life?" She tried to lighten the mood, but maybe now wasn't the time to tease him.

"No, I don't, but it might be relevant."

They were obviously still on the same wavelength because she knew what he was implying. "Because he waited for revenge until he knew I was in a serious relationship to cause me maximum pain?"

"Exactly… so?" he prompted.

"Nothing serious or long term. A few dates here and there, but Paul put me off dating for a long time." She felt the tension easing from his body, that her back catalogue of boyfriends wasn't long.

"So, where does Shona fit into this?"

"Well, tomorrow, we can ask her."

Chapter 34 - Jack

He'd done his best to keep his emotions in check, but asking about Lou's sex life, as she'd so eloquently put it, had tested him to his limit. Of course, it was none of his business who she'd slept with before him, but he was only human, so it was a relief when she'd confirmed her dating life had been pretty tame. Plus, it meant he didn't have to hunt down any other ex-boyfriends but could concentrate on her loser ex-fiancé.

Soon after, she'd fallen asleep. He'd quickly undressed down to his boxers and pulled the duvet over them both, letting her snuggle into him like the koala bear she always was in bed. She'd woken up an hour later and gone to check on Annie. She hadn't come back.

His own night's sleep had been fitful. He'd missed Lou cuddling him, but mainly he hadn't been able to switch his brain off. There were still questions that needed answering. Was Lou's ex responsible for the fake photos? He certainly had the skill set, but ten years was a hell of a long time to hold a grudge. And where did Shona fit in? He could make an educated guess, but tomorrow would confirm it.

It was still early, but he got up and showered and then went downstairs in search of coffee. The rest of the house was dead to the world, but when he went into the kitchen, Lou and Annie were sitting at the table eating breakfast.

"Morning, sweetie." He ruffled Annie's hair. "What are you having for breakfast?"

"Bobbled eggs" She gave him a cute, eggy smile.

"They're called boiled eggs, darling," Lou gently corrected as he went over to give her a quick kiss. "Would you like some?"

"Thanks, but I'll stick to toast and coffee."

He put two slices of bread into the toaster and set the coffee machine to make an Americano - he'd need a strong one if he was going to face their exes this morning.

"So, what's the plan?" Lou put down her own coffee cup and began cutting up Annie's buttered toast into soldiers.

"God, I hope you're not planning any stag pranks like chaining me to a lamppost or something because I'll rescind both your invites to the wedding if you do." Adam had joined them in the kitchen and had caught Lou's words.

"You look rough." Jack ignored Adam's plea, taking in his dishevelled hair and the dark shadows under his eyes. "What time did you get to bed last night?" He winked at Lou as he handed over his own coffee and a glass of water to his best friend. "Do you want some tablets?"

"No, I'm good. I didn't drink that much … can't say the same for Mordros, though. I've just come down to make her some tea."

"Sorry we didn't stick around last night," Lou gave Adam's arm a squeeze. "Did you have a good time?"

"I think the inflatable willy hoopla game was the lowest point, though rude charades ran a close second." He grinned. "What about you guys? Did you have a good night?"

Jack frowned. "Not what you're implying, but have you got time to hear what's been going on?"

"Yeah, I imagine Mordros has gone back to sleep by now, so carry on."

"You'll never guess!" Lou's lips set in a tight line.

"I'm sure I won't, so how about you just tell me?" He stole a finger of toast off Annie's plate. "Your mama is funny."

"Funny!" Annie mimicked.

Lou gave his hand a gentle tap. "Stop nicking my daughter's breakfast and make your own. Now where was I? Oh yes, just imagine this scenario. Jack's ex and mine being together…"

"You're kidding me?"

"I wish we were," Jack said grumpily.

***

By the time they were ready to leave, Matt and Rosie's young son, Toby, had joined them in the kitchen, as well as Tom and Clemmie. After his coffee, Tom began a class on bread making. It was certainly handy having a baker in the group, and Annie was in her element, waving them off without a backward glance as she kneaded her own dough on a floured board.

He could feel Lou's nerves as they pulled into the gravel driveway outside Shona's flat. It was part of a Victorian house conversion and within easy walking distance of his office. He'd been here a few times during the brief period they'd dated, though that felt like a lifetime ago now.

"There's nothing to be nervous about." He squeezed her hand.

"It's just so weird, though, isn't it? I mean, your ex and mine… together."

Yeah, it was definitely weird, but he'd long since accepted that life was sometimes stranger than fiction. "Come on, let's get this over with and then we can get back and try some of Annie's bread. It should be infinitely better than the supermarket stuff I ate earlier."

"Don't count your chickens. Annie and I had a go at baking bread once, and it was so hard I almost broke a tooth."

"That bad, huh? Still, since Tom's in charge… have you tried his sourdough or walnut bread? Not to mention his croissants. Never tasted one better. He's getting quite a reputation in the area."

"He should employ you as his publicity agent, but you're right. Mum's addicted to his doughnuts. She's asked him to supply the hotel with baked goods over Christmas until …" she trailed off.

"Until?" He prompted.

"Until the hotel's sold."

He could have kicked himself as her expression crumpled. "I'm sorry."

"Not your fault." She gave him a weak smile. "Is your offer to look over the sale contract still open?"

"Of course. Just send it to me."

The look of resignation on her face was heartbreaking. But maybe there was a way to save the hotel… he just needed to think of it. Or if Lou was on board, they could pool ideas with the group back at the house. The more heads, the better.

But that was for later. Right now, they had to face their exes.

***

Everything about the flat was familiar. Lots of inspirational wall prints, hearts, and big pink fluffy cushions on a sofa they'd made out on a few times.

He needed to erase that from his memory banks immediately.

"Would you like a drink - tea, coffee, something stronger?" Shona asked as they all found seats. He avoided the sofa and instead guided Lou to a small window seat, which overlooked the driveway. It was a squash, but better than having Lou sit on the sofa where he'd… *No, absolutely not!*

"Baby, it's only eleven o'clock in the morning." Paul smirked.

"Coffee would be great," Lou spoke for them both as if sensing that he was still stuck in his head. "Would you like a hand?"

"No, I'll just be a minute." She disappeared into the kitchen, which he remembered was just across the hallway.

"Do you think we'll have a white Christmas?" Paul asked as they waited for her to return with their drinks.

He inwardly chuckled…it was such a stereotypically British thing, bringing up the weather to fill the awkwardness and distract them from the uncomfortable conversation still to come. "I hope so. We didn't have any snow last year, and I can't wait to show Annie."

Chapter 35 - Lou

Yep, this was officially weird, and not just because she was in Jack's ex-girlfriend's flat where he'd… *Nope, she wasn't going there!* But all this polite talk about the weather was setting her teeth on edge and, to make matters worse, Jack had now brought up Annie.

"Annie's your daughter, right?" Paul asked.

"No," he gritted out. "She's not."

And there went her stomach, folding in on itself like one of those origami paper fortune-telling games she used to love playing as a child. She imagined opening up the flaps to reveal the message…

TELL JACK THE TRUTH! In six foot-high letters and probably neon lights for good measure.

I will…stop nagging, she told her conscience off.

Paul had shifted his gaze from Jack to her, his intense blue eyes observing her, and had he somehow read her mind?

"Here we are." Shona came back into the room carrying a tray of coffee and a plate of chocolate biscuits.

Thank God! She took one of the chocolate digestives – not quite the same as a yummy bar of Cadbury Dairy Milk, but, as an emergency fix, it would get her through the next few minutes.

***

Shona cleared her throat and began. "When Paul and I started dating, neither of us knew the other's connection to you. I mean, why would we? But then for Paul's birthday, I booked a weekend in London, and got us tickets to see Lion King at the theatre. It was during the intermission, and we'd gone to the bar … and well, there you both were, looking all loved up. It was such a bizarre coincidence, realising we'd both dated you and neither of us had come out of it well."

"Let's cut to the chase, shall we?" Jack growled, obviously losing patience. "You hatched a plan to get revenge on us by faking those photos, didn't you?"

Shona exchanged a look with Paul. "The photos were supposed to be a prank."

"A prank?" Jack swiped his fingers through his hair in disbelief. "A fucking prank?" he repeated, clearly trying to rationalise her words.

She nodded, not meeting his eyes. "It was a laugh… a way of getting back at you. It just went wrong."

"You can say that again," Lou muttered. "Did you know we split up because of them?"

"Umm, no."

"Oh, come on - of course you did." Jack glared at her. "Why didn't you own up at the time?"

"You're both cowards…that's why!" Lou hissed, not waiting for her to answer.

"Yeah, you're right. No more excuses." Shona got up and faced them both. "I'm sorry."

"So why tell us now?" Jack demanded, and wasn't that the key question, because it had been nearly three years since their little payback scheme?

Shona's eyes darted to Lou. "When you came into the office the other day, I guessed you were back together. Then last night, at the restaurant, seeing you both, we just knew we had to tell you because we regretted what we did, and we wanted to make it right."

Paul nodded. "I've changed, Lou. I'm not excusing my behaviour, but I just wanted to get back at you for dumping me. The photos were a joke, albeit a sick one, but I never thought you'd split up over them. Then when you did," – he blew out his cheeks – "it seemed a bit late to say anything."

Lou couldn't believe what she was hearing. "Sorry – you wanted to get back at me for dumping you? Maybe if you hadn't cheated, I wouldn't have dumped you." Her breath shuddered. "You hurt me, and you made me distrust every man I met after you. And as for sending me those photos, that was outrageous and unforgiveable."

The room quietened, the air shifting back and forth between the past and now. All the *'what ifs'* – ghosts and dreams of a life with Jack that never was, because she'd believed those photos. An ocean of regret seeped into her as she finally broke the silence. "I hope no one ever does anything so shameful to you."

Shona nodded. "Sending you those photos was a terrible thing to do. And Paul knows he behaved badly when he was with you, but he was young and immature and made mistakes. I see a different side of him, and I truly believe he's changed. We've talked, and I trust he won't cheat on me. I think everyone deserves a second chance, and I'm willing to give him one, because we love each other." She gazed adoringly at Paul.

"Shona's my soulmate." Paul smiled back.

"How terribly romantic, and now you're after our forgiveness." Lou's voice dripped with sarcasm.

Shona ignored her and turned to Jack. "We want to wipe the slate clean because we're getting married and moving away, so I'll be handing in my notice on Monday."

"Where to?" Lou couldn't help asking. Even Australia wouldn't be far enough, in her opinion.

"We're going to Australia. We thought it was a great place to make a fresh start."

"Bloody hell!" she mumbled.

***

"What a load of hooey," Lou launched as soon as they were back inside the car. "We want to wipe the slate clean," she mimicked in Shona's voice. "And as for Paul saying he's changed. Does a leopard ever change its spots? Of course not!" She felt steam whooshing out of her ears from the boiling rage inside her. "I'll tell you something for nothing - she's a fool, and in for a shock when he cheats on her, which he will. And another thing—"

"Hey." Jack leant over the console and cradled her face in his hands. "Take a breath, okay?"

"Sorry. I'm just so riled up."

"I can see that." He nudged his nose against hers and kissed her slowly. "Better?"

"Umm, much, but I think to be sure, you'll need to kiss me again."

He grinned. "My pleasure."

Chapter 36 - Jack

'Driving Home for Christmas' sang out of the radio as they drove back towards Broadsham. Nostalgia swept over him. It was a classic song and always reminded Jack of the start of the Christmas holidays when he was a boy. His parents would collect him from school, and they'd sing along to the Chris Rea lyrics as they drove through the holiday traffic, excitement mounting as they got nearer to home. Family Christmases spent with his parents and Clemmie growing up had been magical. The sort of Christmases he'd like to replicate with Lou and Annie.

In later years, Adam joined them for the holidays, since his subpar mother frequently abandoned him to go off with her latest boyfriend. He cringed when he remembered Adam had spent one Christmas entirely alone. He'd made sure it never happened again.

There were other memories, too. Adam had once asked him to show him how to throw a punch because Elizabeth's latest lowlife boyfriend was an abusive bully, and he wanted to teach him a lesson. Adam's childhood had been the complete antithesis of his own.

Over the years, they'd become like brothers, and Jack's family had become Adam's. In fact, Jack couldn't remember the last time Adam had seen his own mother… years, probably. But now Elizabeth was coming to the wedding, like the prodigal son – or in her case, mother – returning. Jago would be there too, and, with their shared history, there was potential for fireworks going off, and not in a celebratory way.

"You look a million miles away. What are you thinking about?" Lou leant over and squeezed his thigh before resting her hand there.

"I was thinking about Adam's mother and whether she'll kick off at the wedding."

"Now I'm intrigued. Is that likely?"

"I hope not, but with Jago being there…"

When she looked blank, he clarified. "Jago Trevellyan is Mordros's dad."

"Jago Trevellyan - the Cornish landscape artist?"

"Yep, that's the one."

"Wow, I didn't know Mordros had a famous dad."

"Well, I guess to Mordros he's just her dad."

"Yeah, of course. And now I remember she mentioned something about her dad and Adam's mum being a 'thing' once. Apparently, that's the reason he wants to stay at the hotel during the lead-up to the wedding, so they don't bump into each other at Adam's house."

"I don't blame him."

"Have you met Adam's mum?"

"Yeah, a few years ago. She was a pretty rubbish mother to Adam growing up - always hooking up with different men and leaving Adam to fend for himself while she swanned off with her latest one. She's married multiple times, and Adam used to complain that each of his stepfathers was worse than the previous one."

"Maybe she's changed."

"I thought you said leopards don't change their spots?" He couldn't help grinning.

"Yeah, well, there are exceptions. But getting back to Adam's mum… maybe the wedding's a perfect time for him to hold out an olive branch? Maybe Jago, too? It's Christmas after all and a time when families try to get along."

"Forgive and forget, you mean?"

"Maybe not forget, but move on from the past."

"Hmm, well, I can't speak for what Adam thinks, but some people don't deserve forgiveness."

"Why do I think you're not talking about Adam's mum anymore?"

"Oh, I'm including her too, but you're right. I'm thinking about our exes."

There was no damn way he'd ever forgive them for faking those photos. Because of them, he'd almost lost Lou, and for that, they could rot in hell as far as he was concerned… or more precisely, Australia. He'd told Shona not to bother working her notice. Goodbye and good riddance.

Adam wouldn't be happy. With Christmas looming, it wasn't a great time to find a replacement receptionist, but they'd manage. He'd take a shift on reception himself if he had to.

"You're in your head again," Lou complained as they turned into the driveway of their weekend house. "Do you need a distraction?"

Yeah, he could definitely get on board with Lou's version of a distraction. But before he could tell her that, Adam and Annie came out of the front door and began walking towards them.

***

They all congregated in the main living room and over coffee and Tom's homemade chocolate brownies, still warm from the oven, they took turns recounting their visit to their exes.

"It sticks in my craw that they've got away with it and won't face any consequences. But at least they're disappearing off to Australia," Jack finished.

"The good news is that we're back together." Lou beamed at everyone.

"Yeah, we're going to put the past firmly behind us and concentrate on our future." He pulled her in for a quick kiss.

"What a pair of scumbags," Mordros said what everyone else was thinking.

Nick nodded. "I wouldn't bet on their marriage lasting, not with Paul's track record."

"I hope they stay in Australia," Adam muttered.

"Yeah, I agree, but we'll need a new receptionist." Jack underlined the obvious just in case Adam hadn't realised.

"We'll manage until after Christmas, and then we'll advertise."

"What about me? I can do it?" Clemmie piped up.

"You?" Jack turned to his sister. "You're an accountant, not a receptionist."

"I know that, but since I'm taking a hiatus from my old job, I could fill in until you get a replacement."

Jack looked at Adam, who shrugged. "Well, I guess if you're up for it, then consider yourself hired." He noticed Tom trying to puzzle out why Clemmie would take a temporary job as a receptionist when she was an accountant. *Sorry, mate, not my place to say.*

"Oh my God, these are heavenly." Lou's eyes rolled back in rapturous delight as she bit into a brownie.

"I've just eaten my third. I'll never lose my baby weight at this rate. And no, don't you dare say you love me just as I am!" Rosie nudged Matt, who held up his hands in surrender.

"But it's true," he smirked before taking a bite of his own brownie.

"I'll just get a cloth for Annie." Lou got up from the sofa and headed swiftly towards the kitchen.

"Come here, little chocolate monster." Jack picked Annie up before she could put her sticky fingers all over the cream leather sofa she was sitting on. Chocolate smeared her face too, making her look adorable, even if she was a little chocolate monster.

"Chocolate monster," Annie repeated, giving him a wide chocolate grin.

"Yes, you are, sweetie, but we'll soon get you cleaned up." He took the damp cloth from Lou and began gently wiping her face before setting her down again.

"There are more brownies ready to come out of the oven if anyone wants another one?" Tom announced as Nick pinched the last one.

"I can't believe how lucky we are to have you bake for us and supply the hotel over Christmas," Lou said between mouthfuls.

"Talking of the hotel…" Jack looked at her for permission, and when she nodded, he continued. "Lou's mum is thinking of selling–"

"She doesn't want to," Lou interjected. "But the roof needs replacing, and the bedrooms on the top floor are all unusable because of the leaky roof and… well, you get the picture. We don't have the money to pay for the repairs, so our only option is to sell. We've already had an offer, so unless we can come up with an alternative plan…"

He squeezed her hand. *Damn, he'd sell his flat if it would help, but they'd need more than the proceeds from that to pay for a new roof and all the other repairs that needed doing.* "So, if any of you have any bright ideas – other than winning the lottery – we'd love to hear them."

There was quiet in the room as everyone considered the problem until Nick joked. "What if your mum marries someone stinking rich and then bumps them off?"

"Like a black widow killer? Isn't that the term used when you murder your husband to collect the life insurance or inheritance? Maybe I'd better watch my back." Sam snickered.

"Hmm, and Mum would just love to be in prison for the next however many years once she's caught. But thanks for your helpful suggestion," Lou said sarcastically. "Anyone else?"

"Maybe you could start a village campaign to save the hotel?" Mordros suggested.

"We've only just had one, and I don't think the village is ready for another one just yet. And besides, it's money we need, and the odd tenner donation from the locals won't help much."

"Perhaps there's a local builder who'd be willing to do the job for free," Rosie offered.

"If they did jobs for free, they'd soon be out of business." Matt shot down that idea.

"Or you could rob a bank," Nick teased, "and I'll drive the getaway car."

It felt like they were all clutching at straws. "Your ideas are shit," Jack growled.

Chapter 37 - Lou

They'd drawn lots to decide who'd go to the pub and who'd stay home and cook. The girls won … plus Nick, because he'd insisted on being on the girl's team. They left the guys peeling potatoes and making Christmas dinner for their return. And in Matt's case, looking after his grizzly baby daughter.

The pub was only a short walk away from the house. A thatched picture-perfect one with a roaring log fire to tempt customers in on a freezing December afternoon. The bar was pleasantly busy with regulars and tourists enjoying the festive season, but the lounge area was quieter. They peeled off their coats, hats and gloves and chose a couple of sofas nearest to the fire to relax and gossip on.

"We got the better end of the deal." Lou sipped her G&T smugly.

Rosie nodded. "I feel bad about leaving Matt with Mae, though. She didn't sleep well last night, and she's overtired and grumpy."

"She's probably napping by now." Lou tried to sound confident, but from her own experience with Annie, babies rarely did what they were supposed to, and an overtired baby was horrible. Thankfully, last night Annie had slept soundly, and she'd almost risked sneaking back into Jack's room to carry on what they'd started before Shona's message had interrupted them. But then the '*what ifs*' had kicked in. She hadn't wanted Annie to wake up in a strange bedroom without her being there. Motherhood was just one big, long guilt trip.

"Can't you drug her or something?" Nick teased.

Mordros looked horrified. "You can't drug a baby, Nick."

"Well, you say that, but I remember Sam's mum telling me they used to give him extra Calpol when he was a baby and wouldn't sleep. Or maybe it was a tot of whiskey?"

"The whiskey was probably for the mother," Clemmie sniggered. "Sam mentioned you both want to have a baby. How's that going?"

"We're looking into adoption, but it's a long road. Lots of red tape, but we won't give up."

"Good for you. Better not mention your idea of drugging babies, though."

"Funny!" Nick drawled before switching focus to Mordros. "What about you and Adam? Are we going to hear the pitter-patter of tiny feet soon?"

"Are you really going to take that receptionist job?" Mordros asked Clemmie, ignoring Nick's nosiness and changing the subject.

"Yes, I am. A change is as good as a rest, as they say, and it'll tide me over until I find something else that I really want to do."

"Like what?" Nick asked.

"Well, if I knew that, I'd be doing it, wouldn't I?"

"You were getting on well with Tom last night. If you're staying local, maybe you'll see more of him?" Lou kept her voice casual, pretending she wasn't matchmaking.

"Are you matchmaking?" Clemmie wagged her finger. "Tom's nice, but I'm not looking for a relationship. Been there, done that, got the T-shirt."

She wanted to ask what she meant, but it was probably too soon for that kind of in-depth sharing since they'd only just met, and she didn't want to come across as prying. "You'll see a lot more of Jack if you're working at his office," she said instead.

"Yes, I'll love that, and seeing more of you and Annie, too, since you're dating my brother. Annie's so gorgeous, and Jack adores her… I mean, we all do. But now he'll have a ready-made stepdaughter, and I'll be an auntie if you two decide to get married."

"Steady on. We've only just started dating again. We're nowhere near the 'getting married' stage." She chuckled, trying to shake off the feeling that she was on a runaway train hurtling towards a cliff edge, because she still hadn't told Jack her secret. She caught Mordros looking at her, and she was definitely sending a message that it was high time he knew. *I'll tell him soon; she silently communicated back.*

"Let's have a toast, shall we? To weddings, babies, and brand new jobs." Nick raised his glass. "Cheers, everyone."

***

Lou sent Jack a WhatsApp:
Lou: How's the cooking going?

Jack: The turkey's resting.

Jack: Are you having a good time?

Lou: Yes, I am. Nick's keeping us entertained.

Lou: Let me know when the turkey's finished its nap and we'll head back.

Jack: Funny! Dinner should be ready in about an hour.

Lou: Great, I'm starving!

Lou: The guy behind the bar says that the village has a Victorian Christmas market this evening, and an illuminated walk.

Lou: Maybe we could go after dinner and show Annie?

Lou: Hope Annie's okay? Sorry, I should have asked that first.

Jack: She's fine. She's helping Toby build some Lego.

Jack: Well, when I say helping… but he's being very patient with her.

Jack: The market and walk sound fun.

Jack: I've got a mountain of sprouts to peel, which is ironic because I hate the bloody things!

Lou: Good luck

Lou: Be back soon xxx

Jack: xxx

Lou put her phone away.

"Jack says the turkey's resting and dinner will be in an hour."

"I hope it's not snoring," Nick quipped.

"That's a terrible joke," Mordros hiccupped, giving him a lopsided grin.

"Maybe we should go before we end up carrying you home."

The others agreed. "I'm not that bad," Mordros slurred before closing her eyes.

Nick raised an eyebrow. “Hmm, let’s see whether you can put one foot in front of the other before we make a judgement on that.”

Chapter 38 - Jack

"Who the hell likes sprouts, anyway?" Jack said to no one in particular as he finished peeling and cutting a cross on the bottom of the last one.

"Nobody likes them, but you've got to have them at Christmas. It's tradition." Adam grinned. "And why are you cutting a cross on them? You don't need to do that."

"It's supposed to drive evil spirits away or something like that. Anyway, Mum always did it."

"I didn't know you believed in evil spirits."

"I don't. But it's not worth the risk, is it?"

The girls and Nick had arrived back and were getting ready for the Christmas meal the others had prepared. The dress code was 'naughty or nice' Christmas jumpers, and dinner was at six o'clock, so the children could eat with them. Those who wanted, could go to the Victorian market and on the illuminated Christmas walk in the village afterwards.

Finally, he escaped the kitchen and headed upstairs to change. There was no sign of Lou and Annie, and he presumed they were also getting ready in their room, but when he opened his bedroom door, Lou was sitting on his bed waiting for him.

"That's a nice surprise." He smiled as she got up and walked towards him. "But where's Annie?"

"Don't worry, I haven't left her unsupervised. She's with your sister. Annie said she loved the gold sparkly shoes she was wearing last night, and Clemmie asked if she'd like to try them on. Annie wouldn't pass up an opportunity like that."

"How long do you think they'll be?" He tried to do a mental calculation.

"Are you looking for a distraction?" She teased.

"Look at it this way. It'll give us both an appetite."

"Hmm, well, I wanted to talk to you about something, but your idea sounds much more fun."

***

They were late for dinner, but nobody seemed to care since they were all making fun of each other's jumpers.

"I didn't know there were so many puns around Christmas stuffing," Adam remarked as Mordros dissolved into a fit of giggles.

"Or nuts." Sam winked at Nick.

"I'll never look at a candy cane in the same way." Clemmie gently prodded Tom's jumper as he blushed.

"Come on, let's eat before I die of embarrassment," Tom pleaded as everyone took their seats around the big dining table. A green garland decorated its entire length, and Christmas tableware and linen complemented the festive look.

"Thank you for coming to our Christmas pre-wedding getaway." Adam raised his glass.

"And for being such wonderful friends," Mordros added.

Jack clinked his glass against Lou's and offered her a Christmas cracker to pull. Now that they'd dealt with their vindictive exes, it was turning into a great weekend. He watched his sister pull a cracker with Tom and laugh at the corny joke inside. He wasn't the only one having a great time.

"Stop matchmaking." Lou followed his gaze.

"There's definitely chemistry there."

"Maybe, but your sister made it very clear earlier that she wasn't interested in Tom like that."

"Really? Well, the evidence in front of my eyes would say otherwise."

"You're incorrigible. Now switch your lawyer's brain off and let's eat before I die of starvation."

The meal was delicious, but no one touched the mountain of sprouts he'd prepared. Even Annie rejected his attempts at persuasion. "Why did I spend an hour peeling the blooming things if no one wants them?" he grumbled at everyone.

"Because it's Christmas," they all chorused back.

"I told you," Adam grinned.

For dessert, Tom had made a baked Alaska, and Toby and Annie's eyes lit up when they discovered it had ice cream in the middle. "Ice cream is awesome," Annie told him as she finished hers and began eyeing up second helpings.

He chuckled. Ever since the Santa train ride, her new favourite word was awesome, and she used it as much as possible.

"Maybe I should make sprout ice cream for tomorrow? It would use them all up," Tom suggested.

"You're kidding, right?" Nick looked horrified.

"It could be the next gourmet sensation." Tom ducked as everyone aimed their cracker debris at him.

They all helped clear away and stack the dishwasher, and then it was time for the Victorian market in the village…except Mordros was yawning.

"I think we'll stay at home," Adam said as Mordros snuggled into his side on the sofa. "We'll babysit Mae … well, I will, since Mordros will probably be asleep in a minute."

"We'll help babysit too," Nick offered. "It'll look good on our adoption application if we say we have some babysitting experience."

"Wow, I've never had so many offers of babysitters." Rosie beamed.

While they bickered over which film to watch – Nick wanted Die Hard whilst Mordros preferred Home Alone - the rest of them bundled up against the chilly night air and went outside. They made their way towards the pretty village high street, following the signs to the Victorian market. Jack pushed Annie in her pushchair, and Lou walked beside them, chatting and pointing things out along the way.

"See those people carrying lanterns, Annie? We're all going to a special market where people dress up. And there's a little park with some pretty Christmas lights."

Jack let her words drift over him. He'd never felt happier or luckier. He loved Lou, and she loved him back, and after this weekend, he'd ask her to move in with him. Her tiny flat, with its temperamental boiler and 70s vibe, really wasn't suitable for a growing toddler. And if his flat didn't work either, then he'd sell it and buy a house with a garden in Broadsham, like Adam had.

Life was going to be perfect.

***

They browsed the market and bought roasted chestnuts and mulled cider from stallholders dressed in Victorian costumes. Another stall sold candyfloss – not very Victorian - but he'd bought some for Annie anyway, which was a mistake because she got sticky and had to be cleaned up.

There was even a Christmas carousel, and Lou and Annie sat on a little sleigh and waved to him every time they passed by. Annie had loved it and wanted to go on again, so this time, he'd sat with her, and Lou snapped photos on her phone.

At the end of the village, there was an illuminated trail through a small park with carol singers and street performers along the way. Annie wanted to get out of her pushchair, and he'd lifted her onto his shoulders so she could get a better view, holding onto her securely so she wouldn't fall.

Of course, it was way past her bedtime, and according to Lou, she'd be a grump in the morning, but they were all having far too much fun to worry about that tonight. Just as he finished pointing out the lights, lanterns and cutout reindeer to Annie, Clemmie came to stand next to him. "How're you doing, sis?"

"I'm great. How about you?" She looked up at him, and he noticed the green of her eyes – the same green as his – sparkling in the light. It was good to see her looking so happy.

"I'll probably have a bad back tomorrow since Annie's given up walking but won't sit in her pushchair because she prefers to be carried."

"She's got you twisted around her little finger."

"She has." He chuckled because it was true.

Annie's little ears were obviously listening. "What does twisted little finger mean?"

"It means I'd do anything for you, even if it means breaking my back so you can have a free ride home."

Clemmie suddenly squeezed his arm, and when he looked at her, there was something in her expression that he couldn't read. "What are you thinking?"

"Oh, nothing. I'm probably just imagining it," she said mysteriously.

Chapter 39 - Lou

Tom, Matt and Toby were at a stall along the trail, queuing to buy everyone hot chocolate.

It was getting colder, and Lou couldn't feel her fingers through her mittens. Then Rosie shivered and said what Lou was thinking. "I'm so cold."

"Me too. My hands are like blocks of ice, but hopefully hot chocolate will warm us up."

"I thought the mulled cider would do that. Well, it did for about five minutes, but it's like the North Pole out here." Rosie inclined her head towards Annie sitting on Jack's shoulders. "Annie's having a good time, though."

She looked over to where Jack and his sister were standing. Annie was clearly enjoying her elevated view, though she'd taken off her bobble hat and Clemmie was holding it in her hand. She really should go over and insist she put it back on.

"They look great together, don't they?" Rosie interrupted her thoughts. "All three of them kind of match with their similar hair colouring. I don't know why I haven't noticed before."

Her heart stuttered and stopped, her freezing body becoming an inferno of heat as she watched Rosie observing them. Was she going to work it out? *Please, please, please don't guess — at least not until I've told Jack.*

Perhaps the gods were listening, because Rosie remained quiet, and so she found her own voice instead. "Come on, let's go over and help the others with the drinks."

***

"How did you sleep?" Jack asked as she sat staring into her coffee cup the next morning.

It was seven o'clock and, despite a disturbed night, Annie had woken up bright and breezy and demanding breakfast. In fact, it hadn't been Annie keeping her awake. It had been her own conscience buzzing around in her head, like an annoying fly, refusing to let her sleep because of the close call she'd had with Rosie last night. What if she'd already put two and two together and realised Jack was Annie's father? And Clemmie had given her an odd look on the way home, too… why was that?

Yesterday she'd gone to his room determined to tell him about Annie, but then one thing had led to another, and he'd distracted her… well, more precisely, they'd distracted each other. Whatever happened, she needed to tell him today.

"Lou?" he repeated.

She let out a deep, exhausted breath. "Not great. But I'm hoping a strong cup of coffee will sort me out."

"I bet the candyfloss didn't help matters… all that sugar?"

It hadn't – Annie had plummeted from a sugar high to having a meltdown as she'd put her to bed, but she didn't want him to feel guilty when he'd been trying to be nice. "Well, no, but it was a one-off." She turned to watch Annie, who was eating a croissant from a tray Tom had baked earlier and left out for them.

"Why don't you go back to bed for a bit? Annie and I can walk into the village after breakfast. I noticed there were a couple of baby swings in the park last night."

"I'm not a baby," Annie grumbled between mouthfuls of croissant, and he nodded.

"No, you're not. But even big grown-up girls like swings." She considered this for a moment and nodded before going back to her croissant.

"So?" Jack prompted. "You can catch up on some sleep, and Annie can tell you all about her swing adventure when we get back."

"What swing adventure?" Clemmie asked as she came into the kitchen.

"I'm taking Annie to the park to play on the swings for a bit. Do you want to come?"

"Have you looked out of the window? Because I don't think you'll be going anywhere for a while."

She was right. Snow was falling in thick swirling sheets, making visibility almost impossible. He slid the French doors open a bit - a hushed stillness filled the air, and a white blanket was quickly covering the garden outside. "Look, Annie, it's snowing." Excitement edged his voice as he turned to look at her.

"Snowing," she repeated as she toddled over to him, and he lifted her up to show her the winter wonderland outside.

"Would you like to make a snowman later?"

"Swings, peas, Jat."

"Sweetie, I don't think we can walk to the park in this, but let's do something just as fun."

Chapter 40 - Jack

He'd finally persuaded Lou to go back to bed and to stay there until she felt better. The others slowly drifted downstairs, and they sat at the kitchen table eating Tom's croissants – *they really were the best he'd tasted* - debating what to do with their morning since going out was impossible.

"Annie and I are going to make a gingerbread house," he announced to the room.

Nick put down his coffee. "That sounds fun. Do you want any help?"

No, he didn't. He was looking forward to making it with Annie – an activity just for the two of them - but it seemed churlish to turn down his offer. "Okay."

"Would you like to make a gingerbread house?" Matt asked Toby, who nodded between bites of croissant.

"Why don't we turn it into a competition?" Nick suggested. "Jack and Annie, Matt and Toby, Sam and me, and anyone else who wants to join in?"

"Do we have enough ingredients to make multiple gingerbread houses?" he asked Tom because he was the baker amongst them, and even though they hadn't expected him to, he'd kindly taken charge of the kitchen.

Tom rolled his eyes. "I'd be a poor baker if I didn't bring sufficient supplies with me." A smirk crossed his lips. "Actually, I packed more food than clothes this weekend."

"Can I join in?" Clemmie's eyes landed on Tom.

"Of course, why don't we team up together?"

Jack smothered a grin – despite what Lou had said, it was obvious there was *something* between them, but before he could take the thought any further, Nick grumbled. "That's not fair. You're bound to win if Tom's on your team."

"Don't be ridiculous." Sam nudged him. "It's not Bake Off. It's supposed to be fun."

In the end, they nominated Tom as judge, and Clemmie teamed up with Rosie. That left Mordros and Adam together, which seemed perfect since they were the ones getting married.

"I hope everyone likes gingerbread because we're going to be eating it for days," Sam stated the obvious - but then Tom pointed out that since everyone was going home later, they could take their gingerbread houses with them.

***

Tom gave them a list of ingredients, basic instructions, and a template for the house itself. He also provided a selection of sweets they could use to decorate.

Jack helped Annie measure out the ingredients, and then she'd watched as he'd melted the butter, muscovado sugar, and syrup into a pan. That had been the first tricky part because she'd been eager to taste the golden syrup and ended up in a sticky mess. He'd cleaned her up, and then they'd both mixed in the flour and ground ginger to form the dough.

Using the template Tom had made, he supervised as she rolled out the cooled dough to make the sides, front and back walls, together with the two roof panels, to form the structure of the house.

There wasn't enough oven space, so they'd taken it in turns to bake and then cool their gingerbread. For the next part, they needed to make icing and spread it along the wall edges to construct the house. By the time they were ready to decorate, Lou had come back downstairs, and she pulled up a kitchen stool to watch.

"Look, Mama, isn't it awesome?" Annie proudly showed off her wonky gingerbread house.

"It really is. Well done."

"Jat helped me."

Three words … but it choked him up, his heart flying that she didn't want to take all the credit. "It's a miracle it's standing up," he joked gruffly.

"I think you've both done brilliantly."

"The best bit's still to come. Do you want to help decorate it?"

***

His sides ached from laughing.

It turned out Annie had very firm and non-negotiable ideas about decoration. They used icing to stick sweets and chocolate fingers on to make a door. Chocolate buttons became tiles on the roof, and more random sweets were stuck on for no particular reason, other than Annie wanted them there.

"It looks a bit like the hotel roof." Lou eyed the crooked pattern of chocolate buttons, which were stuck in at odd angles.

Compared to the others, it honestly looked a mess, but to Jack, it was the clear winner.

"And the winner is…" Tom made a drum roll sound. "Matt and Toby, because they went the extra mile and crushed up boiled sweets and melted them to make into windows."

"What's our prize?" Toby asked eagerly.

"Washing up," Matt teased.

"Dad! Surely the winners don't have to wash up," Toby grumbled.

"You bet they do." Rosie ruffled his hair. "But then we can all try some."

Chapter 41 - Jack

By the time they'd got the kitchen back to some semblance of order, it was lunchtime. They ate turkey sandwiches made from leftovers, but no one wanted to destroy the gingerbread houses.

It had finally stopped snowing, and when Nick slid open the French doors, there was a blanket of virgin white covering the lawn, which sparkled like silver glitter in the weak sunshine. A red-breasted robin resting on a bird feeder and the silhouette from the trees made it a perfect Christmas scene.

"It's beautiful," Mordros murmured as they all admired the view.

He picked up Annie to show her. "What do you think? Do you want to go outside and make a snowman?"

"Look, white icing, Jat." She pointed a chubby finger, her green eyes shining with excitement, and yeah, it looked exactly like the white icing they'd used to cover the cake board in a thick snow effect.

The enchantment in her voice made his pulse-rate rocket because she'd already captured his heart, and he'd protect her with his life if he had to. *Where had that thought come from except… God, he already loved this little girl.*

"Anyone up for a snowball fight?" Nick challenged the group.

"If you're going to have a snowball fight, do it down the garden away from our snowman," he instructed. "Come on, Annie, let's go outside."

***

"No headshots or hard snowballs and definitely no ganging up," Adam bellowed, giving Nick and Sam a sharp look.

They watched for a while as the others threw snowballs at each other, and Annie whooped with excitement. There was too much rough and tumble to allow her to join in, but he let her throw snowballs at him, and every time she hit her target, he'd fall over with an exaggerated thud to make her giggle.

Then he showed her how to make a snow angel, lying on his back and moving his arms and legs to create an impression of an angel's wings and body. By the time they'd finished rolling around, they didn't look like angels at all, but she didn't seem to mind.

The others were now playing a different version of a snowball fight. They split into teams to defend their own area and tried to capture the other team's flag. No one had a real flag, so they tied one of Adam's socks to a stick and used that instead.

Finally, they broke off for hot chocolate, and Rosie and Clemmie took one for the team by breaking up their gingerbread house for everyone to eat in the kitchen. They'd certainly worked up an appetite, but Annie wasn't content to stay indoors for long, reminding him they still had a snowman to build.

"Dad, can we make one, too?" Toby pleaded with Matt.

"I'm tired, buddy." Matt winked at Rosie to show he was teasing.

"Please, Dad."

"But I'm so tired." He sighed dramatically.

"Dad, please."

"Matt!" Rosie jabbed him in the ribs.

"Ouch!" He held up his palms in surrender. "I think your mum's had enough of my kidding around. Yes, of course, we can make a snowman."

Adam and Tom went off to shovel snow from the driveway since they were all leaving later. The main roads were already clear, but the smaller countryside ones would be trickier. It was going to be an interesting journey home.

He took Annie outside, and between them, they made a passable version of a snowman – maybe it wasn't as professional looking as Toby's, but it had a fat body and a smaller head with two stones for eyes and a carrot nose. He gave Annie his scarf to tie around its neck and added a pair of sunglasses. By the time they'd finished, the others had joined them outside, and everyone said their snowman was a cool-looking dude.

"Dad, what shall we call him?" Toby took a few steps back to admire their handiwork. "What about Chilly Willy because he doesn't have any pants on?" He snorted at his own joke.

"Dad, what shall we call him?" Annie repeated.

"What did you just say?" It was a cliché, but his mouth fell open with shock; but Annie was too busy picking up more snow to reply.

***

She's just repeating what Toby said, that's all. It means nothing, and you're an idiot for reading anything into it.

They'd named their snowman Frosty, but Annie had immediately got distracted when Nick and Sam started up another snowball fight, and Lou had taken her over to watch from a safe distance.

"Did you hear what Annie called me?" he whispered to Clemmie.

"Yeah, I did," she replied in a normal voice.

He grinned because there was no reason for him to act all cloak and dagger, simply because she'd called him dad. It was just a slip of the tongue because she'd heard Toby say it so much this weekend. "I know she's only repeating the word, but I guess I'm flattered."

"Jack." Clemmie slipped her arm through his and looked up at him.

"What?"

"Just take a moment to think."

"Think about what?" He felt like he was being stupid. She was certainly looking at him as if he were, but he didn't know what she was hinting at.

His eyes wandered over to Annie. She'd taken off her bobble hat, and the sun caught the red highlights in her hair against the brilliant white of the snow. Her cheeks were pink, and her green eyes sparkled with mischief as she threw a handful of snow and Lou pretended to fall over.

"Do you see now?" Clemmie asked softly.

***

It was his 'aha moment' when all the puzzle pieces finally slipped into place. While everyone around him was still snapping photos on their phones and larking about, his world had stopped, frozen in that moment, as he finally realised Annie was his.

Of course she was.

He'd escaped the garden, and now he was in his room sitting on his bed, raw pain tearing him apart, his heart shattering into a thousand pieces at all the milestones he'd missed: Annie's birth, her first smile, her first word… *her first everything.*

His shoulders slumped with the weight of grief – too heavy to bear – that he'd missed so much. All the days, months and years she'd been his, and he hadn't known.

Why didn't you tell me I have a daughter? The question spun in a loop in his mind. A world of pain in each word.

A gentle tap on his bedroom door broke into his thoughts, but he ignored it. He didn't want to talk to anyone, least of all Lou. The handle of the door turned slowly. Damn, he'd forgotten to lock it.

***

"It's only me." Clemmie walked in and sat down beside him on the bed. "I'm sorry."

"There's nothing for you to apologise for." A single tear rolled down his cheek, but he didn't bother wiping it away.

"I shouldn't have said anything."

"You didn't. You just let me work it out."

"I know, but still."

"I'm glad you did." He finally raised his head and faced her. She looked as devastated as he was.

She squeezed his hand. "What are you going to do?"

"Talk to Lou, I guess. But I need to get out of here first. Clear my head."

"Is that a good idea? I mean, wouldn't it be best to stay and sort this out?"

She was right, but he was too focused on his anger and hurt to have a coherent conversation with her at the moment. Besides, he needed to process the bombshell that he was a father.

A father… the words would change his life forever.

He got up and began packing.

Chapter 42 - Lou

"When?" Lou stopped packing and turned to face Mordros, who was standing in the doorway of her bedroom.

"About twenty minutes ago. He gave us Annie's car seat so we can take you both back to Broadsham."

"But I don't understand. Why didn't he tell me he was leaving?"

"I don't know."

"Mordros?"

"Honestly, I don't, but Clemmie might. She was with him when he told Adam he was leaving, and they both looked pretty upset."

She sat down on the bed and tried to process what Mordros had just said. Maybe there'd been an emergency, and that was why they'd both looked upset. But it still didn't explain why he'd left without saying goodbye.

She checked her phone for messages, but there weren't any, and when she tried to call him, his mobile was switched off.

What on earth was going on?

***

Clemmie was tight-lipped. "It's best you talk to my brother."

"Well, I would, but he's not here, is he?" Lou watched as she squirmed. They'd only met this weekend, and the last thing she wanted was to jeopardise a budding friendship, especially since she was Jack's sister. "Sorry, that was rude of me. I'm just worried, that's all."

Clemmie shrugged. "I'm sure he'll be in touch tomorrow. He just—"

"Just what?"

"He needs to think some things through."

"What things?"

"Just … things. Look, I don't mean to be unhelpful, and I'm sure he'll contact you soon."

Lou let out a frustrated sigh. "Okay, I guess I'll wait then."

"I'm sorry," Clemmie called out as Lou walked out of the room.

***

Lou knew he'd found Annie to say goodbye before he'd left, because Rosie had wandered into the kitchen and found them together. *So why hadn't he said goodbye to her?*

She sat in the back of Adam's car as they made the slow journey home, contemplating what Clemmie had said… or rather not said. Of course, she was Jack's sister, so her first loyalty would be to him. But what exactly did she need to be loyal about?

Jack still had his phone switched off, and other than hightailing over to his flat in Cheltenham, she couldn't think what else she could do except wait for him to contact her.

Something was wrong… very wrong, her intuition fluttering helplessly like butterfly wings against a windowpane, trying to work out what it was.

Chapter 43 - Jack

"Earth to Jack!"

"What?"

"You're clearly not on this planet at the moment, so where are you?" Adam smirked from the doorway before coming into Jack's office and shutting the door.

"I'm just thinking, that's all."

"And does this thinking have anything to do with Lou?"

It had everything to do with her, but he wasn't ready for a heart to heart. Over the last few days, the only thing keeping him from going mad had been shutting himself away in his office to work. He gave Adam a look that said, bugger off, and went back to staring at the email on his laptop that he'd already read a dozen times and still couldn't make sense of.

"Look, I know it's none of my business, but–"

"You're right."

Adam walked around the back of his desk and turned his laptop off.

"What the hell did you do that for?" he growled as the screen went blank.

"Because, like it or not, we're going to talk."

"Fine. What do you want to talk about… the crappy weather? The state of the economy or - I don't know - the fact I found out that Annie's my daughter."

"Was it a shock?"

"Of course it was a shock. Okay, now looking back, it seems bloody obvious, and I feel stupid for not guessing, but … wait… did you know?"

Adam looked uncomfortable, but then shrugged. "Of course I knew."

"What? How? When?"

"Lou told Mordros and…" Adam waited for him to fill in the blank.

"Mordros told you." Jack tilted back in his chair, studying him.

"Yep."

"And you didn't tell me because…?"

"Because it wasn't my place. This is between you and Lou."

"You're supposed to be my best friend."

Adam rolled his eyes. "Come on, give me a break. Anyway, I thought… well, hoped she'd tell you herself this weekend."

He blew out a breath. "Fine. So, Clemmie guessed, and you both know. What about the others?"

"I imagine they've probably worked it out. I mean, Annie looks like a mini version of you."

He couldn't help the pride in his voice. "She really does."

"So why are you sulking then? Surely, you're happy about it."

"I'm not sulking. I'm just bloody hurt that Lou didn't tell me."

"And rather than talk to her about it, you're hiding away in your office."

"I'm not hiding. I'm processing."

"What's there to process? You're Annie's dad and, okay, Lou should have told you sooner, but she must have had her reasons."

"Easy for you to take the high road and act all reasonable. But why would she deliberately keep it from me?"

"I don't know, and until you ask her, you won't know either."

"You're an arse."

"You know I'm right."

"You're a sanctimonious arse."

"I'm still right."

"An annoying, sanctimonious arse."

"Still right, though," Adam chuckled as he threw a paperclip at him.

Chapter 44 - Lou

"Do you think Jack will look over the contract and act for us on the sale?" Sylvie handed over an A4 envelope containing a stack of paperwork.

Lou swallowed. She hadn't seen Jack since he'd left the hire house so abruptly on Sunday afternoon, but he'd finally sent a short, cryptic message saying they needed to talk. "I'm sure he will, but I'm seeing him later, so I'll ask him."

She took the envelope but didn't bother taking out the contract because she didn't care who was going to buy the hotel. More than likely, it was someone who'd turn it into another one of those impersonal, faceless hotels scattered across the country that didn't have any character. If only she could come up with the money to fix the roof and all the other things that needed doing. But she'd racked her brains over and over and, besides Nick's ridiculous idea of robbing a bank, she'd drawn a blank.

"Are you okay?" her mum asked gently. "You seem a bit preoccupied."

"I'm just tired, but nothing an early night won't cure."

"Is Annie keeping you awake?"

She thought about lying, but that didn't seem fair to Annie. "No, actually, she's sleeping a lot better lately."

"And is everything okay with you and Jack?"

She realised her mum was gently probing. "I think I've upset him. That's why he's coming over later so we can talk."

"Have you told him about Annie yet?"

She shook her head, letting her shoulders slump with the weight of her conscience that she hadn't, and maybe he'd found out, anyway. Why else would he have left on Sunday without saying goodbye? "I think he's worked it out, and that's why he's upset."

"Oh, darling." Her mum sucked in a sharp breath, her disappointment obvious. "Would you like me to babysit so you can talk to him without small ears overhearing?"

"No, actually, I think Annie should be there. If he already knows, then we can tell her together."

The time for secrets was over.

***

She'd been a nervous wreck all day, but now her nerves had taken on a life of their own as she clock-watched waiting for him to arrive.

From the moment she'd received those fake photos, she'd made one terrible decision after another. Not trusting him enough to tell him was bad enough, but to make matters a million times worse, she'd kept her pregnancy and Annie's birth a secret. God, why hadn't she just sat him down and told him everything?

At six o'clock, she heard his familiar knock, and she tried to interpret what his mood might be. It definitely wasn't a hesitant knock, but it didn't sound angry, either. *Just open the stupid door.* Her nerves made her tongue run away with her. "It's great to see you. Annie's been so excited all day. I hope the traffic wasn't too bad. At least the roads are back to normal. Are you hungry?"

"Lou, take a breath." He shrugged off his jacket, and there was a slight tug on his mouth which could have been a smile. She noticed he didn't kiss her, though. She followed him into her tiny living area, where Annie was sitting on the sofa.

"Hi Annie." He bent down to give her a quick peck on the cheek.

"Hi Jat." She pointed to her bowl. "I eat nana and boobies. Boobies best. They like sweets."

Lou watched him translate her toddler speak to banana and blueberries in his head, then nod. He sat down next to her, and they began chatting. It was kind of nice, as if he'd just arrived home from work and they were catching up with each other's day. She boiled the kettle and made tea. "Have you eaten?"

"I'm fine, thanks."

"Are you sure? It's no trouble." *Just stop talking.*

"I'm good." He gave her a brief smile. "I've got a present for Annie, though."

She watched as he handed her a small wrapped package she hadn't noticed he'd been holding.

"Mama?" Annie's eyes were shining with excitement as she waited for permission to open it.

"Go ahead, sweetheart."

Annie tore off the paper, and she leant over the sofa to see what it was. A small framed photo of Annie and Jack stared back at her. Snow covered their coats, and Annie had a fistful of snow in her hand, about to throw it at him, her eyes sparkling with mischief as he grinned back at her. The photo perfectly captured the moment.

"Mama, look, it's me and Jat."

She couldn't trust herself to speak because it was so obvious that Annie was his daughter, and this was his way of telling her he knew.

"I think it's about time we told Annie, don't you?" he said softly.

***

They put her to bed together, and he placed the small photo frame on Annie's bedside table so she could look at it, but her eyes drifted closed almost immediately.

"I'm so sorry." She blurted out, forgetting the words she'd rehearsed as they went back into the sitting room. "I should have told you sooner. I'm so sorry."

Finally, the truth settled quietly between them. For almost three years, she'd kept his daughter a secret from him. Caring for her, keeping her safe, nurturing her body and soul. Not just the big moments but the ordinary insignificant ones too. She'd taken it all away from him.

"Why didn't you?" His voice was brittle.

"It felt such an overwhelming thing, and the longer I put it off, the harder it got. I'm so sorry."

"Keeping her from me … I can't even put into words how angry I'm feeling right now. I actually can't believe you've done this. It was beyond cruel."

She felt his fury vibrating through every word. "I'm so sorry–"

"I don't want to hear you're sorry. Not only did you keep Annie a secret, but you lied about it to my face. Sorry doesn't cut it, Lou."

"I know," she whispered, but he wasn't listening.

"You had no right… absolutely none to keep her a secret from me. But now I know I want to amicably co-parent with you, which means creating a stable environment for her. Obviously, she'll continue living with you, but I'll want regular contact visits and eventually overnight stays."

"What?"

He exhaled slowly, his tone softening. "I want to co-parent with you. We can work out a schedule of visits, but ultimately, I'll want to work towards fifty/fifty time with her."

"Jack, please."

"I'll also backdate all maintenance payments. I won't shirk my financial responsibilities."

"Please stop." Tears were sliding down her cheeks now.

"I'll be flexible and work with you, so we're consistent over Annie's routines. Her needs will always be my priority. However, if we can't agree, I'm prepared to go to mediation." His face remained impassive as he carried on his barrage of words. "I don't think I can forgive you, but I will try to keep things amicable between us for Annie's sake."

"What about us? You and me?" she spluttered through a blur of tears.

"There is no us, Lou."

Stunned, she watched as he picked up his jacket. He barely glanced at her as he left the flat, as if she were no longer of any consequence to him. The room became silent, but her head screamed his words over and over as she sat frozen in misery.

There is no us, Lou.

She lost track of time, but at some point, she must have dozed off. When she woke up, daylight was pouring in from the window and, through the fog in her head, Annie was calling her. She got up slowly, stiff from lying on the sofa all night, and made her way into her bedroom.

"Hello, sweetie. Did you sleep okay?"

Annie pointed to the photo. "Daddy and Annie," she said slowly.

"Yes, Daddy and Annie." She swallowed, trying hard not to cry.

***

Two days later, Lou went to see Mordros. They were sitting in her kitchen drinking coffee before she tried on her bridesmaid dress.

"Do you want to talk about it?" Mordros looked over the top of her coffee cup at her.

"I look that bad, huh?"

"No, just not your usual polished self."

She snorted. "Very tactful, but also a lie."

She couldn't blame her for noticing her unwashed hair and the dark shadows under her eyes. Ever since her fight with Jack – was it a fight if only one person did the talking? – whatever it was, she'd been unable to sleep, tossing and turning each night, as she'd relived the hurt and anger in his voice as he'd shredded her with his words.

"So?" Mordros squeezed her hand.

"I didn't tell Jack about Annie, but he found out anyway." She forced herself to take a steadying breath.

"Oh God, I wondered if that was the reason he left so abruptly on Sunday. How's he taken it?"

"He's very upset." She hesitated. "Actually, he's broken up with me."

"What?" Her eyes widened with shock.

"He wants to co-parent, but in his words, there is no us."

"Oh Lou. I'm so sorry."

She sniffed. "It's totally my fault. I kept putting off telling him, and now he's furious with me, and I've got no one to blame but myself. I should have told him, and I didn't, so…"

"He'll come round. Jack's not the type to hold a grudge for long."

"You didn't see him. I've really hurt him, and he said he didn't think he could forgive me."

"Things get said in the heat of the moment, but once he's calmed down…"

"I don't think so, and I just feel so sad about it all. I've really messed up."

"Just give him time. Maybe Adam could talk to him?"

"No. This is between me and Jack. There is something you can do for me, though." She fished out the hotel sale contact from her bag. "Can you ask Adam to look over this? Jack was going to, but because of the way things are…" she trailed off.

"Sure. I'll give it to him tonight." Mordros took the envelope from her. "Right now, Jack's angry and lashing out, trying to hurt you as much as he's hurting. But he'll get over it. Besides, he's head over heels in love with you."

She shook her head. "I don't think he loves me anymore, and to be honest, I don't deserve his love."

"Of course you do. He'll come around - just give him a bit of time."

She knew Mordros was being the voice of reason and trying to make her feel better, but… *you didn't see the hurt and pain in his eyes.* "I hope you're right." A flicker of a smile brushed her lips.

"How about you try on your bridesmaid dress so we can see if it fits?"

Lou nodded. "That's a lovely idea."

***

Lou did a twirl in front of the long mirror in Mordros and Adam's bedroom. The dress was a simple floor-length, A-line style with a front and back V-neckline. On one shoulder were two tiny embroidered butterflies in ivory white thread.

"I love it, especially the two butterflies, and plum is the perfect colour for this time of year."

"In Chinese art, two butterflies flying together symbolises love and marital bliss." Mordros studied the dress critically. "Good, it's not too low, but it still shows off your amazing figure. Jack will love it."

"Hmm. Well, I don't know about him, but I think it's beautiful."

"We're ditching morning suits. We want our wedding to be relaxed, so we're telling everyone to wear what they like, though Adam's warned Jack not to take that too literally. Imagine if he turned up in his gym kit!" she giggled. "Oh, and I've spoken to the florist along the high street, and she's suggested pale pink, white and purple cyclamen for the tables. What do you think?"

"That's a lovely idea… very Christmassy, and they'll go with your colour scheme."

"Yes, that's what I thought." Mordros went to the wardrobe and took out another garment bag. "Now let me show you Annie's dress."

Annie's flower-girl dress was a princess design in ivory white with a scoop neckline, bodice and matching ruffle cap sleeves. A wide waistband wrapped around to a large bow at the back, and the tulle skirt was perfect for twirling and dancing in.

"It's absolutely beautiful." Lou stared at the tiny plum-coloured butterflies Mordros had painstakingly sewn onto the tulle skirt. They perfectly matched the colour of her bridesmaid dress.

"Can you get Annie to try it on and let me know if it needs altering? The sash and bow are removable if she doesn't want to wear them on the day."

"You're kidding! She'll never take it off. The butterflies must have taken you hours to do."

Mordros nodded. "I loved doing them, but I need to start on my dress sharpish otherwise I'll be walking down the aisle in just my bra and pants."

"Don't even joke." Lou giggled.

Chapter 45 - Jack

It was three days after their big argument, and he'd arranged with Lou to take Annie to the local café for tea. Lou would only be a short distance away if anything went wrong, but since they'd only be gone an hour, hopefully it wouldn't.

"Why is it so cold in here?" he grunted as he walked into her flat.

Lou rolled her eyes. "The boiler's packed up again. I've tried to do the same fix you did, but it didn't work, so I'm getting someone out to look at it."

"It needs replacing."

"I know, but since neither mum nor I have the money, we're hoping it's repairable."

"What about keeping warm tonight?"

"I've borrowed a couple of fan heaters from mum, but Annie can sleep with me tonight. I'll keep her warm."

"That's not good enough. You knew the boiler was on the blink, so you should have got it fixed sooner."

"Easy for you to say when you're earning a six-figure salary and living in a posh flat with all mod cons. Try living in the real world," she fired back.

He scowled, but ignored her dig. "Can't your mum put you up for a night or two?"

"She offered, but I'm an adult and shouldn't keep running to her every time something goes wrong."

"So, you'd rather our daughter froze to death because your ego prevents you from accepting help." *Our daughter … the two words slipped easily from his mouth, and he liked the sound of them on his lips. But maybe he shouldn't be focusing on that at the moment since they appeared to be fighting again.*

"Oh, stop exaggerating. Years ago, people didn't have heating. We'll manage for a few days," she snapped back.

Yep, definitely fighting.

"You think going back to the old days without heating is a good thing?"

"I didn't say that. I just said… oh, it doesn't matter."

"Hello Daddy." Annie gave him a wide grin, making his annoyance melt away instantly.

"Hello gorgeous. How's your day been?"

"I've been to nursery, and we sang our nutty songs."

"Nativity songs," Lou gently corrected.

"And we've got to hurt them every day until we get them right."

"Rehearse them." Lou grinned.

"That sounds a fun day. What songs are you rehearsing?" He tried to keep a straight face.

"Jingle Bells and Away in a Manger. And when we know them, we can sing them to our patients."

"I've got this one… parents," he said triumphantly.

Will you come, Daddy?

"Try keeping me away."

***

It was weird taking Annie out alone. Lou had given him a bag full of stuff 'just in case' with firm instructions to call her if Annie got upset or needed her. He'd almost asked her to join them, but they weren't a couple now, so presumably didn't do '*couple-y*' things. Besides, he was irritated that she hadn't had the forethought to get the boiler fixed, and the flat was like a bloody fridge, but then her words echoed, pricking his conscience.

Easy for you to say when you're earning a six-figure salary and living in a posh flat with all mod cons. Try living in the real world. Yeah, he'd been an arse, hadn't he?

To Lou's credit, she'd chivvied Annie through the door and even though she'd looked confused and asked why mama wasn't coming with them, they'd both convinced her that beans on toast at the café were preferable to staying inside a cold flat. Which it was, except it felt all wrong going without Lou.

Looking back on their terrible fight the other night, he realised his anger and hurt had fuelled much of it. Of course, she should have told him about Annie sooner. But a part of him knew that the secret she'd carried since leaving him in London had been an enormous burden, and the only reason she'd held onto it was because she'd been terrified of his reaction. And he'd proved her right, because he hadn't handled the news well at all.

He'd taken Lou's lead, as she'd gently explained to Annie that he was her father. For him, it had been earth-shattering news, and he'd expected some questions at least, but she'd carried on eating her blueberries and then begun yawning. It had certainly put the whole thing into perspective.

He watched Annie pushing her beans around her plate and every so often looking at the café door as if she was hoping Lou would walk in. He'd tried to make their little outing fun, but from the look on her face, he'd failed miserably. *Lou would be here if you hadn't acted like an arse and let your pride get in the way.*

He suddenly felt weary. "Let's go home, Annie. We can call in at the bakery on the way and buy some cakes to share with your mama."

She immediately put down her spoon and grinned. "I love cake, Daddy."

"I had a feeling you did. Now what sort of cake do you think your mama would like?"

***

The bakery was closed.

Frustration and annoyance rolled over him. Where was the damn cake when you needed some? He'd be having a word with Tom about his short opening hours, though since it was almost seven o'clock, he supposed he was being slightly unreasonable.

It didn't help that Annie was looking at him expectantly, as if he could somehow magically produce cake out of thin air. And he could hear Lou in his head telling him off for making a promise he'd failed to keep.

The café would have cake, though. He should have thought of that in the first place, except Tom's cakes were far superior. But by the time they'd trudged back to the café, there was a closed sign taunting them both on the door.

Okay, what now? Annie was looking decidedly unimpressed, and her bottom lip was sticking out in a pout. Surely there must be somewhere open in Broadsham selling cake at this time of night? Well, maybe there was, but it was freezing, and he couldn't trawl around with Annie trying to find somewhere in this temperature.

"Sorry, sweetheart, looks like everyone's sold out of cake. I can get you some tomorrow, though." His heart almost broke when he saw a single tear roll down her cheek. She didn't have a tantrum though, but somehow that made it worse because she was trying so hard to be grown up about it. He picked her up and gave her a hug. "I'm really sorry, Annie."

"It's okay, Daddy," Annie's muffled voice answered from his coat.

He breathed out slowly. Single parenting was hard, and he'd messed up on his first go at it.

Chapter 46 - Lou

Doing things separately with Annie was obviously their new reality, so she'd better get used to it and try to co-parent amicably. The thought of it – just seeing Jack at pickups and drop-offs was like a gut punch. He was right about one thing, though. Ego, stubbornness or sheer bloody-mindedness had prevented her accepting her mum's offer to stay the night, so now they were stuck in this freezing flat. No wonder he'd felt irritated.

She wondered how Annie was doing. He hadn't called, so she was obviously fine. Of course, she was… whatever the difficulties between them, he would take care of her and make their time together fun. She wanted to be there too instead of sitting alone and feeling left out.

Fragments of their weekend replayed in her head. Laughing until their sides ached as they'd watched Annie decorate the gingerbread house until it looked like a wacky piece of modern art. Snowball fights and larking about. *All her dreams and imaginings of the life they might have shared … yet through her own stupidity she'd lost him.*

Time dragged, but finally there was a gentle knock on the front door, and she rushed to open it. Jack was standing under the porch light, carrying a sleeping Annie in his arms.

"I've already put the fan heater on in my bedroom. Hopefully, it's taken the edge off the cold." She led him down the hallway towards her room.

He didn't even bother putting Annie down because the small heater hadn't made the slightest difference to the bitterly cold bedroom. "Lou, it's freezing in here. I know you want to be independent, but please come home with me tonight. My flat's warm, and you'll both have a much better night's sleep."

She was about to argue… to tell him she had extra blankets and could probably find a hot water bottle somewhere. But there wasn't any smugness on his face, just genuine concern, so to argue further would be more stubbornness on her part. "Okay," she nodded, as a fluttery feeling of hope wrapped itself around her heart.

***

Not only did his flat have underfloor heating, but there was a constant supply of hot water, which she happily took advantage of by having an extra-long soak in the bath. She even found some posh lime, basil and mandarin bubble bath, which he said belonged to his sister, Clemmie, though she wasn't sure she believed him.

They took the cushions off the sofa and made Annie a temporary bed in the guest room. It wasn't ideal, but it would do for one night. Jack stayed with her until she'd fallen asleep, and then he'd ordered a pizza delivery for them to share.

Sitting together on the floor, eating pizza and looking out at the twinkling town lights in the distance, it was easy to pretend they were still together. She stole a look at him, and he was staring just as intently at the night sky as she was. "I don't think I'd ever tire of this. It's beautiful."

"Yeah, I've done a lot of thinking, looking out at this view over the last few days." His face hardened for a moment but then relaxed. "Thunderstorms and lightning across the night sky are spectacular to watch."

"The last few days have felt like being in the eye of a storm."

"You could say that." There was a hint of a smile on his face. He cleared his throat. "I've added you to my insurance so you can use my car in the morning to take Annie backwards and forwards to nursery. I'll take an Uber if I need to go into the office, but I can just as easily work from home."

"You don't have to…"

"Lou, please."

"Okay. Thank you."

"I'll also get a proper bed sorted out for Annie tomorrow. She'll need one here anyway for when she stays. Maybe you can help me choose one?"

"Yes." She bit her lip. "What I did…keeping Annie a secret from you was cruel and wrong. I'm truly sorry." She almost reached for him. *Almost.*

His face tensed. "I know you are."

She sucked in a deep breath. "Annie's so lucky to have you as her daddy." She hesitated… "Umm, would you like to look at some photos of her when she was born?"

"I'd love to, but do you have any photos of your pregnancy, too?"

"Yes, of course." She found the folder on her phone and began scrolling… photos of her pregnancy bump and then the first ones of their daughter as she'd come into the world bawling, a head full of chestnut hair just like her dad.

Photos of her first and second birthdays – her first hesitant steps and smiles – all the milestones he'd missed… *because of her.*

They were so close, their foreheads nearly touching as he stared at each photo. "I'm sorry I didn't deal with the news about Annie well." He looked up, and their eyes locked.

Was he going to kiss her? Yes, yes… but he pulled away, and the moment was gone.

There wasn't much else left to say. Tonight, there'd been a small thaw in their relationship, and maybe they could work towards becoming friends at least. He got up, but she stayed where she was, and she heard him stacking the dishwasher in the kitchen.

"I love you," she whispered into the bright lights in the distance. "I love you."

***

She sat at the edge of the bed in the guest room. The mattress was so comfortable and not at all like the lumpy, cheap one in her flat.

Jack hovered in the doorway. "Is there anything you need?"

She shook her head. She'd packed a small overnight bag for them both, so she had everything. "I've hardly slept the last few nights, so I'm looking forward to crashing out."

For a moment, they both gazed at Annie, who was fast asleep on the cushions. Only her little face, with her chestnut hair splayed out on the pillow, was showing from under the duvet.

"She's had a busy night, so hopefully she'll sleep too," he whispered. "Goodnight, Lou. Sleep well."

The door shut softly behind him.

She brushed her teeth and got into bed, but the urge to sleep had gone. She lay on her back, staring at the ceiling. *Jack's ceiling.* She was in his flat, in his guest room, and he was right next door… only a few feet away. Her body ached for him.

What if she got out of bed right now and went into his bedroom?

She tested the idea out in her head. What would he do if she crawled into bed with him and sank her fingers into his hair…ran her hands over his arms and down his hard body? Would she feel his breath hitch before she kissed him? Would he hold her close and press their bodies together, his weight pinning her to the mattress?

Heat and lust had pulled her fully awake now, and she blinked at the ceiling, her fantasies playing on.

Would he whisper her name as he trailed kisses down her body? Tell her he loved her - had never stopped loving her - and that he wanted her back?

She hugged her pillow, trying to slow her pounding heart. Everything she wanted was in the room next door. But what if he rejected her and looked embarrassed?

There is no us, Lou.

Should she risk it?

She got out of bed, aware that if she made the slightest sound, Annie might wake up. She almost didn't breathe as she made her way across the room to the door. Opening it slowly, she walked out into the softly lit hallway.

Along the passageway, his bedroom door was closed, and she stood for a moment listening. She couldn't hear anything, but nerves still made her hesitate. What if she gave him such a shock that he had a heart attack?

She let out a nervous giggle. *I'm sorry, officer, I didn't mean to kill him.* Perhaps she should just go back to her room? *Yeah, probably best.* She began turning.

"What are you doing lurking in the hallway?" Jack slouched against his door, staring at her. He was wearing sleep shorts and nothing else, and her eyes wandered down and stayed there. "Lou? Eyes up here, please."

"Sorry. I wanted a glass of water. The pizza was salty," she lied. He probably didn't believe her, but he led her into the kitchen anyway. The water was cold and delicious, and they both stood sipping their drinks in the quiet kitchen.

"Do you want to tell me the real reason you were hovering outside my bedroom?" He put his glass down and stared at her, making her skin warm with embarrassment.

"I was just heading for the kitchen."

"Lou?"

She set her own glass down and closed her eyes. "I've ruined things between us, and I miss you so much."

She suddenly felt his touch on her face, and her eyes opened to meet his. They were dark green pools of desire, and he began palming her cheek before his hand slid through her hair. He stopped and waited, and she gave a quick nod.

Hard and demanding, he kept kissing her as he walked her backwards, until she hit the kitchen island. His hands found her hips and lifted her up onto the counter, and she wrapped her legs tight around his waist as he leant into her, never breaking their kiss.

She let herself fall apart beneath his touch as his tongue roved her mouth, swallowing all her moans and shivers as he pressed his hard body against hers. *Was this really happening?* "Don't stop," she pleaded between kisses as she ground against him.

For a blissful moment, there was nothing but their breath mingling, his stubble rough against her skin, as heat pooled inside her. She became light-headed from his mouth and his touch, her heartbeat hammering, desperate, wanton and greedy for more.

But finally, he pulled back, his eyes raking over her vest top. Slowly, he began pulling the thin straps down over her shoulders. "God, you're so beautiful." His voice, midnight dark with desire, made her tremble as he slowly began trailing kisses along her collarbone. It was too much, and she closed her eyes, trying to remember how to breathe.

"Mama, Daddy, Mama, Daddy." An insistent voice drifted in from the bedroom.

They both froze until she started giggling. "Since we're co-parenting now. I think it's your turn."

Chapter 47 - Jack

Jack stared at the hotel sale contract Adam had given him earlier. Everything appeared in order, yet something was nagging at him, and he couldn't put his finger on what it was. No doubt it would come to him when he was doing something else, like making out with Lou.

He closed his eyes, thinking of her perched on his kitchen counter and then Annie's urgent voice interrupting them. Talk about a mood killer, but it would have been a hell of a lot worse if she'd caught them a few minutes later.

That's why bedroom doors have locks on them, idiot!

"Are you asleep? Not that I blame you. Commercial conveyancing is enough to put anyone into a coma." Adam grinned as he came into his office.

"I'm not asleep. But I am trying to work out why this contract bothers me so much."

"Well, while you're figuring it out, I came to tell you we're having a small dinner party tomorrow night, and we're hoping you and Lou will come. Actually, we're begging you to, because our parents will be there, and it's going to be awkward."

"You're inviting us to dinner with your parents, who hate the sight of each other… no thanks." He shook his head.

"Oh, come on. Call it one of your obligations as best man and bridesmaid. Anyway, Nick and Sam will be there too, so it might be fun."

"Fun like having a tooth extraction or an ingrowing toenail?"

Adam grimaced. "Please come, otherwise I'm likely to kill my mother if Jago doesn't do it first."

He sighed. "Hmm, okay, since you've asked so nicely."

"Thanks, I owe you. Dinner's at seven. Oh, and bring Annie, too, if you'd like." Adam hesitated. "How are things between you and Lou?"

Where did he start? "The boiler's broken in her flat, so she and Annie are staying with me for a bit."

"And are you back together?" Adam pressed.

Were they? After last night's events, his head was a confused mess.

"We haven't had time to talk yet."

"What's there to talk about? You love her. She loves you…yada, yada, yada."

"Thanks, that's very helpful."

"Anytime." He grinned. "Now, about that contract."

***

Annie was asleep in her new bed. It was a child's one with removable sides for when she got older, but for now they were there so she couldn't fall out.

They'd both worried she'd hate it, but she'd been as caught up in the excitement as they were. They'd cleared his office since there wasn't enough space in the guest room, and Lou had completed the transformation with a little red reindeer duvet cover, which made Annie's eyes light up.

"Let's celebrate." He handed Lou a glass of wine. "To Annie's first night in a proper bed."

"Don't you think it's a bit early to celebrate? Just wait until the middle of the night when she decides she's had enough of being in her own room."

"Nah, she'll be fine. She sleeps in her own room in your flat, so why wouldn't she here?"

"Good point, but if she wakes up, you're on night duty."

"I did it last night," he teased.

"Yep, and you've got a lot of catching up to do."

"Fair enough." He certainly wouldn't argue about doing his share of night wake-ups. After all, she'd done all of them until now. "Lou, about last night…"

"It's okay. We both got carried away in the moment."

She was giving him a get-out of jail free card if that's what he wanted. "Is that what you think… we just got carried away?"

"I think you felt sorry for me because I said I'd ruined things between us, and I missed you."

"It wasn't pity if that's what you're implying."

"No?"

"Of course not."

"Still, it wasn't our best decision since Annie could have come in."

"I really don't want to think about that." He scrubbed his hand through his hair trying to block out the memory of the close call they'd had.

"Do you regret what we did, though… well, what we were about to do?"

He hesitated, trying to find the right words. "Last night, in the kitchen, I wanted it to happen." He met her eyes as he pressed on. "But I was wrong because I'm still angry at you for keeping Annie a secret from me. I lost so much precious time with her, and I need to work through my feelings… to process everything." He closed his eyes for a second, trying to find the courage to deliver his last words. "So, to answer your question, I regret leading you on last night."

Her violet eyes filled with tears. "Do you think there'll ever be a way back for us?"

Of course, there was a way back for them. But before he could reassure her, she was talking again. "Sorry, that's unfair. But whatever happens, we'll always be friends, right?"

A pain punched his stomach at her words. *Could he ever just be friends with her?*

"Best friends?" She pressed.

"Sure. Best friends." He pulled her against his chest and wrapped his arms around her, resting his chin on top of her head.

"Good," her voice vibrated softly against his shirt. "Because I couldn't bear us not being friends."

Long after she'd said goodnight and gone to bed, her words were still haunting him.

What had he just done?

Chapter 48 - Lou

"Mum, this is Jack. Jack, this is my mum, Sylvie." Lou made the introductions as they shook hands.

"Oh, I think we can do better than a handshake." Sylvie pulled him in for a hug. "I'm so pleased to meet you, Jack, and welcome to the family."

"It's great to meet you, too, and thanks."

"Annie's such a sweetheart, isn't she?"

"She certainly is. You know, last night she sang most of the ABC song to us. She's learning it at nursery."

"Amazing."

"We got her some letters to play with in the bath, and she can already pick out the correct ones to spell her name."

"What a clever girl." Sylvie beamed, and he nodded.

"Oh, come on, you two, this isn't an Annie appreciation party. Jack's here to talk about the hotel sale contract."

"Yes, yes, of course. So, what do you think? Should I sign the contract?"

They all took their seats in her mum's office, and Lou watched a frown appear on his face. "What is it? Is there something wrong with it?"

"No, not wrong exactly. I've perused the contract, and everything appears to be in order."

"There's a 'but' in there somewhere." She picked up the contract and began scanning it.

"Like I said, there's nothing wrong with it, except…"

"Except what?"

"The buyer is someone you used to work for."

"Who?" She looked at the name on the contract. "I don't recognise it."

"No, you wouldn't. Neither did I at first, but then I did a search at Companies House, and the main shareholder of the company is Barret Fortesque."

"Who's Barret Fortesque?" Sylvie's eyes flicked between them.

Chills raced up her arms. "He owns the hotel I used to work at in London. Jack saved me from him – that's how we first met?"

"What do you mean, saved you? Was he …"

"No, nothing like that. He was a bit handsy, that's all."

"I think you're minimising," Jack said gently.

"Oh, come on, it happens all the time. Older male bosses taking any chance to rub up against younger female employees." She shuddered. "It's a power thing, but you get used to it."

"You shouldn't ever have to get used to that." Sylvie's voice was icy, and anger curled into each word.

"Your mum's right. You're talking about sexual harassment."

Sylvie nodded. "You know, when I started my first job as a junior in a small office, I remember two older women taking me to one side and warning me to be careful because the boss couldn't keep his hands to himself."

"Mum, I had no idea." Now it was Lou's turn to be shocked.

"Well, it was the 1970s. Wolf whistles, bottom pinching, unwanted touching, were all very commonplace, but I thought things had changed."

She scoffed. "No way. There's still far too much gender inequality in the workplace. Most female junior staff would never report their male manager because they know they have control over their career progression and job security."

"Is that why you didn't report Fortesque then?" Sylvie dragged a hand down her face as she absorbed what Lou was saying.

"There wasn't any point. He had too many friends in high places, and I would have lost my job."

"Well, that settles it then. Jack, please tell the buyer that I won't be selling my hotel to him or his company."

"Mum, you can't–,"

"Why can't I? I couldn't live with myself if I sold your dad's hotel to a sleazeball like him."

"But you said yourself that selling the hotel would solve all your financial problems. What about the roof?"

"We'll just have to find another buyer. Someone who has morals and who'll treat the female staff properly. Your dad built up this hotel… he loved it, and I couldn't live with myself if I sold it to such a horrible man."

Jack was already putting the contract back in his briefcase as Lou got up and began pacing. "Mum, please think about this. You might not get another buyer, but even if you do, they're unlikely to offer the full asking price. You don't like Barret Fortesque – I don't, either - but it's just a business transaction."

"No, I'm sorry. It's not just a business transaction," Sylvie said firmly. "Look, I accept I'm not a businesswoman, and we're probably in this mess because of that. And maybe I should just sell and walk away, but I can't. Actually, I don't want to sell the hotel at all. There's got to be another way."

"Mum, we've been over and over this. There isn't a magic money tree."

"I'm not selling, and that's that."

Lou recognised the stubborn look on her face and sighed. "Okay, then we'll have to think of something else."

***

"I like your mum," Jack said as they sat in the hotel lounge, sipping coffee and eating one of Tom's fruit scones. Sylvie had been called away to deal with yet another crisis. This time because one of the oven fans was on the blink.

"She likes you, too."

"She did the right thing, you know." His voice was soft as he reached over to squeeze her hand.

"Really? She had the full asking price within her grasp. She just needed to put her signature on a piece of paper, and all her money problems would have gone away. Instead, we're back to square one."

"She didn't want to sell, and I don't blame her. The hotel is brimming with old-fashioned charm and character. Just look around. It's like one of those elegant hotels from bygone days or out of an Agatha Christie film. You can't put a price tag on that."

"Fancy a grand tour, because I think you might change your mind when you see the state of the top-floor bedrooms?" Her stomach twisted, because what on earth would they do now?

"Well, look who it is?" He ignored her, getting to his feet and walking towards a man wearing a Panama hat who had just come into the lounge. "Jago Trevellyan, as I live and breathe."

"Hello Jack. What a lovely surprise!" Jago took off his hat and Lou watched as they embraced.

"What are you doing here?"

"Well, I was just about to order some coffee."

"Come and join us and meet Lou." Jack beamed.

Lou thought what a striking man Jago Trevellyan was. Tall, with a shock of white hair, he was no longer young, but there was an air of confidence about him that was compelling. A weathered face, probably from all his time spent in Cornwall, and mischievous eyes… he was a very attractive man.

So, this is the world-renowned Cornish artist and father of Mordros. She stepped forward. "Hello, I'm Lou."

"Lou's mum owns the hotel," Jack explained. "And Lou and I have a daughter. Annie's at nursery this morning, but you'll meet her soon."

"Do you work here, too?" Jago's piercing eyes fixed on her. *I bet those eyes have broken a few hearts.*

"Yes, but only part-time. I'm helping to organise Mordros and Adam's wedding at the hotel. It's going to be very special."

"It's about time they finally got hitched. Never known a couple take so long," he grumbled.

"You're not staying with them, then?" Jack asked, although Lou already knew the answer.

"No, Elizabeth's there, and the less time I spend with that woman the better."

Considering the conversation they'd just had about misogynistic men, she felt obligated to defend Adam's mother despite not having met her. "I'm sure she's not that bad."

Jack snorted. "Let's see if you still hold that opinion after the wedding."

"Are you both coming to dinner later?" Jago's eyes darted between them.

"Yes, we wouldn't want to miss the fireworks," Jack teased as she kicked his ankle.

"Ouch! What was that for?"

"For being mean."

He grinned. "All I'm saying is leopards and spots."

"Crisis averted," Sylvie announced as she finally joined them, and Jack began the introductions again.

"Please call me Jago, and I hope I may have the pleasure of calling you Sylvie." Jago took her hand and kissed it lightly.

Lou watched as her mum's cheeks flushed pink and she began fussing with her hair. "Welcome to the Broadsham Arms Hotel, Jago. I hope you'll enjoy your stay with us."

"Oh, I'm sure I will." He finally let go of her hand. "Now how about we order cocktails, and you can tell me more about your hotel? I remember reading somewhere that it used to be an old coaching inn. I imagine it has a fascinating history."

She smothered a grin. Was Jago flirting with her mum? She'd never really thought of her mum being attractive to men before. But Jago obviously thought so.

"It does, and I'd love to hear about your latest exhibition in Paris. I believe it was a runaway success."

"My dear lady, I'd be absolutely delighted. Let's both play hooky this afternoon and enjoy a long, leisurely lunch."

Sylvie beamed, "I can't think of anything I'd enjoy more."

Jack winked at her. *Yep, definitely flirting.*

Chapter 49 - Jack

They'd made their excuses and left the two lovebirds, as Lou called them, sipping cocktails in the hotel lounge while they went to the pub instead. Over sandwiches and more coffee, they debriefed on the morning's events.

"Jago and my mum, who'd have thought? They're both well over sixty." Lou giggled. "Did you see the way Mum was hanging on his every word?"

"They were just enjoying some innocent flirtation over a cocktail or two. And being over sixty shouldn't stop them. Your mum's very attractive, and Jago obviously thinks so too."

"Wouldn't it be lovely if they had a Christmas romance? Well, at least until Jago goes back to Cornwall."

He couldn't help chuckling. "Are you matchmaking?"

"Since Dad passed, Mum's never been interested in dating, so it's rather nice to see her having a bit of fun."

"I agree. I'm sorry about the hotel sale, though, because I know you're disappointed."

She frowned. "I think Mum's making a big mistake not going ahead. I know Barret Fortesque is a horrible man, but at this stage, she can't afford to be choosy."

"I don't think she ever really wanted to sell, and finding out about his questionable ethics was the excuse she needed. Honestly, I can't blame her."

"Yes, but what about the roof and all the other work that needs doing?"

"Something will turn up. And if it doesn't, we can always hope for a Christmas miracle." He attempted a half-hearted joke.

"Do you think a Christmas romance and a Christmas miracle are too much to ask Santa for?" she teased.

"It's probably pushing our luck." He relaxed back in his seat, enjoying her company. It was like old times. All the awkwardness between them had gone, and they were having a good time - until her next words hit him like a sledgehammer.

"You and me being just friends isn't so bad, is it? It's quite fun, actually. For one thing, I don't need to shave my legs or lady bits… only joking," she added hastily. "But I've never had a best male friend before – not like Mordros has Nick - and I kind of like it." Her eyes shone with amusement.

His heart thundered in his chest. *Is that what she wants… to be just friends? Had he blown his chance with her by being stubborn and saying he wasn't ready to forgive and forget?*

"I'll always have your back," he grunted.

***

There wasn't much point in driving back to his place when they'd have to come all the way back again for Mordros and Adam's dinner party. They stayed in the pub for a while longer and then walked over to Lou's flat so she could grab some more things. The heating engineer had messaged to say that the boiler would need replacing – not really a surprise - so their current living arrangements would remain unchanged at least until he could fit a new one. Jack secretly hoped it wouldn't be soon, and with the Christmas holidays looming, he was probably right.

"Bloody hell, it's like an icebox in here." He shivered as he waited in the kitchen while Lou packed some more clothes for her and Annie. More than ever, the flat looked stuck in the seventies, but at least when Lou and Annie had been living here, they'd breathed some life into the place. Now, staring at the burnt orange kitchen cabinets, bold geometric tiles and brown linoleum flooring, it just looked old and depressing. Of course, Lou had done her best to turn the place into a home for the two of them, but even with a new boiler, it needed completely renovating. He hated the thought they'd return to live here.

"Won't be long," she called from her bedroom, and he walked across the small bare hallway to find her filling a suitcase. "I just need to get some stuff for Annie. She wants her Simba and the photo you gave her."

She flew past him heading for Annie's bedroom, but he stayed where he was as memories of making love to her came flooding back. That afternoon had been incredible, and afterwards it had felt like they'd finally put the past behind them, and nothing would ever tear them apart again. Yet here they were, just good friends.

"Lou," he began as he tried to find the words to tell her he'd made a mistake. He didn't want to be friends – good friends, best friends or any other sort of friends.

"Sorry, I won't be a minute," she hollered. "I can't find Simba."

A minute later she was back, holding up the lion cub like a trophy. "He'd slipped down the side of her cot." She began zipping up the bulging suitcase before glancing at the time on her phone. "We need to collect Annie from nursery. If we're going to walk, we should leave now."

"Okay, I'll just put your case in the car." He began hefting it off her bed.

"Did you want to say something earlier?" She gave him a soft, questioning smile.

He did… but not here in this dingy cold flat. "No, it's fine. Come on, we don't want to be late for Annie."

***

After they'd collected Annie from nursery, they went back to the hotel. Sylvie had offered to babysit so they could have a child-free evening. He knew Lou was intrigued to meet Elizabeth after everything she'd heard, and, if he only admitted it, he was too. It had been fifteen years since he'd last seen her. For Adam's sake, he hoped she'd changed.

"Did you have a pleasant lunch with Jago?" Lou asked her mum casually.

"I did."

"Oh, come on. I need more than that."

Sylvie laughed. "He was a very interesting and captivating lunch companion."

"And are there any more lunches planned?"

"As a matter of fact, he's invited me out tomorrow. I'm going to show him around our neck of the woods and in return he's treating me to a pub lunch."

"Do you like him?"

"Yes, of course, I like him. He's an excellent conversationalist, and he doesn't talk with his mouth full."

"Mum, you know that's not what I mean. Do you fancy him?"

"Lou, really? I'm not twelve years old."

"Yes, I know, but…"

Jack looked up from his prone position on the floor, where Annie was bouncing on his chest, pretending to be a lion. "It's nobody's business but theirs."

"Spoilsport." She grinned.

"ROAR! ROAR! ROAR!" Annie was really getting into it now, and he held on more firmly to her little body so she wouldn't fall off his chest.

"Are you Simba, sweetheart?"

She nodded as she gripped his shirt. "GRR! GRR! GRR!" she growled.

She really was the cutest, funniest, smartest … and all the other 'ests' he could think of, and she was looking at him with eyes that would have him doing anything for her.

"Santa, bring me lion Christmas, Daddy?"

"Not a real one, sweetie."

"Yes, Daddy, real one." She gave him the biggest smile *(another 'est' for his list)*.

A real lion… Umm, that was a stretch even for him. He smothered a laugh. "Let's see what Santa can do."

Chapter 50 - Lou

Air kisses are weird, thought Lou as she accepted one from Adam's mother. She guessed Elizabeth was in her early fifties since she'd had Adam very young. Everything about her, from her styled blonde hair, the colour of which may have had a helping hand, to the diamonds dripping from her ears and fingers, spoke glamour and money. In comparison, Lou felt like an unkempt mongrel in her jeans and Christmas jumper.

"How lovely to meet you." Elizabeth sashayed past, leaving an overpowering smell of perfume in her wake.

"I'd bet my flat that her dress is top-end designer, and did you notice her amazing cheekbones? I can't decide which I envy most," Lou whispered as she and Jack sat down on the sofa.

"No one would want to win your flat." He chuckled.

"Do you think her bling is real?"

"Yes. She probably got them as part of her many divorce settlements, poor buggers."

"Diamonds are a girl's best friend," she answered flippantly, remembering Elizabeth had been married multiple times.

"Personally, I'd prefer a happy ever after," he scoffed, instantly turning her flippant remark on its head.

"I didn't mean—"

"Relax, Lou." His eyes crinkled at the corners, and a whisper of hope swept over her that maybe he was talking about their happy ever after. She reached for his hand and squeezed, but this wasn't the right time to have *that* conversation, especially as Nick and Sam had just arrived. She watched Elizabeth air kiss them both and then completely blank Jago as he came into the room after them.

"Awkward," Jack muttered, and Lou sniggered because the evening hadn't properly started, but plainly Elizabeth was still holding onto whatever grievances she had against Jago.

"Dinner's about ready, so if you want to take a seat around the table, I'll start bringing in the plates," Adam announced.

"What are we having?" Nick asked as everyone filed into the dining room.

"I've made a chicken and leek pie."

"That's an interesting choice, darling." Elizabeth raised one perfectly plucked eyebrow.

"Is it?" He looked confused. "No one's veggie or has allergies, so I thought it was quite a safe choice. But if you'd rather have something else?"

Mordros caught Lou's eye and winked. "I can always open a can of tomato soup."

"No… no, of course not. I'm sure your home cooking will be delightful, and it will make a change from the Michelin star restaurants I'm used to. Sorry, that probably sounds quite pretentious," she tinkly laughed.

"Every time I've eaten at Michelin star restaurants, I've had to take out a bloody mortgage and I've still left hungry," Nick shot back, and Lou smothered a grin. Trust Nick to call her out.

Jack followed Adam into the kitchen. "I'll help you dish up. We can always lace hers with arsenic."

"Don't tempt me."

Mordros nudged Lou. "Come on. We'll need to make sure Elizabeth and Pa sit as far away from each other as possible, otherwise they'll kill one another."

Lou assumed Mordros was joking, but from her serious expression, she wasn't entirely sure. They guided Jago to one end of the table and Elizabeth to the other. Mission accomplished.

***

"Here we are." Adam began putting plates with generous helpings of chicken and leek pie in front of them. "Help yourself to roast potatoes and veg."

Lou took three crispy golden potatoes and placed them on her plate. "Good job Annie's not here because she absolutely loves roast potatoes. She's our daughter, by the way, and Jack's her dad," she shared with Elizabeth because she was the only one who didn't know.

It was such a novelty saying *our* daughter instead of *my* daughter… like a surprise gift that you didn't expect to receive. She caught Jack's eye, and he winked — and that was another lovely thing — the way they were both getting on so much better.

"And are you married?" Elizabeth's eyes flitted between them.

"No," Jack began helping himself to a selection of vegetables. Elizabeth was clearly fishing, but he obviously didn't feel the need to explain. Quite right too, it was nobody's business but theirs what their relationship status was… or wasn't. Just like it wasn't any of her business about her mum's budding friendship with Jago. Still, it would be nice if things developed between them. Her imagination leapt into overdrive…potentially, she and Mordros could become stepsisters. She smothered a grin at how premature she was being. Still, you never knew.

"You're so brave," Elizabeth twittered as she clasped Lou's hand. "I'd simply fall apart if I had to raise a child on my own."

"With all those stepfathers I had, it might have been better if you had," Adam muttered as he finally sat down.

"She's not raising our daughter alone." Jack's jaw tightened.

"Well, I can't wait to tuck in." Nick nudged Jack as Jago stood up at the head of the table.

"To my beautiful daughter Mordros and my soon to be son-in-law Adam. I wish you both a long and happy marriage." Jago toasted, and everyone clinked glasses.

Elizabeth made a face. "What on earth is this plonk we're drinking? Was it a supermarket offer? My last husband was a wine connoisseur, so I'm afraid I'm used to the very best. Do you know it's important to pair wine with the right food… which of course Jago never did." She tinkly laughed again, and Lou thought how annoying it was.

"Oh, for goodness sake," Jago muttered.

"What else would you like?" Mordros asked sweetly.

"A gin and tonic would be lovely, dear."

While Mordros went off to fix her a fresh drink, Elizabeth turned to Nick and Sam. "The world's so accepting now, isn't it? How long have you two been married?"

"Four wonderful years." Sam beamed at Nick.

"And do you have children?"

"We're hoping to adopt, though it's early days."

Elizabeth's smile was brittle. "Isn't it confusing for children being raised in your sort of relationship?"

Nick snorted. "You know, that's a pretty inappropriate thing to say."

"I'm afraid it's all far too modern for me, but love is love or whatever people say these days."

Adam looked mortified. "For God's sake, they're not here to justify their relationship to you."

"It's okay." Nick's expression hardened, and Lou could tell he was trying to hold back his temper.

"No, it really isn't. I think you'll make amazing parents, and any child you adopt will be very lucky," Adam growled.

Sam smiled his thanks, but Nick still looked irritated. Lou couldn't blame him if this was a little taste of the prejudice they faced every day.

"Here you are." Mordros smiled serenely as she handed Elizabeth a gin and tonic. "Now what have I missed?"

***

The meal limped along as everyone tried to make polite conversation. Both the chicken and leek pie and the chocolate log dessert that followed were delicious, and now they were onto the cheese board. Lou felt stuffed, but who could turn down cheese? She could always diet tomorrow.

In contrast, Elizabeth had barely touched her food, though she had drunk a great deal. Lou did a quick calculation. That must be her third gin and tonic plus a couple of glasses of prosecco she'd guzzled even though she'd declared she didn't like the stuff.

"You know, Jago and I nearly got married. We were this close," Elizabeth slurred as she held up her thumb and forefinger. "Just imagine if we had?"

"I'd be in prison for murder," Jago grunted.

Elizabeth glared. "You always had a peculiar sense of humour, but I suppose we all make mistakes in our youth. Do you still dabble in oils? I remember those awful, moody seascapes you used to paint. I must say they looked very amateurish."

Lou's eyes widened. He was one of the most significant and influential contemporary artists of his generation, and she'd accused him of being an amateur. But credit to him, he didn't react to her goading. "This is a dinner party to celebrate our children's marriage. Let's set aside our differences until the wedding is over," he said calmly.

Jack squeezed Lou's hand and whispered, "Told you there would be fireworks."

Elizabeth turned to Mordros. "I'm dying to know which fashion house you chose for your wedding gown. I'm imagining a classic Chanel design, or perhaps something more modern like Stella McCartney?"

"Umm, neither, actually. I've made my wedding dress."

"I beg your pardon!"

Lou let out a very unladylike snort because she sounded so outraged. It was definitely time to jump in and support her friend. "Don't you think she's clever? She's made my bridesmaid dress and Annie's flower girl dress, too, and they're beautiful."

Elizabeth completely ignored her. "You can't walk down the aisle in a homemade monstrosity." Her lip curled in disgust.

"What the hell!" Adam barked.

"Being a home seamstress differs completely from haute couture, darling."

"Whatever my fiancé wants to wear on our wedding day is fine by me, and if you don't like it, you can always stay at home."

"I second that," Nick grunted. "And FYI, Michelin star food isn't all it's cracked up to be. Pairing wine with different courses might work if you don't swig the stuff back so fast you can't taste it. Oh, and last but certainly not least, gay marriage is just marriage."

"Well, really," Elizabeth glared at them both.

"Coffee, anyone?" Mordros leapt up, clearly wanting to escape the atmosphere.

"I'll help." Lou rushed after her. She found Mordros bent over the kitchen counter, her shoulders shaking and her breaths coming in rapid gasps. She gently squeezed her shoulder. "Oh sweetie, please don't cry."

Mordros slowly straightened. "I'm not crying. I'm laughing. Honestly, I'm going to throttle that woman if she carries on like this."

"You had me worried there for a moment. But you're right, she's not the easiest person to like." They were both still laughing when Adam came striding into the kitchen, his face like thunder.

He pulled Mordros into his arms. "If she's upset you, I'll tell her to leave."

"No, I'm fine, but thanks for having my back."

"Always." He kissed the top of her hair lightly.

Jack was next to arrive in the kitchen. "I wish I'd snapped a photo of Elizabeth's face."

"Everyone okay?" Nick asked as he and Sam joined them, and they all broke into spontaneous applause. Nick took a theatrical bow. "I'm sorry, but it needed saying."

Adam grinned. "You said it well, mate, and no need to apologise."

"Let's hide in here for a bit," Jack suggested. "I think we all need a break from your mother."

Lou certainly didn't want to go back into the dining room. "Good idea. I'll put the kettle on."

Mordros suddenly squealed. "Oh, no!"

"What is it, sweetheart? Tell me what's wrong," Adam asked anxiously.

Everyone turned to look at Mordros and waited with bated breath. What on earth was the matter?

She giggled. "We've just left Pa and Elizabeth alone, and they're going to kill one another."

***

They rushed back to the dining room. Elizabeth lay slumped over the table; face planted in her untouched chocolate dessert.

"Pa, please tell me you haven't murdered her?"

"Wouldn't be worth the prison sentence, love. She just passed out from too much booze. Fifteen years and nothing much has changed." He chuckled.

It wasn't funny really, but everyone looked relieved Jago hadn't killed her. Jack helped Adam carry her up to her room. They removed her shoes, carefully washed the chocolate off her face and put her to bed on her side in case she was sick in the night.

"This is like old times, and not in a good way," Adam grumbled. He placed a glass of water and a bowl on her bedside table before switching off the bedroom light. When they went downstairs, the others were having coffee.

"How is she?" Mordros asked.

Jack helped himself to coffee and sat beside Lou on the sofa. "She's going to feel like shit in the morning, but she'll live."

Adam put his arm around Mordros. "If you've changed your mind about inviting her to the wedding, I wouldn't blame you. Or we could just elope?"

"No way. I want to show off my homemade monstrosity," she giggled, but then became serious. "We really shouldn't have let her drink so much."

Adam nodded. "That's my fault. The trouble is, she can't just stick to one, and once she starts, she gets an acid tongue."

Nick looked embarrassed. "I feel bad about calling her out now."

"No, she deserved it. She's always been hard work, as Jago will testify."

Lou suspected he had lots of unsavoury memories he could share, but he shrugged and remained tight-lipped, which proved what a gentleman he was. Anyway, it was probably time to move on from Elizabeth's antics. Everyone was relaxing. Nick and Sam were curled up together on the other sofa, and Adam sat beside Mordros. She stole a look at Jago. She'd quizzed her mum earlier about him. Now it was time to turn the tables.

"Did you have a pleasant lunch with Mum?"

"I certainly did. Sylvie is excellent company."

"She said exactly the same thing about you."

"She took me on a tour of the hotel afterwards. Obviously, there's a lot of work that needs doing, but there's a great deal of potential too."

"Did you see all the flood damage in the upstairs bedrooms?"

"Yes, but it's all fixable. And when the renovations are done, the hotel will be a goldmine with all those rich American tourists descending on the Cotswolds every year."

Lou sighed. That was the response of someone who had tons of money. Fixing things when you didn't have any money at all was quite a different matter. Still, it would be rude of her to point that out.

"She also showed me the outside of the old servants' quarters at the back of the hotel. You have a flat there, don't you?" Jago regarded her thoughtfully.

"Yes, my flat is the only one that's occupied in the building. It's a bit of a wreck, to be honest. The boiler's broken, so I'm living with Jack at the moment."

"You're not going back there," Jack said firmly.

"Excuse me."

"I mean it, Lou. I'll sort out somewhere more suitable for you and Annie. Somewhere that isn't falling down."

"It isn't falling down. Structurally, it's fine. It just needs to be brought up to date a bit."

Jack snorted. "A bit? It needs gutting."

Admittedly, her flat wasn't great, but she was lucky to have it, and the rents in Broadsham were enormous, so she couldn't afford to move out. Jago was still watching them, and she wondered what he was thinking. "Let's talk about this another time," she huffed.

"Fine, but I'm not changing my mind."

She probably should be cross with him. She was a strong, independent woman, not used to being bossed around, and he'd just gone all caveman on her. But the fact he wanted to look after her and Annie made her annoyance melt away, and maybe it was also a sign that he wanted to be more than just friends?

Stop it. Just because you want to be more than friends doesn't mean he does. In fact, hadn't he shot her down when she'd asked if there was a way back for them? But the way he was looking at her…

"Okay," she said simply.

Chapter 51 - Jack

The week had flown by, but he'd barely seen Lou because she'd been working long hours at the hotel making sure all the arrangements were ready for Mordros and Adam's wedding. They'd messaged of course – mostly about Annie – but he couldn't have the sort of conversation he wanted by text.

With Lou tied up with work, he'd become Annie's designated picker-upper at nursery and responsible for feeding her at teatime. By the time Lou arrived back in the evening, and they'd put her to bed, they were both too tired to have more than a brief chat about their day.

And now it was their friends' wedding day, and he and Adam were at the hotel waiting for Mordros, Jago, Lou and Annie to arrive. Adam had spent the morning pacing and checking his phone for the hundredth time. Jack nudged him. "It's another fifteen minutes, and traditionally brides are always late, so you need to relax. Lou's sending me regular updates… I promise she won't stand you up."

Adam groaned. "Why did we say we'd get married at 4 p.m.? This has been the longest day of my life."

"How about a little Dutch courage?" He pointed to the bar. "Maybe a tot of whiskey for your nerves?"

"Absolutely not. I need to keep my wits."

"Don't worry about Elizabeth. I'll make sure she behaves even if I have to lock her in one of the guest bedrooms."

"How did you know I was talking about her?"

"She's the only one who winds you up."

"I've told her not to drink… though I doubt it'll happen." Adam shrugged, and he suddenly felt sorry for him. Throughout Adam's childhood, she'd been a rubbish mum, yet he still hoped for some spark of maternal instinct to surface, especially on his wedding day.

He glanced at his phone messages. Adam had got him doing it now… checking to make sure everything was okay. He'd have to switch his mobile off in a minute because he didn't want it going off in the middle of the ceremony. "Lou says they're on their way."

***

Mordros looked stunning in her 'homemade monstrosity' - the name had stuck precisely because Mordros found it hilarious, so they'd all adopted the expression as their own. Of course, her dress wasn't anything of the sort. A floor-length ivory silk gown with two plum-coloured butterflies embroidered onto one shoulder, it was simple but beautiful and suited her perfectly. She'd twisted her long mahogany hair into a topknot, adding tiny white flowers, with loose tendrils framing her smiling face.

But it was Lou and Annie that drew his attention the most... Lou in a floor-length plum coloured dress, which showed off her gorgeous figure, and Annie in an ivory white princess dress with a wide bow at the back and tiny plum butterflies embroidered on the skirt. Annie was holding Lou's hand, her face beaming, and every so often Lou would look his way and smile. *His girls. God, he loved them both so much.*

Surrounded by family and friends, Adam and Mordros exchanged simple gold bands and promised to love each other for better, for worse... till death do us part, and he knew they meant every word of their vows. Afterwards, the officiant, a middle-aged woman smartly dressed in a navy suit, pronounced them husband and wife, and Adam, taking that as his cue, pulled Mordros into his arms and kissed her as all the guests clapped and cheered.

Servers began handing round glasses of rosé champagne and wedding cake... well, cakes, since the happy couple had opted to have miniature individual ones in a variety of flavours (lemon and blueberry, chocolate and mocha) for each guest to choose courtesy of Tom's amazing baking skills. And then it was time for the speeches to begin.

Jago made everyone laugh with funny anecdotes of Mordros's childhood in Cornwall but when he spoke about her Ma, who had passed away when she was just a baby, they all wiped away tears because she wasn't here to see her daughter marry the love of her life.

Then it was Adam's turn... another heartfelt speech about how he'd met Mordros one idyllic summer in Cornwall but at the end of the summer he'd left and broken his promise to stay in touch. Fifteen years later, by chance, they'd met again in Broadsham... and the rest, as they say, is history.

And now it was time for his best man's speech. He stood up and cleared his throat.

"Ladies and gentlemen, I'd like to thank you all for being here today to celebrate the marriage of Adam and Mordros. I can't believe it's taken fifteen years for them to tie the knot, but they finally got there in the end.

"Now, to give you an idea of the sort of guy Adam is, it's my pleasure to share with you his recent case of a lifetime and the one that finally got him and Mordros to reconnect with each other. No, he wasn't defending an innocent client or taking down a corrupt corporation. It was something far more important: saving a two hundred and fifty year old pear tree.

"So, there he was, spending hours poring over planning laws, citing environmental statutes and arguing about the historic significance of what I'm sure was just a regular tree that occasionally produced fruit.

"Now, most people would have said, 'It's just a tree. Let it go.' But not Adam. He saw it as his duty… no, his calling to protect it. Why? To this day, no one really knows. Maybe it was the principle. Maybe it was nostalgia. Or maybe he just really, really likes pears…"

Adam snorted, looking embarrassed.

"Or more likely, he just wanted to impress Mordros." He looked at his friend because that was exactly what it was.

The room erupted in laughter and applause.

"A toast to the bride and groom – Mordros and Adam – we all wish you a long and happy marriage."

Everyone stood and raised their glasses. "To Mordros and Adam."

Guests began sitting down, and he felt relieved that the speech part of the day was over and he could relax… except Elizabeth had now stood up and was clearing her throat. "I just want to say something…"

"Please don't." Adam groaned, looking worried, and who could blame him? Elizabeth shook her head, looking determined.

"Everyone knows I haven't been the best of mothers. Actually, let's face it, I've been an awful one, always putting myself first and never considering your needs." She smiled at Adam. "I've never been maternal – never been interested in attending school prize giving or playdates or whatever it is you're supposed to do with kids. Motherhood was never for me. But somehow, despite this, you've grown up to be an amazing lawyer but, more importantly, an amazing human being." Elizabeth's eyes teared up. "I'm sorry for all my past behaviour, and I just wanted to say how proud you make me."

She turned to face Mordros. "I also remember telling you in Cornwall many years ago that you weren't good enough for my son, and I'd like to take that back because I was wrong. I think you're perfect for my son, and I wish you both a lifetime of love and happiness."

The room erupted in loud applause as Adam jumped to his feet and hugged her. "Thanks, Mum, that's made our day."

"Bloody hell! Miracles will never cease," Jago muttered. He began playfully poking at his ear. "I think my ears might need testing."

"Mine too," Jack smirked because he couldn't believe what he'd just heard. Maybe there was a glimmer of maternal love in Elizabeth's heart… maybe?

Chapter 52 - Lou

Lou couldn't find her mum anywhere. Jack was missing too. In fact, come to think of it, she hadn't seen Jago, or the bride or groom for a while. Where was everyone?

She left Annie with Clemmie and Tom happily eating a chocolate wedding cake. The four-piece string quartet was playing traditional Christmas music, and Matt and Rosie, and Nick and Sam were dancing, as well as several other couples. She did a quick scout around the room. Nope – no sign of them.

"Henry, have you seen Mum anywhere?" she asked the elderly maître d'hôtel as he came into the room carrying a tray of canapes.

"She's gone outside to the courtyard. There's quite a group of them out there." He chuckled. "They'll need hot water bottles and blankets if they stay out there much longer."

What on earth were they doing outside in the dark and freezing cold? She made her way to the back of the hotel and, yep, there they all were, staring at the old servants' quarters where her flat was.

"Can I join the party?" The rest of them had clearly had the foresight to put coats on, but she'd been in far too much of a hurry. She shivered, and Jack shrugged off his jacket and wrapped it around her shoulders.

"Yes, of course." Her mum came over and hugged her before going to stand next to Jago. "I… no, sorry, I mean, we have some exciting news."

"News?" Her teeth began chattering, so Jack pulled her closer. "What kind of news?"

Her mum beamed at Jago and then back at her. "Jago has made me an offer I can't refuse."

The others were smiling too, so they clearly knew what the offer was. "Umm, does he want to buy the hotel, because that would be amazing?"

Her mum shook her head. "No, sweetheart. He doesn't want to buy the hotel."

She pulled away from Jack's arms just enough to look at them all. They were all still smiling, but if he didn't want to buy the hotel, then what on earth was there to smile about?

"Jago, you tell her." Her mum could hardly contain herself.

Jago shook his head. "Not here. Let's go back inside, and then we won't all freeze to death."

***

They were all crammed into her mum's small office.

"Come on then. Tell me what you're all smiling about." Lou leant against her mum's desk looking at them all.

"I've asked Sylvie if I can buy the old servants' building and turn it into an apartment to live in and an art studio. My architect has already begun drawing up plans, and because it's not a listed building, unlike the hotel, there shouldn't be any problem with planning laws. However, that's why Jack and Adam are here, so they can deal with all that side of things."

Her mum was beaming. "When Jago asked me if I'd consider selling the old servants' quarters to him, I thought he was joking, but… well, he wasn't. I can't believe it, really."

Jago smiled and continued. "I'll still keep my place in Cornwall, but since Mordros and Adam intend to live in Broadsham, I want to have a base here so I can visit but not get in their way either. Buying the old servants' quarters is the ideal solution. And once my apartment and studio are ready, I'll turn the rest of the building into a gallery - not just for my paintings but for local artists to display their work too."

Her mum was crying happy tears, and she rushed over to hug her. "Honestly, darling, it's like a dream come true. There will be enough money to carry out the roof repairs and refurbish the flood-damaged bedrooms. Plus, with Jago having a gallery in Broadsham, the hotel is bound to benefit from art lovers wanting to stay and visit."

Lou felt her own tears sliding down her cheeks because it was exactly like a dream come true. She caught Jack's eye and wondered if he was thinking the same, because she'd desperately wanted a Christmas miracle to save the hotel, and now they'd got one.

"What do you think?" Her mum was waiting for her approval, and there was no reason not to give it… except for one tiny thing. Where were she and Annie going to live? Still, she'd be terribly selfish if she put her own needs above her mum's, especially after everything her mum had done for her.

"I think it's a Christmas miracle," she managed before her mum pulled her in for another hug and everyone began cheering.

***

Yesterday had been a wonderful day – a day full of miracles.

First, Elizabeth's impromptu speech, when for a few minutes she'd behaved like a loving mum. Okay, the cynic in her didn't quite believe she'd turned over a new leaf, especially as a bit later she'd found her in the bar snogging one of the other hotel guests, who turned out to be a rich Texan widower who'd drawled at anyone who'd listen that he'd made his money in oil. They'd disappeared up to his room for the night, and the next day 'rich Texan guy' had checked out with Elizabeth in tow, and … well, who knew where they were now. She tried picturing Elizabeth on a horse wearing a cowboy hat and failed.

The second miracle was Jago's offer to buy the old servants' block. Once the repairs to the roof and the refurbishments had been done, there'd be enough money left over for her mum to retire and maybe go on some holidays - with Jago as her holiday companion if things worked out between them, because if you couldn't do a little matchmaking at Christmas, when could you?

And now it was Christmas Eve, and this afternoon she and Jack had been to watch Annie's Christmas nativity concert at her nursery. They'd both wiped tears from their eyes as their daughter had sung Jingle Bells and Away in a

Manger faultlessly along with the other children in her class. It had been the perfect start to Christmas.

On their way back, they'd stopped off and bought a large Christmas tree, and Jack had hauled it up to the apartment, and then the three of them had decorated it – Annie carefully putting baubles on the lower branches, while they'd decorated the higher ones singing along to Christmas songs as they'd worked. Then, Jack placed the glitter bomb star he and Annie had made on top, and Annie had clapped and been just as excited as two-year-olds can be.

Christmas Day was tomorrow, and Lou had just one more Christmas wish to go.

Chapter 53 - Jack

Christmas music played softly in the background so as not to wake Annie. They'd put out a glass of milk and a mince pie for Santa and a carrot for Rudolph, and when Annie asked how Santa would get into the apartment since they didn't have a chimney, they told her he'd use the lift just like they did.

"You look miles away." Jack sat down next to Lou on the floor as she stared at the town in the distance. Since coming to live with him, it had become her favourite place to sit in the evenings, watching the lights twinkle like fireflies against the night sky.

"I love this view."

"I know you do, but I'll have to move in the new year. Annie needs somewhere with a garden, so she can run around, and if your mum wants to retire, you'll be doing more hours at the hotel, so it makes sense to live in Broadsham rather than here."

"I guess you're right. I really should start looking for a place too since I won't be able to go back to my flat."

"I've been wanting to talk to you about that, but this week's been so manic, I haven't had a chance."

Lou nodded. "There's been a lot going on, like awkward dinner parties and weddings."

"Yeah, and going to nursery concerts and decorating Christmas trees… just normal life, I guess. But now we're here and Annie's asleep in bed – at least for a bit - and it's almost Christmas. Would it be too corny to say I've only got one Christmas wish?"

"I don't think having a Christmas wish is corny at all. Doesn't everyone make one on Christmas Eve?"

That was probably true, but it wasn't just any Christmas wish – like he might wish for a new watch or the latest gadget that he didn't really need. This was far more important. The background music played on… *Have yourself a Merry Little Christmas* …and he followed Lou's gaze as she looked out at the lit-up night sky. "Lou…" her name was a whisper that drifted away. "When we were together, I was so happy."

"Me too, until I ruined everything." He watched her flinch, and he desperately wanted to pull her into his arms to comfort her, but first…

"The thing is, even when I was hurting and angry that you'd kept Annie a secret, I didn't stop thinking about you… missing you." Slowly, she turned her head from the window, her violet eyes searching his. "We still could be together," he breathed out slowly, but his stomach tightened when she stayed silent. "Lou, please say something."

"Do you want to get back together because we have a child together? Because if that's the case…"

"No, of course not. I love you… I've never stopped loving you, and I can't tell you how much I want us to be together." She was still searching his face… but for what, though? "Please tell me you want to be more than just friends," he blurted out.

She was smiling as she reached for his hand. "Of course, I want to be more than just friends. I just said that to make myself feel better because I'd messed up." Her voice lost its playful edge, becoming serious. "I've always loved you, even when I didn't want to."

He finally breathed out the tension in his body, and pulled her in for a slow, gentle kiss, which became anything but because she was his everything and he needed to show her. Her lips tasted of love and home, with the promise of tomorrow as she melted into his touch. When she tugged on his shirt, whispering his name between kisses, he swallowed her moans, losing himself in her desire as their bodies aligned. *This is us. This is forever,* he silently promised as the Christmas tree lights twinkled joy and hope across the darkened room.

***

Much later, Lou lay tangled up in his arms in bed. She really was like a koala bear, he thought as he shifted them both a little so he could stretch out.

"Hmm, watcha moving for? I'm all nice and comfy." Lou flung her arm over his chest.

It was a clear night, and moonlight bathed his bedroom in soft silvery shadows. It had just turned midnight – Christmas Day. "Happy Christmas, Lou." He kissed her, his lips gently brushing against her tousled hair.

She lifted her head slightly so she could see him. "Happy Christmas, Jack. I got my Christmas wish," she mumbled sleepily.

The moonlight slipped across her body, and he could just make out her smile. He'd remember this moment forever… the perfect start to Christmas. A second later he heard soft snuffling sounds coming from her as she drifted back to sleep.

His voice was softer than a secret. "Me too," he whispered.

THE END

Dear Reader

I hope you enjoyed reading The Christmas Secret - Jack and Lou's story - as much as I enjoyed writing it. If you did, please leave a review as it helps other readers discover my books. You can also visit my author page on Facebook: Celia Tandy books and Instagram: @celiatandybooks. I'd love to hear from you, and it's where I'll share teasers about new books and events.

My next book will be Clemmie and Tom's story, and I can't wait to share that with you.

Acknowledgements

There are a few people to thank:

Katie for my amazing book cover design.

My advance readers and also to Barbara and Emma for their helpful edits and encouragement.

Mark and Liya for your constant support. You are my world.

Printed in Dunstable, United Kingdom

71170565R00170